THE BALANCE
OF TIME

Book 2 of the *TIME CHAIN* series

S T E V E N   D E C K E R

Quotes of scripture are from the World English Bible.

ISBN 979-8-9873940-2-1 (print)
ISBN 979-8-9873940-3-8 (eBook)

Library of Congress Control Number: 2023901787

Book Cover by Sabrina Milazzo
Interior design and formatting by Sabrina Milazzo

First edition 2023

Visit the author's website at www.stevendecker.com
Published by TIER Books LLC

Novels by Steven Decker

Distant Finish

The Time Chain Series:
  Time Chain
  The Balance of Time
  Addicted to Time

The Another Kind Series:
  Child of Another Kind
  Earth of Another Kind
  Gods of Another Kind
  Genesis of Another Kind

Walking Into Dreams

Chapter 1

1801

Dani and Aideen popped into existence just outside the town of Claddaghduff, hoping their arrival from 2022 attracted no attention from random bystanders. It was around two in the afternoon, cloudy, but not raining. Dani could see Omey Island across the bloated causeway, full of water and impassable on foot until the tide emptied it. She scanned the area to see if anyone had noticed them, knowing the microsecond time stop that accompanied any time jump—whether from the old Time Chain method used by Charles or the new, state-of-the-art technology utilized by Sadiki—would cover their entrance. People always got a little foggy about their surroundings when travelers jumped in nearby, so the risk of being discovered was minimal.

Dani saw little to be concerned about. A farmer on a cart being pulled by an old horse was heading out of town on the muddy lane and was already well past them. A few people working in the fields across the road didn't even look up. A smooth arrival, so far. Dani and Aideen were dressed in clothing that was normal for that era and locality—a thick, ankle-length skirt, a linen undergarment, a heavy blouse, a shawl made of wool, a linen headscarf, and heavy leather shoes.

Since they hadn't taken the pill that would make them look thirty years old yet (they were saving that until they retrieved Orla from 1801) Aideen still looked to be a woman of middle-age, in good shape, with only a hint of gray in her fiery red hair, while Dani was a woman in her mid-twenties, tall and fit, with the broad shoulders of a swimmer, and dark hair that just touched her back. Based on their age difference, they could be mother and daughter, but that's not what they were; they were best friends and lovers, and always would be.

They left the field where they'd appeared and walked along the road toward town, trying to avoid the mud and puddles as much as possible. Dani realized Orla wouldn't mind if they tracked mud into her home because once she saw them, she'd understand they'd arrived to fulfill their promise to her—to whisk her away from 1801, forever, bring her to 2022, and make her young again. They'd all take the pill to make them look and feel like a thirty-year-old and Orla would no longer be sixty-two, Aideen would no longer be sixty-eight, and each of them would look nearly as young as twenty-four-year-old Dani, who, upon reaching the age of thirty, would remain so for around ninety years, according to Annette.

They took their time, on the lookout for the travelers Sadiki had warned them about. Annette Li, the Minister of Time Management in 2253, had told them before they left that era that a team would be dispatched to 1801 to look for Charles, and Sadiki had confirmed that the team he was assigned to in 2022 had jumped from the Giza station a few days before Dani and Aideen had arrived there. Their mission was to apprehend Charles and bring him to 2253 to stand trial for murder and a number of other crimes, business that Dani and Aideen hoped to avoid. They just wanted Orla, and then to be free of all the chaos time travel had wrought, living the simple life on a nearly deserted Omey Island in the year 2022.

The two women made it into town and Dani eventually led them to Orla's house, all based on her memories from the trip she'd made here with Charles a few months ago. Dani was surprised when young Ciara answered the door. Ciara was Orla's granddaughter and resembled the younger Orla. She was short, with dark hair and a pretty face. Ciara had been part of Charles's Time Chain until his time station was decommissioned by the department of Time Management. She used to live in a house nearby, with her mother and father, but both of them were dead now, a terrible tragedy that Dani remembered well. Dani and Charles had arrived in 1801 during the rape of sixteen-year-old Ciara by her drunken father, who had killed Ciara's mother when she'd tried to stop him, and then Charles had used a weapon from the future to kill the father. Ciara remembered Dani well.

"Well now!" she said, in Irish. "Hello there, Dani! And who's this you've brought with you?"

Ciara spoke no English, and Dani had no Irish, so Aideen took over, introducing herself and translating for Dani. While Aideen and Ciara were speaking, Dani noticed that Ciara had a bump on her belly that suggested she was pregnant, and Dani feared this was the baby from the incestuous rape she'd witnessed four months previously, which Aideen confirmed.

"Ciara is married now, and obviously pregnant. Her husband thinks the baby is his, but it's not. It's from the rape by her father, as I'm sure you suspected. Ciara was lucky enough to entice a man to marry her soon after news spread regardin' the deaths of her parents. He's a fisherman from Omey Island and was more than happy to marry young Ciara and move in here with her and old Orla, whose drunken husband died a few months back. The house her parents lived in remains empty. Ciara can't bring herself ta' go back in there again."

"Where's Orla?" asked Dani.

"Now that's the question, isn't it?" said Aideen. "I've already asked Ciara that and the news is not good."

"What?" asked Dani, beginning to get nervous.

"Orla hasn't been seen for several days."

"Oh no," said Dani, shaking her head.

"As I mentioned, Ciara's husband, James, is a fisherman from Omey Island. He frequents the same pub your old friend Liam Murphy goes to every day. James doesn't stay there until closin' time like Liam does, as he's a good husband and always makes it home in time for dinner. But Liam's always there. Normally arrives in early afternoon, and by the time the fishin' boats come in and the fisherman enter the pub, Liam is bollocksed and holdin' court with anyone who'll listen. James overheard him tellin' a tale of man named Charles Burke, who was from the future and who'd shown him a piece of black stone that was from a prison Liam claimed to have been held in underground, many years ago."

"Did Liam say anything about Orla?" asked Dani.

"No, he did not. But we can infer that if Charles is here, and Orla's missin', that Charles has her. We know he used young Orla to get here from 2253, so it makes sense that Charles would capture old Orla when he arrived, especially if he has the black stone. Once he gets his time station operational, he can use Orla to go to 2022 or 2253, or any other time she's traveled to. But no matter what era Charles is in, he's trouble. More trouble than the world can bear I'm afraid."

"What do you think we should do?" asked Dani.

"I think we should go and have a talk with Mr. Liam Murphy," said Aideen.

"In the pub? They don't let women in pubs in 1801."

"Then we'll just have ta' look like men when we go in there, won't we?"

Chapter 2

W e're both as tall as most men here in 1801, so we can make it work," said Aideen. "We'll use James's clothes."

Ciara helped the women pick out the appropriate attire. Surprisingly, there was plenty to choose from since James had taken possession of her deceased father's wardrobe. Both women ended up wearing linen shirts, breeches that came to just below the knee, wool stockings that covered their calves and heavy, leather shoes. They used twine to cinch the breeches tight around their waists and covered everything with long heavy coats. Next, they tied their hair up in buns and covered their heads with wool tweed caps. The only remaining issue was how to get hair on their faces, but Ciara had an idea.

Charles had given Orla a big bag of coins when she'd agreed to become a time link and send Charles and Dani back to 1751, to her twelve-year-old self. Ciara knew where Orla kept the money and they used it for day-to-day expenses, but the right amount of money could buy almost anything. She told Dani and Aideen to wait for her, then left the house in a rush, with plenty of coins in her pocket. Around half an hour later she returned with a burlap sack, full of something.

"What's in there?" asked Aideen, in Irish.

"Gruiag," said Ciara, the Irish word for hair, explaining to Aideen where she got it.

"The local barber sold it to her," said Aideen. "Of course, it was going out in the trash anyway, but a little money kept him from asking any questions."

Ciara opened the sack and emptied the contents onto the floor of the house.

"That's disgusting!" said Dani. "No way any of that is touching the skin of my face."

"I'll have to agree with you on that," added Aideen.

Ciara looked crestfallen, disappointed she couldn't help and even more so because she had no other ideas, but as always, Aideen had one. First, she explained it to Ciara in Irish, then, as Ciara rushed out of the house on another errand, she explained her idea to Dani.

"Ciara's on her way to buy some coal. We'll say we're miners from Maam who've just made a delivery to the port, stoppin' in for a pint before we head back to Maam. We can smear coal on our faces, hands and clothes to make it look like we've been handlin' coal during the delivery. When we're in the pub, a few extra coins on the bar should stop the barkeep from askin' too many questions."

"Fine," said Dani. "Let's do it."

When Ciara returned with the coal, she smudged it onto their faces and they each held a lump of the black rock in their hands, making sure it marked them. Ciara resisted when they asked her to rub the coal on their clothes, since they belonged to her husband, but Dani reminded her that all of Orla's coins would fall to Ciara when Orla departed for 2022, meaning that buying new clothes for James would be no problem. Ciara relented and got to work on their clothes. By the time she was done, they looked a mess and might be able to pass as men inside a dark pub with few windows. Now they needed to hurry because the fishing boats would be coming in at four in the afternoon and it was already half past two. They wanted to confront Liam before the crowd of unruly fisherman entered the pub—more eyes to discover their ruse. The tide was out, so it was a good time to cross the causeway over to Omey Island. Ciara accompanied them in case they encountered obstacles along the way that she might help with. She also put together a few things to eat in case they were delayed.

When they reached the causeway, Dani noticed there were no posts to show the way across, but because the population of Omey Island was much higher than in 2022—nearly 500 people—there was a lot of foot traffic back and forth, including horse drawn wagons carrying supplies and food. But Aideen and Dani didn't need a guide. They could find the way across the channel in the dark, and had done so many times, going to and from Charles's original time station, which had been hidden below the bottom of the channel. When they arrived on the island, Aideen was amazed at what she saw there.

"There's at least a hundred homes here on the island!" she explained. "There's less than a dozen in 2022."

"Yes, it changed quite a bit from now to then," said Dani. "And wait till you see the town. Hard to believe it was ever here, but it is."

They entered the town square. It was full of shops—there was a tailor, a general store, a store for fishing supplies, and even a small post office—and Aideen's head was on a swivel, marveling that all of this was once here, only a few hundred meters from where her cottage would be built in a hundred years or so. They located the pub and walked toward it.

"We'll just go in and see if Liam Murphy's there," said Aideen. "If he's not, we'll leave immediately. If he's there, we should approach the bar and get as close to him as we can. Then we'll talk to him and see what we can find out. Does that sound all right?"

"Sure," said Dani. "I just hope this coal miner stunt works."

Ciara stayed outside while Dani and Aideen entered the pub. It was dark, with no windows and nothing but whale oil lamps lighting the area. It was also filthy, the plank floors covered in mud tracked in from outside and the air dank with the stink of sweaty, dirty men. A few patrons glanced up at them, but then settled back into their conversations, enjoying their ale and food. The pub was roughly half full. They spotted an old man at the far side of the bar, a man who was older, by far, than anyone else in the pub, and they knew it must be Liam Murphy. He was holding court with a tall man with long, dark hair and a beard. The dark-haired man seemed to be just finishing his lunch. Liam wasn't eating. When they were about ten feet away, Dani grabbed Aideen by the arm, pulling her to a stop.

"That bearded man beside Liam looks familiar," whispered Dani.

Aideen peered closely at the man, then Dani saw Aideen's eyes widen. She took Dani's elbow and pivoted her in the direction of the entrance to the pub, pulling her with some force and urgency.

"Did you recognize him?" asked Dani, as they exited the pub.

"Indeed I did," said Aideen. "It's Charles Burke."

Chapter 3

W hat do you think we should do?" asked Dani.

"I think we should wait," said Aideen. "Ciara can go back home before the tide comes in, but the two of us need to stay here until Charles comes out of that pub. Then we'll follow him. Agreed?"

"Okay," said Dani.

"And remember," said Aideen. "If there's trouble, just push the button on the location device Sadiki gave you. I'll do the same, and we'll travel back to 2022. You still have the device, don't you?"

"Sure do," said Dani. "I'd say it's pretty important, wouldn't you? I mean, if we lose it, we're stuck here forever, right?"

"I don't think so," said Aideen. "Sadiki said that he'd set the time station to retrieve us if we aren't back in three days."

"Oh, that's good," said Dani. "I must admit, I prefer 2022 to this."

"Indeed," said Aideen. "But we've work to do before going back. A lot more work than I'd hoped for."

Aideen spoke to Ciara in Irish. Ciara handed her the sack of food, hugged them both, and left. Dani and Aideen sat down on a stone wall on the other side of the square from the pub and waited. Aideen pulled some bread from the sack, broke off a piece and offered it to Dani, who declined. Aideen took a bite of the bread and as she was chewing, Charles Burke emerged from the pub, alone. It was obviously too early for Liam to go home—he was just getting started—and Charles appeared to have been at the pub primarily to get something to eat. He turned in a northerly direction and moved out of the square. Dani and Aideen jumped up and hurried after him. They kept their distance so as not to alarm Charles if he looked back. The good news was that with only a hundred or so houses on the island, it shouldn't be difficult to find out where Charles was staying.

Charles turned left off the main road and headed up a slight incline to a grouping of houses that bordered Fahey Lough, the freshwater lake in the center of the island. He then turned right down a small lane and made his way to a tiny cottage at the very end of it and went in. The cottage had no windows.

"What should we do now?" asked Dani.

"There's not much we can do at the moment," said Aideen. "But we know where Charles is staying. My guess is he's got Orla in there too. I'd also bet this is Liam's house."

Dani thought back to the discussions she'd had with Annette Li in 2253. Annette had told her quite a bit about how OIM—Organic Intelligent Material—worked. It could grow nearly anywhere—in seawater, underground, above ground—as long as it had raw material to work with, and virtually anything with mass served that purpose.

"Charles is probably growing his new time station right underneath the cottage," she said. "The dirt and rock below it will be fine as raw material, and he doesn't need the station to remain hidden for a long period of time. I'm sure all he wants is to use Orla as a time link to get to either 2022 or 2253, and after that, he might not even plan to use the station anymore."

"Well, you know more about how the time stations are built than I do," said Aideen. "But assuming that's true, I'd say he'd go to 2022 if he's decided to simply disappear, never to be seen again. If he goes to 2253, it'll mean he still wants to go through with his plan to destroy the future. Do you know how long it takes for the black stone to grow?"

"No idea," said Dani. "But I think it takes a while. I bet the station isn't close to being ready yet. I mean, if Orla disappeared only a few days ago then Charles has only been here that long. So really, he's just getting started."

"We need to stop him, if we can," said Aideen.

"We have to get Orla out of there," said Dani. "How are we going to do that? Charles most certainly has one of those Ticklers. That's probably how he's getting Orla to cooperate, but he can also use it to kill anyone who gets in his way."

Ticklers were the cigar-shaped devices from the future that could bend a person's will, or stun them, or kill them, depending on the setting selected by their operator.

"We need to regroup," said Aideen. "Let's go back to Claddaghduff and see if we can talk Ciara into getting James to help us. Maybe she'll let us stay at her old house too, since it's empty."

"Okay," said Dani. "Let's get across the channel before the tide comes back in."

Chapter 4

Dani and Aideen arrived back in Claddaghduff just as Ciara was serving dinner, and she invited them to join her and her husband, James. As always, it was fish stew, with bread on the side. Edible, but Dani was glad she'd taken the immunity pill that Charles had given her a few months back, and she was sure Aideen was as well. After they were seated and had begun eating, Aideen brought Ciara and James up to date.

"I believe we know where Orla is being held," Aideen said, in Irish. Dani knew the plan and assumed Aideen was following it, not needing translation yet.

"Where?" asked Ciara.

"At a cottage on Omey Island," said Aideen. "We don't know for certain, but there seems to be a good chance she's there. We think it's Liam's house."

"Is Charles Burke the one holding her?" asked Ciara.

"Yes, we believe so," replied Aideen.

"What can we do to help?" asked Ciara.

"It will be dangerous, no matter what we do," said Aideen. "Do you remember the device Charles used to kill your father?"

"Yes, I remember."

"We feel certain Charles has it with him and is using it to bend Orla to his will. But it can also kill, as you've seen."

"Can we get it from him?" asked Ciara.

"We need to try," said Aideen.

Dani had been watching James's expression as the conversation unfolded and was happy to see a look of determination in his eyes. James wasn't a big man, shorter in fact than Dani and Aideen, but he was stout, with plenty of muscles. He might be able to subdue Charles, as long as Charles didn't use the Tickler on him. Dani looked at Aideen and nodded her head, indicating she was comfortable with Aideen moving to the next part of the planned conversation.

In Irish, Aideen asked, "Do you think James would be willing to help us get Orla back?"

Ciara didn't have a chance to answer because James spoke up.

"I'll give m'life to help me family," he said.

"I'm afraid there's a chance that might happen, James," said Aideen. "You need ta' understand the man has killed before and will do so again, if given the chance."

"Then we canna' give him the chance," said James. "What's the plan?"

Aideen brought Dani up to date on all that had been discussed, then explained their ideas to Ciara and James. During the conversation, Ciara agreed that the cottage Charles was operating out of very likely belonged to Liam Murphy. Aideen speculated that Charles had probably offered Liam the immunity pill and the pill to make him younger in exchange for his help. Dani hadn't seen Liam Murphy up close, so she couldn't say for sure if he looked younger than a man sixty-six years of age, but she also remembered Annette had told her the pill to make a person younger took about a week to work, and it had been only a few days since Charles arrived. It was also possible that Charles was withholding the pills from Liam until his station was operational, or he might not even have them due to his hasty exit from 2253. But none of this really mattered. The important things were getting Orla back and trying to stop Charles.

The plan was to return to Omey Island tomorrow afternoon around lunch time, hoping that Charles would be in the pub. James would go to his captain early in the morning to tell him he needed to be off work, to help with a family emergency. Part of the plan was for James to enter the pub to see if and when Charles arrived there for lunch. Once James confirmed both Liam and Charles were in there, he would accompany Dani and Aideen to the cottage and help them to free Orla, if she was there. Ciara would stay in the square, a good distance north of the pub, and rush to warn them if either Liam or Charles came out.

When all the plans were finalized, Ciara led Dani and Aideen over to the cottage where she'd grown up, and where her father had raped her and killed her mother. As she unlocked the door, Ciara assured them the cottage was clean and the bed was made before returning home. Dani and Aideen entered the cottage and lit some of the lanterns, as night was falling.

"Too bad Ciara has to stay in this time" said Dani. "This era is pretty miserable, don't you think?"

"I think it's what she knows," said Aideen. "And since she was a time link, she understands that she has a role to play, just as Orla did, in bearing the children and raising them so the family can continue on, all the way to me."

"I hope so," said Dani, thinking already about their other objective. "What are your thoughts about Charles, Aideen?"

"That one is fairly clear to me," said Aideen. "The first thing we must do is rescue Orla and remove her from this time. When we do that, Charles's only means of getting far into the future will be gone. So, I'd like to send you and Orla back to 2022 together, immediately after we find her. I'll remain here to finish some important business."

Dani was shocked and upset to hear Aideen say this. "That doesn't work for me. I'm not leaving you here by yourself."

"I want you to," said Aideen.

"Why?"

"Because murder is a difficult thing to do."

"What?" asked Dani. "Are you going to murder Charles? I thought the idea was for him to be put on trial in 2253?"

"That was Annette's idea," said Aideen. "But we can't leave Charles alive back here. He can still do quite a bit of damage, even without the ability to travel forward through time."

"Like what?" asked Dani.

"For example, if he kills Ciara, out of spite, I'll never be born. And there are other things he can do to disrupt the future as well. You know that, Dani."

"Yes, I do. And that's why I'm going to stay until Charles is either captured, or dead."

Chapter 5

There was no more argument between Dani and Aideen about who should stay and who should go. Dani knew Aideen would insist on staying if the circumstances were reversed and she had a good point, anyway—Charles needed to be stopped. There was just too much at stake, for all of them, in the past, present and future, for him to remain free. Capturing him was still the best option, but if the only choice was to end his life, Dani would have to find something inside herself that would enable her to do it, although she wasn't sure it was there to be found.

Around noon of Dani's and Aideen's second day in 1801, the four of them—Dani, Aideen, Ciara, and James—set out for Omey Island. The two women from 2022 were dressed in suitable clothes—the ones they'd arrived in—as it was no longer necessary to appear to be men. A light rain was falling, but it wasn't a soaking rain and barely accumulated on their clothes and heads. James kept a rowboat near the shore of the channel, for crossings when the tide was in. He rowed the boat through the unsettled waters while the three women remained mostly silent. The plan was set and each of them knew their role.

The first step was to visit the pub and have James check to see if Charles was there. He went into the pub around 1 p.m. and came out about ten seconds later.

"Both Charles and Liam are there," he said, in Irish, nodding his head. Dani needed no translation.

Ciara took a seat on the wall and the other three walked briskly out of the square and made their way to the cottage where Charles was staying. They approached the front door and Aideen knocked. There was no answer, and no noise from inside. She tried the door handle, but it was locked. The three went around back to try the door at the rear of the cottage and found that it was unlocked. They entered the home and quickly determined that Orla wasn't there.

"Well, that's a disappointment," said Aideen.

"But we haven't finished looking yet," said Dani.

Aideen held her tongue while Dani inspected the floor of the cottage. Surprisingly, it was made of wooden floorboards rather than simply hard-packed dirt. She stopped at a section of flooring and knelt, pushing on it with her hands.

"Aideen, can you ask James to give me his knife?" she asked.

James didn't own a gun but had insisted on bringing his knife along, and now it came in handy. Dani pushed the knife down between the floorboards and levered it sideways to pry the board up. It came up easily, as did the next one and the next one. Below the floor was a substantial hole in the ground. All three of them leaned down and peered into the hole. Dani pulled out her cell phone and turned on the flashlight, shining it down into the opening. There was no reflection coming back at them but it was clear they were looking at a chamber made of black stone—OIM—which didn't reflect light and was the material time stations were made with. The chamber was empty.

"I'm going down," said Dani.

"Me too," said Aideen. She spoke to James in Irish, telling him to stay alert and to bar the doors to the cottage in the event Charles returned.

James helped the two down into the hole—which was only about five-feet deep—then moved away and began his work to prevent easy entry into the cottage. Once in the small, four-sided chamber Dani and Aideen stooped over and used their flashlights to scour the walls. They saw nothing but black stone.

"I've got an idea," said Aideen. "If this chamber is made from the same black stone material of the original time station, it should still recognize us, wouldn't ya' think?"

"Let's try," said Dani. "You start on that wall and I'll start on this one."

The two women separated, crouching to keep their heads from hitting the ceiling above them, which was the floor of the cottage. Dani placed the palm of her hand on one wall and Aideen on the other. They slowly changed the location of their hands, and after nothing had happened for either of them, they each moved to another wall. Suddenly, Aideen spoke.

"Here!" she said. "It's opening up!"

Dani rushed to join her as an opening that was the full height of the wall appeared. There was a drop off of about two feet to the floor of the tunnel in front of them, so the tunnel was nearly seven feet in height and could be easily negotiated without having to bend down. The two followed the dark passage, using their cell phones for light, and noticed that the floor gradually descended, just as the floor of the tunnel of the original station had done. They followed the tunnel for about 100 feet and encountered another wall. Aideen quickly placed her palm on the wall and an opening appeared which led them into the time station itself. The chamber was fully formed, with a height of at least twenty feet and a light source somewhere up in the ceiling, just like the original time station chamber. But there was only one time cradle in this chamber, and lying on it was Orla, securely bound to it by strong rope.

The two rushed up to her.

"Orla, can you hear me?" asked Dani.

The old woman opened her eyes and it was obvious she was not herself. There was a vacant look in her eyes that suggested she was under the influence of something.

"He's used that Tickler on her, no doubt," said Aideen.

"Orla," said Dani. "It's Dani and Aideen. We're here to take you to 2022. Can you hear me?"

Orla nodded her head weakly.

"I can't believe how far along he is with this station," said Aideen. "I wonder if it's already operational?"

"I don't know," said Dani. "But it really doesn't matter. If we can get Orla away from here, he won't be able to use it to go forward in time. Help me undo these straps."

They unfastened the straps and helped Orla to her feet. She was struggling to stand but with both of them supporting her, the three exited the chamber together and slowly ascended through the tunnel to the small chamber below the cottage. When they arrived there, Aideen called out to James. There was no answer.

A shape appeared above the opening. The shape of a man. But it wasn't James.

"Your friend is dead," said Charles Burke. "And soon, you will be too."

He raised the Tickler and pointed it toward them.

Chapter 6

'"ve got Orla!" screamed Aideen, reaching out to take Orla's hand. "Push the button on your device!"

Dani reached into her pocket and latched her fingers onto the time location device Sadiki had given her, and pushed the button. After a few seconds of disorientation, she regained her senses and found herself in Sadiki's time chamber. Aideen and Orla were there too. They were alone in the chamber.

"We made it!" she shrieked. "We've got Orla, and we made it!"

Aideen was less enthusiastic.

"But James is dead, and Charles is still in 1801. And that means he can still do some serious damage to the future, and to us. I've just figured out that there's still a way for him to go forward in time."

"How?" asked Dani.

"He can use Liam to go as far back as 1751. It doesn't matter if he goes back that far, however, because all he has to do is go to a time when Orla is still there, and he can recapture her and use her to travel forward."

"Do you think he knows that?" asked Dani. "He was always a bit lame when it came to time travel."

"We can't take the chance, and he can cause disruption, even from 1801. We need help."

"What about the men from Sadiki's station that went back to find Charles?" asked Dani. "We can use them, right? We just have to get Sadiki to bring them back and we can work together with them."

"They're dead," said Orla, who seemed to be regaining her senses. "Charles killed them and threw them into the black stone chamber and it used their bodies to make more black stone, just as it does with everythin' else it touches."

"Oh no," said Dani. "Is the station operational?"

"Almost," said Orla. "He's started the final AI infusion, to turn it into a time station. It'll only be a day or so more, maybe less, and he can use it."

"Let's think about all of this," said Aideen. "First, let's not forget that poor Ciara is sitting in the square on Omey Island waiting for us to return. Her husband's dead and she has no idea we're gone from that time. Plus, Charles will undoubtedly want to get his hands on her because she can take him forward in time, at least to 1851, which is where Dani first met her. Or he might just want to kill her and end my family tree, including me. That could have serious implications for the future as well."

"What are you saying?" asked Dani.

"I'll go back and get Ciara and bring her here for safekeeping. You and Orla need to rush to 2253 and get some help."

"I don't want to split up!" said Dani.

"It's a good plan," said Orla. "We need to do it, Dani."

Dani knew Aideen and Orla were right. Ciara was in danger, Charles was still on the loose, the men from Sadiki's station were dead, and it was clear that the three of them couldn't stop Charles on their own.

"All right," she said. "Let's see if Sadiki will help us."

"I'll make sure of it," said Aideen.

Chapter 7

S adiki's station was the newer technology from the future that didn't rely on human time links to make the transfer. Instead, it was based on a complex merging of quantum theory and relativity with the B theory of time, which postulates that the past, present and future are all happening at the same time. The tech was developed by the Community of Minds, sometimes called the Mind Upload Community by biological humans, because these minds had no bodies. The Community was composed of 100 million uploaded minds, housed in the Time Management building Dani, Aideen and Orla had visited previously, in the year 2253.

The time chamber in which they found themselves at the moment was a simple box, with no need for time cradles or time links. The time coordinates—a combination of the date and location where the Travelers were to be sent—were simply input by the operator, in this case, Sadiki. An energy field directed at such coordinates was fed into the chamber and the transfer followed. The location devices allowed the operator to pull the Travelers back when necessary, and also permitted the Travelers to initiate the return process on their own, which Dani and Aideen had just done. Aideen's physical contact with Orla had insured that the energy field pulled Orla along with them. There was also a failsafe time setting which gave the traveler's a predetermined amount of time at their destination, after which they would be automatically pulled back if they hadn't already returned. The location devices did not need to be on the person of the traveler for the failsafe to work. This way, if a traveler lost their location device, they could still be brought back to their natural time.

The operator's room was behind a glass wall next to the transfer chamber and was obviously empty at the moment. But Sadiki carried a device of his own that alerted him when an unplanned arrival had transpired and, as if on cue, a door in the chamber materialized and Sadiki entered. He'd obviously come down from his tent, located near the pyramids at Giza, which was directly above the time station. Sadiki was of Arab descent, a tall and healthy thirty-year-old since he'd taken the pill from the future. He wore the traditional robe and headdress of his people, as his father Asim had, now passed away from natural causes, having decided not to take the pill. Sadiki spoke English with only a slight accent.

"You must be Orla," he said, bowing slightly. "Welcome back to 2022. I've heard most of your story and find it all quite fascinating."

"Thank you," said Orla. "I'm glad to be here, but I'm worried about what's going on in 1801."

Sadiki turned his gaze toward Aideen, looking for an explanation as to what Orla had been referring to. He'd risked his job, at the very least, by agreeing to send her and Dani to 1801, and Orla's concern had raised an equal level of unease in him. But Aideen knew how to handle Sadiki.

"First, I'll say that it was a good thing you sent us to 1801," she said.

Sadiki frowned. He would need some convincing.

"Your men are dead," said Aideen. "Killed by Charles, before we arrived."

Sadiki raised his eyebrows. "That's bad news. I'll have to inform 2253. But I'll also need to explain to them how I know that."

"Wouldn't their location device signals turn off when the men died, especially if they were absorbed by the black stone, which is what Orla tells us happened?" asked Aideen.

"The devices continue to work even when the bodies are dead. This way we can retrieve the bodies. But if the devices themselves are destroyed, then of course, their signal would be lost to us. The fact is, however, that I'm still receiving the signal."

"Which means the devices are still working," said Dani.

"And that Charles has them," said Aideen.

"That's bad," said Sadiki. "I'll need to be prepared if he comes here."

"Yes," said Aideen. "But he won't do that unless he has no choice, because he has to believe you'll be ready for him."

"I certainly will," said Sadiki.

"But Charles has other options, Sadiki," said Aideen. "He can use Liam Murphy to go back it time and grab a younger Orla, then use her as a time link to go forward in time as far as 2253. Or he can capture Ciara in 1801 and use her to send him forward as far as 1851, where he can keep moving up the time chain by finding and using former time links."

"So he must be stopped," said Sadiki.

"Yes," said Aideen. "But your people have tried and failed, and Dani and I have tried and failed. We need help, from Annette Li, and we need it now!"

"It's all a lot to take in," said Sadiki. "I don't know if I can help you at this very moment."

"Sadiki, there's more than your job at stake here," said Dani. "If Charles upsets the balance of time too severely, no one's life is safe, including yours."

"I can understand that," said Sadiki. "What do you propose?"

"Aideen will make a quick trip back to 1801 to bring Ciara here for safekeeping," said Dani. "Orla and I will go to 2253 to seek help from Annette. We need to hurry, Sadiki."

"All right," he said. "Who's going first?"

"Me," said Aideen. "I need to get to that square before Charles does. It might already be too late."

"Very well," he said, raising his arm and beckoning Dani and Orla. "The two of you follow me."

Sadiki approached the glass wall that separated the control room from the time chamber itself, placed his palm on it and an opening appeared in its surface. He rushed through and waved to Orla and Dani to follow him through the opening. They stood to the side while Sadiki approached the console and began typing furiously. Aideen was now alone in the chamber.

"How long for the failsafe?" he asked.

"What's that again?" asked Dani.

"It's when we bring her back if she doesn't come back on her own."

"Just make it six hours," said Dani. "She can't need longer than that."

"Fine," he said, still typing into the console.

Dani looked up and saw Aideen mouth the word "Hurry." Sadiki must not have bothered to turn on the sound system between the two rooms.

"She says to hurry!" urged Dani.

"I am!" yelled Sadiki. "The program is complicated. I need to concentrate. If I mess this up, she could end up stuck in a rock somewhere before the beginning of civilization. Or they could end up not making it back to this location and this time frame. The proper time coordinates must be entered. We normally triple check our entries before initiating a jump."

"There's no time for that!" screeched Dani. "If she doesn't get there soon, Charles will have enough time to get to the square. It's only a ten-minute walk from the cottage."

"But why would Charles rush back there?" asked Orla. "He doesn't even know Ciara's there." In the frenzy of the moment, no one seemed to hear her.

"Okay," said Sadiki, pulling two location devices from the programming station and handing them to Dani. "Please give these to Aideen. There's one for her and one for the other person, I can't remember her name. And take the one she has from her so she doesn't use it by mistake. The location devices can only bring you home once and then need to be reprogrammed."

Sadiki pushed a button on the console which created an opening in the glass wall for Dani. She rushed through the door, handed Aideen the two devices and asked her for her old one. Aideen gave it to her and the two shared a quick embrace. No words were necessary. Dani returned to the control room and the opening in the glass sealed up.

"Here we go!" exclaimed Sadiki, and pushed a button. The energy field flooded the time chamber and within seconds, Aideen was gone.

"Now," said Sadiki. "Let's get you two to 2253. That's easier. I'll leave it to you to explain to Minister Li why you're there and how all of this mess happened. I'm sure I'm out of a job, no matter what."

Chapter 8

A ideen appeared at the opposite end of the square from where they'd left Ciara. She checked to see if anyone had noticed her entrance back into 1801 and saw no one looking her way. Peering across the square, she spotted Ciara sitting on the stone wall, just where she'd been when Aideen, Dani and James had left her to rescue Orla. Aideen rushed across the square, searching for any sign of Charles. He wasn't there, yet. When she reached Ciara, the girl spoke first.

"Where are James and Dani, and Orla?" she asked, speaking Irish.

"I'll explain later," said Aideen. "Just take this, please. It's not safe here, Ciara."

Ciara took the location device from Aideen.

"On the count of three, push the button on your device. One. Two. Three!"

At first, nothing happened, but then Aideen briefly lost consciousness. When she came to, she was no longer in the square, but she wasn't in Sadiki's time chamber either. She and Ciara were side by side but found themselves deep in a humid jungle. Luckily, it was daylight, but they had no idea where or when they were. For a few seconds, there was silence, no doubt an effect of their arrival, but then, the noise of the jungle returned. The sound of insects chirping, monkeys chattering, and birds trilling surrounded them. Aideen wondered what else was here, watching them, waiting for the moment to strike. She looked up into the trees and saw many of the animals that were making the noises—monkeys, baboons, several kinds of birds—and also saw a few large snakes slithering through the branches, on the hunt.

"Something must have gone awry with the programming," said Aideen. "I have no idea where or when we are."

"Well, neither do I!" said Ciara, appearing frightened. "I've never been out of County Galway, but this is certainly not Ireland."

"Could be sub-Sahara Africa," said Aideen. "Maybe Sadiki got the latitude wrong, but hopefully he got the time right. If we can survive this, we can get back to where we're supposed to be, but the jungles of Africa are still quite dangerous, even in 2022. How are you feeling, Ciara?"

"I feel fine," she said. "I've had no morning sickness during the entire first four months of the pregnancy, so that's something. And I brought some bread for us to eat. Water is another matter."

"One step at a time," said Aideen. "Maybe we'll get lucky and find some water that won't kill us. I'll be fine, because I've had some medicine from the future, but I imagine a lot of the water here is full of parasites. I really don't know for certain. Let's look around. Perhaps there's a path of some sort."

Aideen pirouetted slowly in a circle, seeking any kind of an opening in the foliage. The humidity of the jungle pressed on them heavily. Aideen was already perspiring and imagined Ciara was as well. She pulled off her shawl and dropped it onto the ground. Ciara did the same. Aideen spotted a small opening in the dense undergrowth, a tiny path of some sort, and tried not to think about what kind of animals had made it.

"Let's go this way," she said, pushing forward.

Ciara followed and Aideen wondered when she would ask what had happened at the cottage. She wasn't sure how much she should reveal at the moment, because right now basic survival was the priority. She pressed slowly ahead, pushing leaves and branches out of the way as she went, with Ciara pressed up closely, holding on to her clothing. After only a few minutes, they arrived at a small river.

"Oh feck!" said Aideen. "Lots of nasty beasts live in and around jungle rivers like this."

Aideen whirled her head around, searching for anything that might help them, and her eyes landed on a dead, fallen tree with several branches still attached. She broke two branches off, and with a little more work, fashioned two walking sticks that could also serve as defensive weapons, if needed. Unfortunately, the exigency of defense arose immediately as Aideen spotted the snout of a crocodile coming rapidly their way through the dark water.

"Ciara, get to a tree and climb it, now!" she screamed. "Leave your stick!"

Ciara handed Aideen her stick, moved back into the forest, and found a tree she could climb, grabbing some low hanging branches with her hands and pushing her feet against the trunk. She'd made it a few meters up into the tree when the crocodile emerged from the water, darting at Aideen. It wasn't full grown, but it was still at least two meters long and could easily kill her if given the chance, but Aideen thought she could keep it at bay with the sticks. She whacked it hard on the head with one and jammed the other into its snapping mouth, feeling it contact soft flesh, but the jaws of the animal crunched down. The sound of the stick shattering interrupted the incessant yammering from the other jungle animals. She surmised that some damage must have been done because the crocodile had stopped its attack and was swinging its head from side to side, trying to dislodge the stick from its mouth. Aideen turned and ran back into the trees, handed the remaining stick up to Ciara, and wrestled her way up to join her.

"Let's go higher," said Aideen. "The further up we go, the better the chance we'll see something that might be useful."

The two climbed higher into the tree. They didn't seem to have the company of any unwelcome animals other than a few birds, so that was a positive. Ciara was doing quite well for a woman four months pregnant, but Aideen remembered she was only sixteen years old, and probably tough as nails from the life she'd been leading in old Ireland. Even so, after they were about half way up the tree, Ciara moved aside and let out a deep breath.

"Is this high enough, Aideen?" she asked, seemingly exhausted.

"Yes, you stay here," she responded. "I'll go higher and see if I can get a view of anythin' useful."

Aideen climbed higher and higher, leaving Ciara behind. The further she went, the more her old bones and muscles ached, and the more she wished she'd taken that pill already. She was nearly to the top of the tree, swinging precariously from side to side on a less-than-stable branch, when she finally caught sight of the canopy of the jungle. She held on tightly and surveyed her surroundings, looking for anything other than the endless span of the green forest ceiling. And then her eyes caught something different. It was a city. Tall buildings and smoke rose from it. She guessed it was maybe fifteen miles away. She marveled that civilization could be so close to such natural wildness and danger, yet was also well aware that this jungle wasn't going to allow them to transit fifteen miles through it without swallowing them up for good. It was only a matter of what killed them first, a wild animal, thirst, hunger or some kind of other accident, such as falling from a tree.

And then it hit her. If that was a city, and if Sadiki had made only one mistake in the programming for their return, then this was 2022. They might simply be due south of Giza. How far south she didn't know, but with a city only fifteen miles away, she might have a way of finding out. She pulled her cell phone from her pocket and saw two bars of reception, so she opened up "Contacts," found Sadiki's number, then pressed "Call." Her heart beat rapidly, not only from exhaustion but also from the knowledge that this call was going to make the difference in life or death for both her and Ciara, and a number of other people in Ciara's family tree.

"Hello, Aideen?" came Sadiki's voice. "Where the hell are you?"

"Ciara and I are in some jungle, at the top of a tree. We just escaped from a crocodile and we're not going to survive much longer unless you can bring us in. There's a city about fifteen miles to the west of us."

"I must have inputted the latitude improperly," he responded. "I told Dani I couldn't rush!"

"Can you find us?"

"Probably," he said. "Let me go back to the programming records and figure this out. Give me a moment."

While Aideen waited for Sadiki to come back on the line, she heard a ruckus down below, some kind of hooting from multiple sources. She looked down and saw Ciara fending off at least half a dozen chimpanzees with the stick. Aideen remembered reading somewhere that chimpanzees were highly territorial, but she wouldn't be able to reach Ciara in time to help, and probably couldn't help anyway. She had no weapon and these chimps were angry, baring their teeth and threatening to bite Ciara if she didn't move. Aideen was about to tell Ciara to climb down out of the tree so the chimpanzees could see she was leaving their territory, but then Sadiki came on the line.

"You're in the Republic of the Congo," he said. "Due south from Giza about four thousand kilometers. The city you see is probably Kampala, the capital. Specifically, you're in the Mabira Forest preserve, which is a huge tropical rainforest, undoubtedly populated by a wide variety of dangerous wildlife."

"We know about the wildlife for God's sake!" screamed Aideen. "We're being attacked by a feckin' pack of chimpanzees right now! Get us out of here!"

"Doing it now," he responded.

Aideen yelled down to Ciara to get ready for a time jump, and then they disappeared.

Chapter 9

2253

D ani had asked Sadiki to send them to the concourse outside of the Time Management building in Brussels rather
than inside the building. After all, they'd be arriving unannounced since Sadiki felt he was in no position to explain all
that had happened using the encrypted methodology at his
disposal. Dani wasn't worried because the Minister of Time
Management, Annette Li, knew her. All she had to do was
approach the building as she'd done before, during her first
visit to 2253, and request a meeting with Minister Li.

Dani and Orla walked together toward the Time Management building, the tallest of the cluster of government
structures that dotted the area. The concourse on which they
walked, the food kiosks and chairs that had sprouted from it,
and all the tall buildings that rose high above them, were all
black. Black stone. Officially known as OIM (an acronym for
Organic Intelligent Material, which was pronounced *oym*), it
was one of the many inventions of the Community of Minds
from these times, yet was also the weak link upon which all of
civilization had nearly perished, due to the virus Charles had
planned on infusing into it. But Dani and Annette Li had saved
the day, sending a team just one day back in time to capture

Charles before he'd had the opportunity to unleash his devasting cocktail on the world of 2253.

Orla was old and slow, but Dani and Aideen had left the youth pills at their cottage in 2022, so for the time being, Dani would need to be patient with the old woman, even though time was of the essence. She had no idea if Aideen had successfully removed Ciara from 1801 and regardless, Charles was still on the loose in that time, very likely preparing to use Liam Murphy to capture Orla in a time before 1801 and use her to come forward in time, if Ciara was gone from his grasp. And if all that failed, he still had the location devices from the two travelers from Sadiki's station that he'd killed.

When they arrived at the building, the pleasant female AI voice addressed her from the black stone wall of the Time Management building.

"No one is permitted without an invitation," said the voice.

"Yes, I know," said Dani. "But I was here, not long ago, working with Minister Li on a critical project, and she is in dire need of the information I bring today."

The AI voice went silent for a moment, then returned.

"Do you have ID?" it asked.

"Yes," said Dani, holding out her passport to the wall, watching the wall absorb it as it had done during her last unscheduled visit.

"And the ID of the woman with you?" asked the AI.

"She doesn't have one," said Dani. "Just tell the Minister her name is Orla."

The AI went silent again, then a doorway appeared in the black stone.

"Go to floor seventy-three," said the AI. "Have a nice day."

"You too," said Dani, taking Orla's hand and leading her to the area of the invisible elevator.

The elevator shot up to floor seventy-three and spoke to them. "Please walk to the opening."

Dani stepped out onto the invisible forcefield walkway, pulling Orla with her, and walked across the open space without looking down. After crossing over, she stepped onto a platform, strode through the opening and was met by two guards who escorted her and Orla to a conference room. Annette Li sat on the far side of a table made of black stone. She was an attractive woman of Asian descent, appearing to be around thirty years old, but Dani knew she was much older than she looked.

"Hello, Annette," said Dani. "Sorry to burst in on you unannounced, but it's important."

Annette smiled.

"I'm sure it is," she said. "Why don't you two ladies have a seat? Who is this you've brought with you?"

"This is Orla, from 1801. When you two last met, Orla was twelve years old. Now she's sixty-two."

"And how did you come to find Orla in 1801, if I might ask?" Annette inquired.

Dani told her the whole story. Their plan to use Sadiki's time station to bring Orla to 2022 for good, Charles's kidnapping of Orla, Charles's killing of the Travelers from Sadiki's station, her narrow escape with Aideen and Orla, Aideen's return to get Ciara, and the tools still at Charles's disposal to come forward in time and resume his apocalyptic plans, including the location devices of the two men he had killed.

"Well, that's a mouthful," said Annette, somehow remaining calm after all the bad news. "And terribly tragic for our travelers. Charles just keeps on killing, it seems."

"Yes, and we're here to ask for your help to stop him, Annette. We need to bring this potential calamity to an end, once and for all."

"I agree we need to stop Charles," said Annette. "But we are limited in what we can do."

Dani had anticipated this response and didn't know how she could overcome it. Nevertheless, she had to try.

"Annette, I know all about your law against time travel to the past. And I realize you set up the 2022 station in Giza before the law was formally adopted. Those men were brave and honorable to accept the mission to go back and work from the Giza base, and now they're dead. Sadiki did what he thought was right in sending us back to 1801, because he hadn't heard from the crew and he felt removing Orla from that time period would help reduce Charles's options. But I'm not here to plead Sadiki's case. That's a matter for you to handle as you see fit. But Charles's time station will be operational in approximately twenty-four hours, or less, and he'll be coming for all of us when it is."

Annette was quiet, something she often did when trying to envision a solution to a difficult situation. But eventually, she spoke.

"What kind of support would you like to have, if I can arrange it?" she asked.

Dani didn't hesitate.

"A team of four soldiers, like the ones we used during the raid of Charles's original time station."

"I'm sure you know what I'm going to say next, don't you Dani?" said Annette.

"Yes," she responded. "You need to seek the approval of the Executive Committee. But Annette, it goes without saying that the balance of time will be disrupted, soon, if we don't stop Charles. He's hellbent on destroying the world, and he's close to having an operational time station and can easily gain access to the time links he needs to unleash his plan."

Dani remembered well the first time she had met Annette, a few months earlier but in the same year, 2253, learning from her that Charles had stolen the time travel technology seventy years prior to that time and had been missing ever since. But then it was discovered that Charles had devised a way of infecting the world's OIM infrastructure and Dani had come up with a plan to stop him. They succeeded in halting his plan, temporarily, but Charles had escaped to 1801 and clearly still had the power to end the world. He needed to be stopped for good this time.

"Give me thirty minutes," said Annette, standing up and leaving the room.

Chapter 10

2022

Sadiki entered the time chamber soon after Aideen and Ciara appeared, having just saved them from their ordeal in the jungles of Africa. But Aideen was still not happy.

"How the feck could you do that, Sadiki?!" she screamed.

"I'm sorry, Aideen!" he implored. "I told Dani it takes time to program this station. I need to triple check the calculations and she wouldn't let me."

"All right, fine," she huffed. "Now get in there and start programming our next trip."

"What? Where are you going?"

"To 2253, of course."

"Why?" he asked.

"To help!" yelled Aideen. "How long ago did you send them there?"

"Less than an hour," he said.

"All right, get to it," she ordered.

Sadiki complied and returned to the control room. Aideen decided that now was a good time to tell Ciara about James. She took Ciara's hands in her own, then spoke to her in Irish.

"Ciara, dear, I'd tell you to sit down but there's no place in here to do that. So just listen to me, carefully, all right?"

"James is dead?" she asked.

"Yes, I'm afraid Charles killed him."

Ciara pressed her lips together, but no tears came to her eyes. She raised her head high and looked straight at Aideen.

"James was a good man," she said. "A brave man."

"I didn't know him long, but of that there is no doubt," said Aideen. "I'm sorry."

"It's all right," she said. "He was going to die anyway."

"And how do you know that?" asked Aideen, already suspecting she knew the answer.

"I know ma' future, up until 1851," said Ciara. "I knew before I married James that he'd die. Just not in the way he did."

"How did he die, in the future that you know?" asked Aideen, a little unsettled by this revelation from Ciara, because the trip to 1801 had obviously already affected the balance of time by changing the nature of James's death.

"He died in a storm at sea. All hands lost."

"And when was that to happen?" asked Aideen.

"Not long from now. A week or so, I think. I was strugglin' not tellin' James to stay home that day, but now I won't have to make that decision."

"No, you won't, but it's a sad thing nonetheless. I can't say for certain what it means that James died a week before he was supposed to. But we're both still here, so maybe the ripples from this change will be small, although still just as tragic. I feel for you, lass."

"Thank you, Aideen, but I'll be all right, if we're able to stop Charles Burke."

Sadiki reentered the room.

"Okay, it's ready. You'll be arriving just outside the Time Management building, just as Dani and Orla did."

"All right," said Aideen. "And Sadiki, I'm sorry for blowin' up at ya'. I know we rushed you through things. That was foolish on our part."

"This transfer will be smooth sailing compared to that one," he said.

Sadiki shook hands with Aideen and gave a slight bow to Ciara, then returned to the control room. After a few minutes, the energy field enveloped them and they were on their way to rejoin their friends—at least they hoped they were.

Chapter 11

2253

Instead of being escorted to floor seventy-three, Aideen and Ciara were taken to the top of the building, to the time station itself, which was the size of a small stadium and capable of sending up to 2,500 people at once on a time jump. It was composed entirely of black stone, OIM. They were brought out onto the floor directly in front of the massive black monolith that housed the Community of Minds. Dani and Orla were there, along with four other people Aideen assumed were soldiers, since they were dressed in the light blue, skintight suits that covered their heads. Annette Li was also there, and Aideen addressed her as she approached the group.

"I'll need one of those suits," she said.

"No, you won't," said Dani. "The four of us are staying here, for now."

"Why?" asked Aideen.

"The soldiers know exactly where and when they're going and what to do when they get there," Dani responded.

"And where and when is that?" asked Aideen.

"They're going to Omey Island, to the moment in time when James comes out of the pub to tell us that both Charles and Liam are in there. At that point, the soldiers will appear in the pub, arrest Charles and return here."

"Won't it upset the people in that time to see these four soldiers, all dressed up in their fancy suits?" asked Aideen.

Dani provided more details. "Two soldiers will be sent directly into the pub. They'll grab Charles, and immediately bring him here. Chances are that very few people will even notice, due to the time stop and the fogginess bystanders experience during a jump. The other two soldiers will be jumped to just outside where Orla is being held, but they'll wait until we save her before they make their appearance."

"And we'll be back there in 1801, with no idea what's goin' on?" asked Aideen.

At that point, Annette took over. "The two soldiers being sent to the cottage know who you are and have been given instructions to let you see them, which should help you figure out that a mission is taking place, and they will answer your questions, if you have them."

"And what will happen to the four of us here, after Charles is arrested?" Aideen asked. "And by the way, I'm all for this plan. You've obviously got a handle on the details. But it's not the way it happened, originally. So, what does that mean for the Dani, Orla, Ciara and myself that are here right now?"

"You will never have been here," said Annette.

"All right, now wait a minute," said Aideen. "That's complicated."

"How so?" asked Annette.

"Because we're already here. When we save Orla and Ciara again, what happens to the Orla and Ciara that are already here?"

"They will never arrive here," said Annette. "And I will have no memory of them, or you, having been here. You will rescue

Orla for the first time, again, but you won't be in danger from Charles, because we'll have him here. As far as Ciara goes, you won't have to rescue her because she will no longer be in danger from Charles."

"What will we remember about this?" asked Aideen.

"I'm not sure," said Annette. "You may experience some vague memories of the incident, and whatever else happened to you after you rescued Orla the first time may come into your mind from time to time, as would a daydream or a déjà vu experience."

"I'd prefer not to have a déjà vu experience of what Ciara and I just experienced in the jungles of Africa!" said Aideen.

"What?" asked Dani, completely thrown by Aideen's statement.

"I'll explain it to you after these four soldiers leave, and I'll try to do it in a hurry, because soon after that we'll be forgetting it, right Annette?"

"Hopefully," Annette responded. "If the soldiers are successful."

"What about the time station Charles is building, below the cottage on Omey Island?"

"The two soldiers who will be dispatched there will destroy it."

"Make sure they wait until we have Orla out of there, all right?" said Aideen.

"They know to make sure of that," said Annette, beginning to show signs of impatience. Annette was a person who liked to get on with things when the plan had been laid out, and approved by her superiors. But Aideen wasn't quite finished.

"And what about you?" asked Aideen. "What will you remember about this?"

"As I said, I'll have no memory of you being here. But I've made notes about it that are in my office, so when the soldiers return, with Charles in tow, they won't have to explain to me where they came from. We know from past experience that basic inanimate objects, such as paper, normally survive a reality change, such as what is about to unfold."

Annette's explanation made complete sense to Dani because she and Annette had already experienced something similar, when Dani sent four soldiers back one day in time to capture Charles's station and free Aideen and Orla from him. The one-day younger Dani was also there in Charles's station, and after Charles abandoned ship and went back to 1801, his plan to infect the world's OIM was derailed, and the future was changed. When Dani, Aideen, Orla and the four soldiers returned to Brussels from that mission, the Dani who had sent the soldiers wasn't there, in fact, had never been there, and Annette remembered nothing of the mission. But Dani remembered, because she had been the time link for the mission, and all that she knew had transferred to the one-day-younger Dani in Charles's station, who then went to Brussels and witnessed Annette's inability to remember that mission. It didn't surprise her that Aideen was confused.

The one thing that never quite made sense to Dani was exactly what had happened to her one-day-older self. Supposedly she'd never been there because the future had been changed, but Dani knew that she *had* been there, so was there another reality where the other Dani was living out her life, just as Dani was living out hers in this reality? She would probably never know the answer, but there was one question, regarding the current mission, that she thought she did know the answer to, and it was good news.

"There's also a silver lining to all of this," said Dani, a big smile on her face.

"What's that?" asked Aideen.

"James won't be killed by Charles, back in 1801."

"Well, that would be good, except…" Aideen trailed off before she finished the sentence. She looked over at Ciara, who didn't speak English, then leaned over and whispered to Dani.

"Ciara told me he's going to die anyway. His fishing boat sinks during a storm. Ciara knows her future and that's part of it. She says she's been struggling about whether or not to tell him to stay home that day."

"I'm so sorry to hear that," said Dani. "But Ciara's struggle is one all of us old time links face. I'm still not reconciled to allowing my parents to be killed in a car accident next year."

Annette gave a little cough, trying to get things back on track.

"Oh my," she said. "What trouble Charles has caused, for all of us. We really need to get him behind bars. Can we proceed, please?"

Dani and Aideen nodded. They all wished the soldiers good luck and accompanied Annette to the control room to watch the time jumps from there.

Chapter 12

1801

Dani, Aideen and Ciara sat on the stone wall at the edge of the square of the town on Omey Island. James entered the pub and emerged a moment later, walking toward them and nodding his head. At that instant, Dani felt her mind wander for a moment, losing touch with what was going on around her.

"Did you feel that?" she asked Aideen.

"Indeed I did, Dani. That felt like a time jump, but I don't see anyone new. I'll ask James to have a peek back in the pub." Aideen gave the instruction to James in Irish. James reentered the pub, then came out, a confused look on his face and shaking his head. Aideen asked him what he'd seen. "He says Charles is no longer in the pub. It's just Liam now."

"Hmmm," said Dani. "I wonder if the time jump had something to do with Charles?"

"Or he went out through the kitchen!" said Aideen. "Let's hustle over to his cottage. We can get there before him if he truly did sneak out of the pub."

"I really don't think he's here any longer," said Dani.

"Great!" said Aideen. "Let's make certain of it."

Aideen told Ciara to remain in the square to see if anything further happened there, and they set off briskly for the cottage. When they arrived, there was no sign of Charles, at least out on the streets. James approached the cottage and knocked. No one answered, so he tried to open it, but the door was locked. They went around back and got in. Seeing no sign of Charles or Orla inside, they inspected the cottage carefully and discovered a concealed opening in the floor, found the time station and rescued Orla. As they were leaving, two soldiers from 2253 dashed past them, and entered the house.

"Well, that explains a lot," said Dani. "There *was* a time jump. And Charles was very likely captured! And now I bet these two are here to destroy the time station."

"Do you think we should ask them?" asked Aideen.

"Yes, I'll go in," said Dani, not giving Aideen time to agree or disagree. She entered the cottage and came out a few minutes later.

"Yippie!" screamed Dani. "Hail, hail the witch is dead!"

Aideen tilted her head. "The Wizard of Oz?"

"You bet!" said Dani. "The two soldiers confirmed that Charles has been taken to 2253 to stand trial. He's not technically dead, but he won't be causing any more trouble for us, or for anyone else."

"So he's gone," said Aideen. "To a place we'll very likely never see again."

"Yes, he's gone," said Dani. "But never say never. We could end up there again, for something we haven't even thought of yet."

"I suppose you're right," said Aideen. "Let's go get Ciara and walk with her and James back to Claddaghduff, so she can say a proper goodbye to Orla."

"Cool," said Dani. "And how about this idea? So, we're fulfilling our promise to Orla, but maybe we should make one to Ciara too. Maybe in fifty years, when Ciara's done with all her child-rearing and raising, we can come for her too. Maybe that will help her to avoid changing things she knows are coming."

"It's not easy," said Aideen. "An incentive like that could help Ciara, but it's still no cakewalk. I've been livin' my whole adult life that way. And it's somethin' you'll have to face soon, with your parents."

"It's true, and I'm highly conflicted about that," said Dani. "But in this case, by trying to encourage Ciara to let her future come, no matter what she knows about her future, because there's a silver lining waiting for her. And I'm also trying to preserve a person I love very much."

Aideen smiled, knowing Dani was speaking about her. Ciara, while only sixteen years old in 1801, was Aideen's great grandmother, and if things changed too much in Ciara's life from the way they were supposed to be, Aideen might not even be born.

"I'm willing to come back for Ciara in 1851, if Sadiki's willing," said Aideen.

"So can we tell her?" asked Dani.

"Sure," said Aideen. "I'll tell her on the way back to Claddaghduff. And then we need to hurry back to 2022, where we belong."

Chapter 13

March 2023

H ave you been having the dreams?" asked Dani.
"About what?" asked Aideen.

"About being together in 2253 right before the mission to capture Charles?"

"No," said Aideen. "But I'm glad they caught him."

"So nothing, then?" asked Dani.

"For me, it's something else."

"What?" asked Dani.

"I've been dreaming about a crocodile and some chimpanzees in the jungle," said Aideen.

"Oh really? That's interesting."

"Why?" asked Aideen.

"Because in my dream, you tell me about the jungle."

"Hmmm. I wonder what that means?"

"I think it means it really happened," said Dani. "But then they changed things when they captured Charles."

"Yes," said Aideen. "Of course it does."

"And you know what else it suggests to me?" asked Dani.

"No, what?"

"That there are separate realities. Different paths for different circumstances."

"Okay," said Aideen. "I can live with that, I think."

"So can you live with me warning my parents about their impending deaths?" asked Dani. "Because this life is our reality. And I can't live with myself in this reality if I let that happen."

"I understand. But you should be subtle about it. Just have them do something else that day, okay?"

"Will you go with me?"

"Of course."

Dani and Aideen were sitting out on the pea gravel patio of their cottage on Omey Island, enjoying some red wine—their favorite Pinot Noir—while they waited for the sun to go down. It was early March and getting a little chilly, so they went inside to warm up, settling down in the living room. Dani was relieved that Aideen had agreed with her about her parents and would accompany her to Chicago when the time came. But there was another matter that was bothering her.

"I was hoping we could speak about Orla. She's out again, at the pub over in Claddagduff."

"She's a grown woman, Dani. She has a right to do that."

"I know, but I worry about her. She's obviously sleeping with a lot of strange men. Do you know if she's taking the birth control pills we got for her?"

"She's not stupid," said Aideen. "Of course she's taking them. And she can't get sick. None of us can."

All three of the women had previously taken the immunity pills from the future, and as soon as they'd returned home after the ordeal of retrieving Orla, around six months ago, they'd finally taken the pills to make them look and feel thirty years old. But Dani was worried about Orla, who'd been sixty-two when they brought her from 1801, and was now a very attractive thirty-year-old. She seemed to be relishing the myriad of freedoms women had in 2023 compared to when she'd come from. Dani was now twenty-five years old, and Aideen and Orla looked thirty. All three were attractive people in their own way, but Orla, while nearly six inches shorter than Dani and Aideen, drew far more stares, from both men and women, when the three of them were together in public.

Orla's green eyes glistened as would the leaf of a palm after a summer rain. Her lightly freckled skin seemed to glow as if she'd just come in from a walk during a brisk winter day. And her wavy, raven hair shimmered when the light touched it. Dani remembered that even as a twelve-year-old girl, Orla's body had been more well developed than normal, and now as a grown woman, it was simply impossible for her to hide her curves. The men at Sweeny's pub must have felt they'd met an angel from heaven when Orla's attentions drifted their way.

But Dani worried about her. Even though Orla was a sixty-two-year-old in the body of a healthy woman of thirty, Dani still thought of her as the girl of twelve who she'd grown to love and care for, not so long ago. "I understand," she said to Aideen. "And it's really amazing how she's adapted to living in our time. It's like nothing phases her."

"She's a special lady," said Aideen.

Just then, there was a knock at the door. Very surprising, considering the tide was still out and there were no visitors on the island that they knew of. It wasn't quite spring yet on Omey Island, and when the sun went down, the cold and the wind could be a hostile combination, certainly not for the faint-hearted. It was so odd to have a visitor this time of year that the two women temporarily froze, trying to determine from the look of the other what should be done. But after a few seconds, Aideen's expression turned to one of annoyance, the fierceness at her core taking over her persona. She rose up from her seat on the sofa and approached the door.

"Who is it?" she said in a loud, aggressive voice.

"Annette Li," a muffled voice returned through the door.

Aideen looked back and Dani nodded. Aideen opened the door and sure enough, in front of her was a woman of Asian descent, about thirty years old, wearing the light blue skinsuit that all employees of the Department of Time Management wore.

"Well now," said Aideen. "Come on in out of the cold, will ya'. What brings you back 231 years in time, Annette? It must be quite important for the Minister of Time Management herself to visit."

Chapter 14

After exchanging pleasantries, the three women sat together in the tiny living room, Annette on the sofa, and Dani and Aideen across from her in two chairs on the other side of the coffee table, on which rested three glasses of Pinot Noir.

"To what then, do we owe this pleasure, Annette?" asked Aideen. "Our old friend Charles hasn't escaped already, has he?"

Annette smiled. "Oh no. Charles is safely ensconced in a high security cell in our building," she said. "The AI watch him 24/7 and have been programmed to shock him if he tries anything. He won't be going anywhere. Ever."

"That's good to hear," said Aideen.

"So what's going on?" asked Dani, feeling a little nervous. Annette's presence here, especially without a military escort, was highly irregular. "Is everything all right in the future?"

"Generally, yes," said Annette. "But Aideen is right. The reason I myself have come is to discuss an important matter with you. There was little risk for me, coming here without an escort, since you live alone on this island. I arrived outside the cottage purely out of politeness, not wanting to just barge in. Anyway, the point of my visit. You see, after the Executive Committee was thoroughly briefed on all of Charles's activities, including his construction of the Time Chain, assembling time links from different eras under false pretenses, certain changes have been initiated."

"Such as?" asked Dani.

"Time travel will soon become more highly restricted than ever before," she said.

"I thought it was illegal already, at least backward travel?" questioned Aideen. "Except for the station you manage in your time and the one Sadiki operates in Giza."

"The Giza station has already been shut down," said Annette. "And travel backward *and* forward from the station in my time is now prohibited, except for this mission itself."

This was a shock to Dani. If those stations were shut down, it essentially meant that time travel would no longer exist. "But why?" she asked.

"The damage done by Charles is the reason," said Annette.

"What damage?" asked Aideen. "I thought we stopped him?"

"We did," said Annette. "But think about all he did to upset the balance of time just from the people he encountered along the way. The time links, for example. All of those people's lives were changed by Charles in ways that will ripple through time forever. Even more disruptive were the missions we unleased to stop Charles, which both of you were involved in."

Dani was moved but not yet convinced. "Do you have evidence, in your time, of time ripples that changed something?" she asked.

"Of course," said Annette. "You and I have both experienced it. When we sent the team back one day in time to stop Charles, for example. And both you and Aideen have been through it again, although you may not realize it. The two of you, plus Orla and Ciara, came to 2253 to warn us about what Charles was up to in 1801 and to help us formulate a plan to stop him. Dani and Orla arrived first, and then you, Aideen, and Ciara showed up, and you told us some story about being stuck in a jungle in Africa and being threatened by crocodiles and chimpanzees. The only reason I remember you four coming to 2253 is because I took copious notes before we initiated the 1801 mission that led to Charles's capture."

Both Aideen and Dani nodded their heads.

"The dreams," said Aideen. "They really happened."

"As we suspected," said Dani.

"But that's the point," said Annette. "We believe these separate realities, as we three have experienced, are not the normal way of things. It's only through time travel that the balance of time is upset, and different realities begin to occur. We theorize that if these disruptions continue to happen, eventually the separate realities will begin to compete with our primary reality for dominance, and there will end up being no safe reality to live in."

"You mean when one reality tries to force itself onto another?" asked Aideen. "What would happen then?"

"We don't know," said Annette. "There might be a physical reaction, such as an explosion, or it could be that the individuals involved, like us, would simply lose their minds."

"So you think stopping time travel will fix this?" asked Dani.

"It will certainly keep it from becoming worse," said Annette.

"But what about all the people who've already been affected?" asked Aideen.

"That's why I'm here," said Annette.

"How so?" asked Dani.

"I'm here as part of an assignment," she said. "To bring all the time links from Charles's Time Chain to 2254."

"Why?" asked Aideen.

"To minimize any damage you might do to the balance of time, if we allow you to continue on in your natural time."

"So you're saying you want us to go there, like, to live?" asked Dani.

"Yes," replied Annette.

"That won't happen," said Aideen.

Just then the front door opened and Orla walked in.

Chapter 15

Orla hugged Annette, then went to the kitchen for a glass and joined Annette on the sofa when she returned. She poured a glass of wine while Dani brought her up to date, and even though she was a bit drunk, she seemed to follow along easily and wasn't the least bit surprised by any of it. Dani marveled, once again, at how Orla rolled with the punches so effortlessly and with such a lack of worry. When Dani finished briefing Orla, Annette took the conversation to the next level.

"The reality is that all of the other time links are already with us in 2254," she said.

"Seriously?" asked Dani. "Did they come willingly?"

"Absolutely," said Annette.

"I don't understand why they would do that," said Aideen, shaking her head.

"Think about the way you did it with Orla," said Annette. "You waited until she was old. She had fulfilled the responsibilities of her life and was simply waiting to die, more or less."

"Are you saying you waited until they were all old, then went and got them?" asked Dani.

"Yes."

"But how does that help?" asked Aideen.

"It helps in two ways," said Annette. "First, it brings an end to all the storytelling of time travel by people such as Liam Murphy, who was more than happy to come forward in time, to get the pills Charles had promised him but never delivered. The harsh reality is that as people get older, stories about the old days are a big part of their life, and even the most disciplined person would have trouble not telling some of the stories the time links have experienced."

"It's true," said Orla. "If I hadn't known Dani and Aideen were comin' to get me, I would have spilled the beans to anyone who'd listen. It's just too much to keep inside."

Dani nodded, beginning to understand. "Is Ciara there?" she asked.

"She certainly is," said Annette. "She was surprised actually, when our people arrived in 1851, not because she was going to the future, but because she was going further in the future than she had expected. It seems two people from your era had promised to bring her there." Annette smiled, and Dani understood she was referring to the promise she and Aideen had made to Ciara before they left 1801.

"Well, thank you for saving us the trip!" said Dani. They had decided to wait to see how Orla adjusted before going back for Ciara, and now it turned out they wouldn't have to go at all, probably couldn't even if they wanted to, since Sadiki's station had been shut down.

"What's the second reason, then?" asked Aideen.

"Politics," said Annette.

The three other women didn't comment, curious looks on all of their faces, so Annette continued.

"A law has been passed to end time travel, and a project to clean up as much of the mess as possible has been initiated.

Regardless of whether it makes sense or not, that responsibility falls on me and my department. Essentially, I'm following orders."

"Well then, why don't you wait until the three of us are old and gray?" asked Aideen.

"That would be a long wait, now, wouldn't it?" said Annette. "Since you've taken the pills already. Also, you three are the most prodigious time travelers of all the time links, by far. You've been involved in the creation of several separate realities that we already know of, and probably many others."

"What about Sadiki's group?" asked Aideen. "They did much more travelin' than us."

"Yes, but with specific protocols not to affect change during their missions. They were sent back to observe, and learn, primarily, until the mission to capture Charles was initiated. But regardless, Sadiki is in the future now. Unfortunately, the two travelers who worked out of that station were killed by Charles in 1801."

"And what about Charles's exploits?" asked Dani. "Think of the damage he's done that can't be changed."

"What's done is done," said Annette. "Charles is in captivity now, so the bleeding has been stopped. All that's left are you three. And think about this: The lives you three are now living are completely different from the ones you were supposed to live. You must know this Dani, and Aideen, because all of those future memories you have will never come to pass in this reality. All the other time links lived out their lives basically as they were supposed to. They understood their responsibility to the future, especially to you, Aideen. They wanted to do their part to make sure you were born, and they did. But you three don't know what's coming. You have memories of your future lives that will never happen, and every move you make in your new lives, the ones based on the new reality you have created by bringing Orla forward, and with the elimination of Charles's time station, will send time ripples forward that were not there before. And we simply cannot let that happen."

"And if we won't go willingly?" asked Aideen.

"You'll be taken by force, I'm afraid. But I'm hoping my visit here can help us avoid that possibility altogether, based on the information I'm providing about how dangerous it is for the future for you to stay in this time era."

"And what about money?" asked Aideen, seeming to soften a bit. "We have plenty of it, here, but none in the future."

"You'll all be given full retirement packages," said Annette. "That's more than enough to live, but there's a way for your money from this time to be there waiting as well."

"How?" asked Aideen.

"Invest it in Bitcoin," said Annette. "Cryptocurrency is the only form of currency in our time. Essentially, Bitcoin, and all other crypto companies in existence 150 years from now, will be acquired by EarthGov when a law is passed to have one world currency, and one currency only. The infrastructure of companies like Bitcoin will be used to rapidly convert the world over to the new currency. But here's the point: I'll make sure you're fully compensated for your shares in Bitcoin if you bring the documentation with you. And if what I suspect about your personal wealth in 2023 is correct, Aideen, you very likely will become one of the richest people in the world of 2254."

Aideen seemed unimpressed by the prospect of becoming a billionaire, but Dani had other concerns. "What about my parents?" she asked. "They're going to die in a few months and I don't intend to stand by and let that happen."

"There's a solution to that as well," said Annette.

"What?" asked Dani.

"We bring them with us to 2254."

Chapter 16

After another hour or so of discussions, sometimes heated, sometimes cordial, Annette departed from 2023 by pressing the button on her time locator and disappearing. The three women who'd been expecting to spend many long years in the little cottage on Omey Island had not yet reached a consensus on what to do, but they agreed it would be very difficult to hide from Annette and her team without dramatic changes to their lives, such as leaving Ireland altogether and taking up residence elsewhere, ideally in a place where they weren't likely to be found. Sadiki wasn't an option because his station had been closed down and he was already in 2254, according to Annette. The three went to bed uncertain about the best course of action, choosing instead to try again in the morning after a good night's sleep. Annette had left five time locators, one for each of the three, and one each for Dani's parents.

The next morning, as the three sat around the kitchen table drinking coffee and eating breakfast, Dani breeched the subject first. "I think we should go talk to my parents," she said.

"And tell them what?" asked Aideen.

"That they need to go to the future with us."

"So now you want to go, do ya'?" asked Aideen. Dani had been going back and forth on what the best solution to this dilemma might be the prior evening.

"I think it would be best for us to go," said Dani. "If we go cooperatively, we're more likely to be treated well. What's causing me to waver is my parents. So if we could talk to them about it, get them to understand what's at stake, for us, and especially for them, it would be a lot easier for me to go."

"I'd be interested in goin' with ya', Dani," said Orla. "I've never been to Chicago after all!" Orla always had a way of injecting humor into an otherwise daunting situation, and it helped.

"It would be an interestin' trip, but we need to do somethin' fast," said Aideen. "Best we get to the future soon, so we don't fall too far behind the others in the orientation program."

Annette had told them that most of the other time links were going through an orientation program of some kind to help them adjust to the future. She said the ones from further back in time would need more time in the program, with some exceptions, like Orla, who'd already been to the future and who seemed to be able to handle anything and everything as just another everyday challenge. Aideen had been joking about the three of them falling behind the others, but underneath the humor was a sincere desire to go forward in time, for good. Annette had revealed that Aideen's mother, Aoife, was there, and she was quite anxious to see her daughter, and Aideen felt the same way. As for Orla, she was intrigued by the idea of reuniting with her granddaughter, Ciara, who was also there. Of the three, Dani had been the most non-committal about going, because she wasn't sure if they could get her parents to understand the whole situation. But during the night she'd convinced herself that it was better than the alternative, for both her and her parents. Unless Dani intervened, her parents would die in a car crash that very summer.

Annette had given them seventy-two hours to make up their minds and use the time locators to bring themselves to the future. She said if they didn't arrive by the deadline, a team would be dispatched to bring them there against their will. Dani knew Annette well enough to know she wasn't bluffing, so she'd resolved that she needed to go to Chicago and tell her parents everything.

"I'll book a flight for tomorrow," she said.

"Don't forget to make it for three!" said Orla, who now had a passport of her own, thanks to Aideen, who knew the right people to make that happen.

"I agree," said Aideen. "I think we can provide moral support, if nothin' else, and we might even be able to help you get them to believe it all."

"It's more than that," said Orla. "The three of us should stay together, until we're certain where we'll be livin' for the rest of our lives."

"A fine point, lass," said Aideen.

"Indeed," said Dani.

"And don't forget to buy as much Bitcoin as you can before we leave!" said Aideen. "That's what I'll be doin'."

Chapter 17

The following day they headed for Dublin to take the Aer Lingus flight to Chicago. Aideen locked the cottage up tight and before getting into the car, she stood and looked at it for a long time. Dani noticed she was crying but didn't realize why. She stepped up to her and put her arm around her.

"What's the matter?" she asked.

"Just sayin' goodbye to the only home I've ever known," said Aideen, wiping her hand across her eyes.

And then Dani understood. They wouldn't make it back by the seventy-two-hour deadline, so if they were going to go willingly to 2254, it would be from Chicago, not from Omey Island. But she thought of something that might comfort Aideen.

"We can come live here on Omey Island in the future," she said. "I saw homes here when I was here in 2253. I didn't have a good enough view to see if this cottage was still here, but we can get something close by if it's not, I'm sure. Annette will help us out."

Aideen smiled. "Thank you, Dani," she said, kissing her on the cheek. "Knowin' that's a possibility will make this whole ordeal easier for me, I do believe. And I'm sure my mother will feel the same way."

Orla was already in the backseat when Dani and Aideen got into the car, ready to go, as always. And off they went. Dani had phoned her parents in advance to tell them she was coming to see them to discuss something important, and when they came out of the terminal at Chicago O'Hare, her parents were waiting for them in a Land Rover SUV. They got out when they saw Dani and rushed over to hug her. It had been a full year since Dani had left for Ireland, and while they'd spoken on the phone several times, they hadn't seen her in person for all that time.

Next, Dani made the introductions.

"Mom and Dad, the redhead is Aideen, and the short one is Orla. Guys, this is Donald and Patricia Peterson, my mom and dad."

"Please, call us Don and Pat," said her dad. "It makes us feel younger!"

Everyone shook hands. Dani noticed her parents staring at Aideen, and she realized they were probably trying to ascertain her age. Dani had told them Aideen was closer to their age—Donald being fifty-four and Patricia fifty-one—than to her own. But now they were looking at woman of thirty, and were obviously confused. Dani realized this would be a good way of breaking the ice regarding time travel and the future.

The three ladies from Ireland got into the backseat of the Land Rover. Dani had explained to Aideen and Orla that her parents were both successful business people. Her mom had made a fortune in commercial real estate and retired a few years ago, and her dad was scheduled to retire from his position as an advertising executive later that year. While Patricia drove, Dani whispered to her friends that her father was a terrible driver, but she didn't mention that it would be him behind the wheel when the fatal accident occurred. They went to a nearby restaurant for an early dinner. It was 5 p.m. After they were seated, Dani's mom tried to get the conversation going.

"Good to see your hair's growing out," she said.

Dani's hair was now shoulder length since she hadn't cut it after arriving in Ireland a year ago with a buzz cut. But now was not the time for small talk, so she jumped into the fire and got things going in the right direction.

"Thanks, Mom," she said. "But you'll remember I said we had something to speak to you about."

"Right," said Patricia, a little shaken by Dani's abrupt segue.

Her dad leaned forward, a concerned look on his face.

"What's up, honey?" he asked.

Don was on the taller side and in good shape from his morning workouts. His gray hair was neatly combed and stylish. Patricia's shoulder length blonde hair had no gray in it and Dani knew that was from coloring, but it certainly helped her mom look far younger than fifty-one, along with her trim physique. Like Donald, Patricia was also a fitness enthusiast.

"Well, Dad, there's actually a lot going on," said Dani. "But first things first, I thought you might want to see Aideen's old passport. The one she used before she became young. Would you mind showing them that, dear?"

Aideen reached into her pocket and withdrew her old passport, then passed it across the table to Don, who already had a bewildered look on his face.

"And why do we need to see this?" he asked.

"I want you to check her birth date," said Dani.

Don opened the passport up, looked at it, and his eyes grew wide. Without saying a word, he handed the passport to Pat. She looked at it, mouthing the number *1954* to herself, which was the year Aideen had been born. She looked up at Aideen.

"So you're sixty-eight years old?" she asked.

"Soon to be sixty-nine," said Aideen.

"But how can that be?" asked Patricia. "You look to be about the same age as Dani."

"We were wondering about that as soon as we met you at the airport," said Don. "We were expecting someone that looked our age. But you look more like Dani's age, yet this passport says you're actually quite a bit older even than us."

"It's all true," said Aideen.

"How can it be?" asked Don.

Dani stepped back in to the conversation. "It's because someone gave Aideen, and Orla for that matter, a pill to make them younger. Orla's sixty-two, by the way."

"We've never heard of any such pills," said Pat. "In fact, I'm certain no such pill exists."

"That's true," said Dani. "In 2023, no such pill exists. But in the future, they do."

Dani watched her parents carefully to see if she was losing them or if they were still in the game. She decided they were still in, although both of them looked very confused. Aideen was obviously seeing the same thing because she made an effort to keep the conversation moving in the right direction. "I know it's hard to believe," she said. "But it's true. Time travel is real. People from the future discovered it. And for a while, they let us in on their little secret."

"And they gave you a pill to make you look younger?" asked Don, in a skeptical tone.

"Yes, they did. And Orla too. And Dani too."

"Why would Dani need a pill like that?" he asked.

"Because now she'll never look older than thirty for the next hundred years or so," said Aideen.

"And this is what you came all this way to tell us?" he asked.

"Not exactly," said Dani.

Chapter 18

It took a while, but eventually they got it all out and on the table. Dani's parents had always been level-headed people, and most importantly, they trusted their daughter. And now they were fully up to date on all that Dani had been up to during the past year. Her girlfriend, Aideen, was nearly sixty-nine years old, their friend Orla was sixty-two and had been born in 1739, and all three of them had taken pills they'd been given by the woman who was in charge of Time Management in the year 2254. It was really Orla who convinced them it was all true. She spoke for a while in Irish, and even though no one but Aideen could understand her, and aside from the fact that it demonstrated her heritage, there had always been something about Orla's voice that was soothing, almost hypnotic. After that, she switched to English and told them stories of her life back then, and how she had come to love Dani when she only twelve years old.

Don and Pat were overwhelmed, yet they were making a genuine effort not to reject out of hand what they were being told, but when Dani explained they would be killed in a car crash this coming summer, they bowed their heads in disbelief.

"We know the future, Mom and Dad," said Dani. "I know *your* future. And it's not a good ending for either of you."

"What are you proposing we do about it?" asked Pat.

At that point, Dani removed the five time locators from her backpack and placed them side by side on the table.

"What are they?" asked Don.

"They're time locators, Dad," she answered. "One for each of us."

"So you want us to go to the future with you, is that it?" he asked.

"Yes."

While both Don and Pat sat back in their chairs, flabbergasted by what they'd just heard, Aideen stepped in.

"The fact of the matter is, folks, that the three of us are going to the future, no matter what you decide to do."

Both Don and Pat directed their gaze at Dani.

"Is this true, Dani?" asked Pat.

Dani nodded. "We have no choice, Mom. The government in the future has decided to close down the time travel operation, permanently. It's caused too many problems, and almost destroyed the future entirely at one point. So they're gathering up anyone who's been directly involved in time travel and bringing them to the future. I've been there, twice, and I'm telling you, it's an awesome place. People live until they're 150 years old, minimum, and they look and feel thirty years old for most of their lives. You can have all of that too!"

It was clear that the idea of being younger, and living longer, appealed to both Don and Pat. And they were obviously rattled by the idea of never seeing their daughter again. But it was a lot to take in.

"How much time do we have to decide?" asked Don.

"About thirty-six hours, maximum," said Dani. "Then they'll be coming for the three of us and we'll be gone, forever."

"I don't know," said Pat, shaking her head from side to side.

"But you believe us, right, Mom?" asked Dani.

"I think I do," she said.

"Well then, I have an idea."

"What?" asked Pat.

"Aideen, Orla and I will leave right now, using these devices. If there's any doubt in either of your minds about this being true or not, that doubt will be completely erased when we disappear in front of your very eyes."

"And we'll leave the remaining two devices for you to either use, or not," said Aideen.

"Are you serious?" asked Don, appearing stunned and hurt by what their daughter had just proposed. "You're just going to disappear from our lives forever, right now?"

Dani looked him right in the eye. She wasn't at all certain she could follow through on the threat she'd just made, but she was determined to get her parents on board. "I'm here to save your lives, Mom and Dad. I know for sure you're going to die this summer. I'm also aware that while you guys have a lot of friends, you're not close with any of them. You won't miss them. And you have no pets to miss either. But you will miss the chance of a lifetime if you don't follow us."

"Please," beseeched Orla. "Dani will not be well, unless you come with us."

Pat and Don looked at each other.

"What about clothes?" asked Pat. "We would have to pack."

"No you won't, Mom. They take pills that make their clothes. And the Minister of Time Management has allotted each of us a full retirement package, meaning we'll have plenty of money to buy anything we want."

"And if you buy Bitcoin shares before we leave, they'll be waiting for you when we get there!" said Aideen. "We've been guaranteed that by the Minister herself."

In spite of the heavy sell by the three of them, it was clear her parents were not yet fully convinced, and her mother confirmed that.

"I don't know," said Pat, slowly shaking her head.

"I think we should consider it, Pat," said Don. "I trust Dani, and her friends seem like honest people too. But we need more time. You said we have thirty-six hours, right Dani?"

"Yes."

"Why don't you three come with us to our house and spend the night? You can explain more about the time and place you want us to go, then we'll sleep on it, and if your mother and I decide to accompany you, we can put our affairs in order and leave tomorrow evening."

Dani, Aideen and Orla looked at each other, and all three nodded.

Chapter 19

After spending the rest of the day and evening with Dani, Aideen and Orla—the shock of the initial revelations about the future, the pills that made people younger, and their pending deaths retreated, yielding to acceptance of the truth of the situation—the Petersons decided to go with them. They called their attorney and explained that they were leaving the country, permanently, and needed documents to transfer ownership of their home and cars to their next-door neighbor. The attorney was surprised but had a short document in their hands by afternoon. They called the neighbor and explained they were going on a long trip, with no intention of returning, and that they would leave documents transferring the house and cars to them if they wanted them. Again, shock and surprise, but also a sense from the neighbors similar to people winning the lottery.

Don called his boss and took a leave of absence, explaining that he was having difficulties coping with life and would be leaving the country immediately, seeking treatment. Next, both Don and Pat invested the vast majority of their savings into Bitcoin—just as Dani and Aideen had done back in Ireland—hoping the money would grow and be there waiting for them when they arrived in the year 2254. It didn't seem likely to the Petersons that this would happen, and they were a little worried about supporting themselves if it didn't, but Dani assured them that a full retirement package in the future would be more than enough to enjoy life, regardless of whether or not their Bitcoin investments paid off.

At two in the afternoon, all five of them gathered together in the Petersons' living room and simultaneously pushed the buttons on their time locators. The next thing any of them remembered was waking up in the stadium-like time station at the top of the Department of Time Management building in Brussels, Belgium. They were alone in the chamber, dwarfed by the massive Community of Minds monolith. Soon, a guard dressed in one of the light-blue skinsuits entered and greeted them, explaining that a message had been sent to Minister Li regarding their arrival. Not long after that, Annette joined them, entering the cavernous room with a pleasant smile on her face.

"I'm so happy you came!" she said, then directed her gaze to the Petersons. "And I presume these two are your parents, am I right?"

"Yes," Dani responded, excited and relieved that the trip to Chicago had enabled her to save her parents' lives and bring them to a place where she felt certain they would thrive. "Annette Li, please meet Patricia and Donald Peterson."

Annette shook hands with both of them. "Welcome to 2254, to all of you. I have no doubt you will love living here in this era of peace, prosperity and freedom."

"Speaking of which," said Aideen. "I know Dani's seen a bit more of how things work here than the rest of us, and myself and Orla have some experience here as well, but the Petersons are a blank slate, except for what we've told them, which is somethin', but not nearly enough. They have a rough understandin' of how we got involved in time travel, and they know what a time link is, and they've heard a few nasty stories about our friend Charles, but they've no idea how things work here in the future. I'm assumin' they'll be enrolled in the orientation program you mentioned the last time we met. Is that right, Annette?"

"I'm glad you asked that," said Annette, "and I'm happy to explain, for the benefit of the Petersons, and you guys as well. All of the other time links are already here, and have either already been released into society or are working their way through various orientation programs. Why don't I start with the present, and work my way back in time? First, there's Leah. She's from this time and was held by Charles Burke against her will in his rogue time station for many years. But she's been free since our successful mission together and is living with her family back in Ireland. Sophie, who was living in an era about 100 years ago, is also back in Ireland and doing fine. Next in the line back are Aideen are Dani, who are here with us. The two of you will go into a class together and we'll get you up to speed quickly on the technology you'll need to live well and prosper in our time era. Next back is Aoife, Aideen's mom, who I'm sure you can't wait to see, and we'll arrange that shortly. She's in a class with Roisin, her mother, and Ciara, her grandmother. Orla is next back in time and we think she would do well in a class with Liam Murphy, who is from her era and who could use her help. His adjustment has been more challenging than the others so far.

"Oh, and I almost forgot," continued Annette. "Eabha, from your time era, is also here, and she's been placed in a class with Sadiki, our Giza time station operator who some of you know. Finally, the Petersons will have a class of their own. We expect that everyone will have a different orientation experience, and there is no pressure to be finished at any given time."

"When can I see my mother?" asked Aideen.

"We've scheduled a group dinner in a few hours' time," said Annette. "But if you can't wait, we can pull Aoife out of her class and you can see her now. By the way, I should warn you that everyone else has been here for at least a week, and they've all taken the immunity and age pills, so each of them now has the appearance of a person who's thirty years old."

"I can wait," said Aideen. "I'd like to surprise her, if it can be arranged."

"Oh yes, I'm sure it can," said Annette. "The group dines together in the same room every night, so Aoife will just think she's coming to another normal dinner."

"Thank you," said Aideen, then Dani brought the subject back to the pills.

"I assume my parents will be given the same opportunity as others to take the pills?" she inquired. "We've discussed it and they're both interested in pursuing it."

"Absolutely," said Annette. "I'll have you five shown to your living quarters here in the building and we can take the Petersons directly to a short course which will introduce them to the benefits of the immunity and age meds, along with any psychological effects for them to look out for, and they are welcome to take them any time after that."

Dani assumed the psychological effects Annette was referring to had to do with the profound shock of seeing and feeling young again after having become older, but she knew that neither Aideen nor Orla had experienced any emotion other than joy at being young again, so she wasn't worried.

"Perfect," she said. "We're all anxious to get started."

Chapter 20

W hy is everything black?" asked Pat Peterson.

They were seated in a large, private dining area somewhere in the vicinity of the time station in the Time Management building. The table had been set for twelve and so far, only the five people from 2023 had arrived, but the table had served them wine while they waited for others to arrive. The Petersons were amazed. The next group to enter the room included Ciara, Roisin and Aoife, Aideen's mother. Aoife noticed Aideen immediately but seemed quite calm, wandering over somewhat casually and giving her daughter a slight hug and a peck on the cheek. The two looked like identical twins, with their wavy red hair, gray-blue eyes and freckled skin, except Aoife was about four inches shorter than Aideen.

"What?" asked Aideen, feigning offense. "You're not surprised to see me, Mam?"

Aoife scoffed. "Of course not! I know my daughter. You must have adventure in your life or you will perish. With Charles's time station gone you would die of boredom on Omey Island."

"That may be so," replied Aideen. "But I intend to find out. Dani and I want to go back there to live when we pass through orientation."

This comment caused Aoife to turn her attention to Dani. She approached her and took both of her hands in her own.

"Well now, young lady, I hope now, finally, you and I will have the time to get to know one another properly, after all the chaos our former employer, Charles, produced in our lives."

"I know we will, Aoife," said Dani. "Also, I'd like to introduce you to my parents, Pat and Don Peterson."

Aoife smiled and raised her eyebrows. "Well, well! I had no idea I'd be gettin' to meet the in-laws!"

Don and Pat smiled and played along.

"I didn't even know they were married!" said Pat.

They all laughed. It was true that Aideen and Dani weren't married, but they might as well have been. They shared future memories of a lifetime together in a reality that seemed to have passed out of existence, and they were fully prepared to do it again here in the future, if given the chance.

Next to arrive were Eabha and Sadiki, who seemed very much a couple to Dani. She was aware that neither had ever married in their original lives, and it made sense that in this new, strange environment, two people from the same time era, both appearing to be thirty years old and unattached, would gravitate to one another.

The final person to enter was Liam Murphy. Liam was wearing clothes from his era—a linen shirt, breeches coming to just below the knees, under which were wool stockings, covering his calves and leading down to heavy, leather shoes— and this surprised Dani, a little. Her parents were still wearing their clothes from 2023 but had promised to switch to the clothes from this era as soon as the pills they'd taken that afternoon had worked their magic on them. Everyone else was already attired in the more modern skinsuits, including

Aideen, Dani and Orla. Even Sadiki had forsaken his robe and headscarf for the clothing of 2254. In addition to the clothing of his time, Liam also held a pint mug of ale in his hand.

"Where on Earth did ya' get that ale?" asked Orla, feigning jealously.

Liam looked Orla's way and raised his eyebrows.

"Tell me it isn't so!" he exclaimed. "Are you the young goddess who freed me from that black stone prison so long ago?"

"Indeed, I am, sir, but not so young anymore."

"Young enough, I'd say!" he responded, and the whole room erupted in laughter.

Liam was obviously drunk. Dani wondered how he could learn anything if he was allowed to drink while he was in class. She leaned over to Annette.

"So, you have your hands full with Liam, I see," she said, quietly.

"Indeed," whispered Annette. "We can't get him to agree to take the pill to free him of his alcoholism. He says it's what he's known his entire adult life and doesn't want to change it."

"But he took the pill to look younger, didn't he?" asked Dani.

"Yes, and he's a good-looking man, too. I hate to see him waste his life drunk when I'm sure he could easily find a partner to help him get comfortable in these times, if you know what I mean." Dani glanced at Annette, who had a sly smile on her face, and realized that Annette was taking a stab at humor, a rare departure from her normally serious demeanor. Dani was pleased to be friends with one of the most powerful people on Earth in 2254, and even more so since Annette was comfortable enough with Dani to let down her guard, if only for a moment.

"Well, I mean you *are* indulging him a bit, wouldn't you say?" asked Dani. "What did it take to get him that ale, for example."

"Just a few words to a kiosk," said Annette. "You remember how easy it is to get things here, don't you, Dani?"

"Yes, of course, but you could have programmed it not to give it to him, couldn't you?"

"We could have, but that would create other issues that we'd have to deal with. Frankly, we were waiting for you three to get here to help us sort out the issues with Liam."

"It might not be an issue, anyway," said Dani, tilting her head toward Orla, whose expression said she was already smitten with thirty-year-old Liam Murphy, who had a full chest and slim waist, wavy dark hair and a tall, sturdy frame. A giant for his time, average height here in 2254. "Orla has no qualms about drinking. It's what she's known her entire life as well."

"Then perhaps they'll be a couple," said Annette. "But we can't let them out into the world until they learn to behave themselves, and more importantly, how to take care of themselves."

"Agreed," said Dani. "I'll speak to Orla and see if we can get her to understand more clearly that we need her help with Liam, settling him into these times. I think she'll understand. She's a quick study."

"Great," said Annette. "Shall we eat?"

Chapter 21

The following day, Dani and Aideen paid a visit to Charles. All the others from the past were in their classes, but Dani and Aideen needed less schooling than their former colleagues, and both wanted to address their mixed feelings about Charles—the person who had changed each of their lives more than any other—by seeing him in person. From Dani's viewpoint, without Charles's rogue time station project she wouldn't have gotten to know Aideen the way that she had, probably would never have met her at all, and she certainly wouldn't have met Orla and the other good people from the past and the future, and never have been able to save her parents' lives.

Annette was happy to arrange for the meeting and actually had a favor to ask of them that Dani found odd. "Please try to find out what is in his heart?" she asked.

"What do you mean?" Dani asked, confused. "Where are you coming from with that, Annette?"

"I knew Charles over seventy years ago, Dani. When I first met him, he was the most inspiring person I'd ever known. Then, he sank into madness. I'd like to know if there's anything left of the Charles I once knew. He's closed off to me now, but maybe you two, having known him more recently, can find a glimmer of hope that he may one day become his old self again."

"All right, Annette," she said, still wondering about the source of Annette's emotion for Charles. "We'll try."

Charles was being held in a high security cell equipped with a bed and private bathroom. His furniture was comfortable, and he had a small kiosk for ordering his own food and drink. Dani assumed they were limiting his menu, but she wondered if they let him drink alcohol as they were doing with Liam. Charles was no alcoholic, but he definitely enjoyed his wine, as evidenced by his voluminous imbibing of Pinot Noir during his visits to the cottage on Omey Island. Dani was rapidly forming the opinion that the people of this future time were more lenient, in general, than those of her time. More forgiving. And it didn't feel wrong.

The two women were allowed entry into the cell, completely constructed of OIM, as was nearly everything in this time. Charles was not bound in any way, but there was no doubt the AI that monitored the room was on high alert and would stun him if he made any aggressive move toward them. He was dressed in an orange skinsuit, denoting his status as a prisoner, and his long, dark hair was tied back in a ponytail, accentuating his sharp features. His hands were folded behind his back. The expression on his face when he saw them was one of surprise, but he smiled as he approached and shook both their hands vigorously.

"You've returned to 2253," he said, his British accent still perfectly polite.

"2254," said Aideen. "Losin' track of time, Charles?"

"Oh dear," he said. "How time flies when you're having fun! Please ladies, do you have time to sit and chat? Perhaps a glass of wine?"

"I was wondering about that," said Dani. "So they let you drink in here? I mean, you're a convicted murderer and time travel felon, Charles. That just doesn't seem, normal."

Charles pressed his lips together. "I can see your point of view," he said. "But you see, they still want things from me. Specifically, they want to know what I know about OIM. So they bribe me with these small favors. I tell them a little of what they want to hear, and they give me wine. So far, it's been a fair trade as far as I'm concerned, but I'm afraid their patience is running thin and they want to know more."

"Can't they just get you to tell them what you know with the Ticklers?" asked Dani.

"Actually, no," said Charles. "I found a way to program my brain to resist the Ticklers. A little touch of OIM with the right programming before bed every night, and my brain made some adjustments. They can't even kill me with those things, but old-fashioned guns still work, and they have those too."

"Well then," said Aideen, wanting to move the conversation away from this morose topic. "Let's have some wine!"

"Pinot Noir?" he asked, remembering.

Both women nodded.

"Three Pinot Noirs," said Charles, and the table they had gathered around produced the wine in shining glasses.

The three sat and raised their wineglasses off the table.

"A toast, then," said Charles. "To one of my oldest friends, Aideen, and to the person who ended my reign as the King of Time Travel, Dani. Let us hope that time can come back into balance, now that I am retired." He raised his glass. "To the balance of time!"

"To the balance of time," the two women toasted, and the three glasses clinked.

The wine tasted good to Dani and she felt the warmth of it traveling into her body, feeling a wave of nostalgia for all they had lost. They were a long distance from when and where she had hoped to live out the rest of her days.

"What happened, Charles?" she asked. "Why did you do it? Was it so important to gain eternal life that you were willing to kill others to achieve it?"

Charles was quiet for a moment. And then a tear rolled down his cheek, and he lowered his head. "I lost myself," he said. "I literally lost my mind. My experimenting with OIM changed me. As you've just heard, I had no hesitancy to try my experiments on myself. Some worked, some didn't. I lost my mind in the process."

"Is the damage permanent?" asked Dani, and Charles brightened.

"The only thing that seems permanent is my resistance to Ticklers," he said. "But the thing about any kind of OIM infusion into the human body is that you always want more. It's a bit like being a heroin addict, I'm afraid. The high always ends, and then you need more."

"So you've gone through withdrawals?" asked Dani.

"Yes, but thankfully those were not as physically painful as what a heroin addict experiences. Mentally, however, it was challenging. I was on suicide watch for about two weeks while I kicked the OIM habit."

"So does Annette know you're, well, rehabilitated, at least regarding OIM?" asked Dani.

"She knows I'm not crazy anymore," said Charles. "But what does it matter? The crimes were committed and I must pay for them. I *deserve* to pay for them."

"I think Annette would like to know if you're really back to your old self, like, all the way back. Like when you two first met."

"Did you know that Annette and I were, together, for a while?" he asked, and Dani's question about Annette's affection for Charles seemed to be answered, but she wanted to make sure.

"I know you worked together," she said. "Are you saying it was more than that?"

Charles paused, reminiscing, it seemed.

"For a while," he mused.

Aideen seemed to care little about what might have happened long ago between Charles and Annette and abruptly changed the subject.

"Do you know why Dani and I are here, in the future?" she asked.

"I believe they've made it completely illegal, forward or backward, haven't they?" he asked.

"Indeed," replied Aideen. "And they had to clean up the mess you made in the past as best they could, so they brought all of the time links to live here in the future. That way we can't change 'the balance of time' any more than we already have."

"Time is indeed a delicate thing, isn't it?" he said.

"It 'tis."

Silence enveloped the room as the three considered all the things they'd done that might have affected the future, each one knowing it was impossible to fully predict the ramifications of even the slightest change to the past. Charles was melancholy, but also seemed happy to be spending time with two people he'd shared any number of adventures with, even though the last few had been as adversaries.

"It wasn't all bad, was it?" he asked.

"How do you mean, Charles?" asked Dani.

"I mean, I did some good too. Look at you two. You wouldn't have had the opportunity to fall in love if not for me."

"True," said Dani.

"And Aideen and her mother got rich because of me introducing them to time travel. That's not so bad."

"Also true," said Aideen.

"And I set some fairly strict rules to prevent the time links from changing the balance of time, didn't I?"

"You did," said Aideen. "But then you went and broke them all yourself!"

Charles laughed at that. "I did, didn't I? What a hypocrite I am. A good for nothing hypocrite." He bowed his head, wallowing in self-pity again, or pretending to. Regardless, Dani didn't want to leave on such a sour note, so she added one more thing to the conversation.

"You saved my parents' lives, Charles."

Charles's head came up, an inquiring look on his face.

"I did? I don't remember that. How did it happen?"

"Because I knew my future, I became aware that my parents would be killed in a car accident in the summer of 2023. But we got them out of that time. They're here with us, Charles. And glad to be here. Without you, we would never have known and they would be gone. Thank you."

Charles was smiling again, energized somewhat by Dani's revelation.

"I am so happy for you, Dani," he said, and his sincerity was evident. "And I'm encouraged that at least a little good came from my foolhardy adventure."

The three finished their wine and Dani and Aideen got up to leave. Charles stood and walked them to the edge of the cell. A door opening appeared in the wall.

"Will you visit me again?" he asked. "Please."

"For sure," said Dani. "It's been good to see you, Charles. I hope someday we can help you make up for some of it. And I sincerely mean that."

"I hope so, too," said Charles. "Thank you. It's a lot of... weight, to live with. I'd like to lighten that load, for me, and for those I have wronged."

Chapter 22

With the exception of Liam Murphy, the transition to 2254 was going well. Because of Dani's prior experience in this era, the adjustment for her and Aideen was easiest. Dani already knew how to use the small device that facilitated travel, shopping, dining and other forms of purchasing, as well as telepathic communication, when desired. She took Aideen on several excursions outside of the Time Management building to familiarize her with how to do all of these things, including a trip to Omey Island. The cottage was gone, replaced by a building made of black stone, as were the vast majority of other homes on the island. Aideen's reaction was one of revulsion and she became resistant to moving back to the island when they obtained their full release, which would come soon. Instead, the two decided to rent an apartment and began looking around Brussels for one that might suit them.

The orientation people working with the group from the past explained that home entertainment was no longer provided by televisions, desktop computers, tablets, laptops, cell phones or augmented reality devices such as 3D viewers. In fact, most of these devices didn't even exist in 2254, except in museums. Once again, the tiny card that allowed for all other forms of activity also provided any form of entertainment one could imagine, directly to the brain. The experience could be tailored to your individual tastes, not only in terms of content, but the intensity of the experience could also be programmed into the device. The exception to all of this was that the walls of any apartment could be commanded to produce a viewing screen, similar to a television of old. And while Dani and Aideen hadn't kept a television in their cottage on Omey Island, they both preferred the viewing screen to a direct feed to their brain, at least at the beginning.

The rest of the group from the past was also doing well, save Liam. Eabha and Sadiki, having arrived a few weeks prior to Aideen, Dani and Orla, were to be released within a day or two and had already secured an apartment in one of the nearby residential areas. They would be living together. The other two individuals from 2023, Pat and Don Peterson, were thrilled, so far, with their adventure to the future, especially since they were now fully immune to disease and looked thirty years old. The technological aspects of 2254 were not beyond them as both had been fully entrenched in the technology of 2023 and could easily understand the purpose of the device that controlled all aspects of living in 2254. Both had actually scheduled to have a device imbedded in their forearms so they wouldn't have to worry about where they put it.

The ease of the transition for the people from further back in the past was a little more challenging, but was easier than one might think since they didn't need to learn how to use a computer. The device that controlled everything could be commanded telepathically, so the focus of their training had been on how to do that properly, so the device didn't mistake their command for something else entirely. The biggest hurdle for the likes of Aoife, Roisin and Ciara—other than learning English for Roisin and Ciara—was understanding how the culture in the world of 2254 worked. The norms of their time had long since been abandoned. For example, there was literally no difference in how people viewed a woman compared to a man, in fact, women could easily become men and vice versa, and no one thought twice about it. Race and country of origin were also of little consequence in how a person was treated in this time. Even religion, which was now embraced by only a small segment of the population, wasn't discriminated against. The goal of society was for all people to be free to choose how they lived their lives, as long as they in no way hurt others through their actions. This concept was somewhat foreign to the older ones, yet it was the singular area where Liam Murphy seemed to excel, without realizing he was doing it.

Liam had maintained his individuality to a degree the others had forsaken, due to their collective desire to adjust to the times and to fit in. Liam, on the other hand, was entrenched in his identity as a man of 18th century Ireland, proud and comfortable with who he was. Yes, he was a hopeless drunk, but he had lived for sixty-six years on the rough, western coast of Ireland during the 1700s and had witnessed the turn of a century while sitting comfortably at the bar of the pub on Omey Island, guzzling ale. The pub was long gone, as were all the people he had known, save the "beautiful young lass," as he had referred to Orla while regaling others about being held prisoner in a chamber of black stone, only to be saved and released by the beautiful young lass.

Liam was still enchanted by Orla, and he followed her as a sheep would follow a shepherd, always wanting to make sure she was okay, and obeying her every command. But Orla was equally smitten, drawn to Liam not only for his handsome visage and muscular physique, but also because he was her contemporary, and even though she loved Dani and Aideen with all her heart, something had been missing for her when she left 1801 to live in 2022, but in Liam she seemed to have found what she was looking for, no matter his faults.

Thus, Orla hadn't been much help in rehabilitating Liam and advancing his adjustment to 2254. Her own acclimation to the new era would have gone much smoother and proceeded far more quickly if she and Liam had been separated, but that was out of the question, for both of them. They spent all day and night together, unwilling to be detached from one another even for an instant. It was true love, and while Dani missed her friend, she was also happy for her, but at the same time concerned about her well-being, and Liam's.

"What should we do about Orla and Liam?" she asked Aideen one night, as they lay together in their room in the Time Management building.

"It's a tough one, for certain," Aideen admitted. "They love each other, without doubt, but that love is holdin' them back from adjustin' properly to this time. On the other hand, everyone talks about how people here are free to be who they are, but poor Liam is being told he can't do that."

"True," said Dani. "But you must admit, Liam will flounder if he remains as he is."

"That may be so, but I don't understand why a person can't choose to be drunk if they want to, as long as they harm no one else."

"You have a point, Aideen. And frankly, I'm sure there are people here who choose to live that way. But the thing about Liam's drinking is that it's getting in the way of him learning about this world. And in his case, because he's from the 18th century, he'll undoubtedly reveal that to anyone who'll listen, and that's not what we've all agreed to do."

The people from the past had all pledged never to disclose the "when" about their origins. The "where" was fine, and a little tap-dancing about the details, when asked about their homes and their lives, was going to be needed. But Liam was a well-known blowhard on the subject of the mysterious black stone, and he'd spent time with Charles himself, just before Charles was captured. So, it would indeed be a problem if he was turned loose without some kind of restraint on his mouth.

"Annette won't release Liam and Orla until they prove not only that they can live in this time, but also that Liam will keep quiet about when he's from," said Dani. "And she might be forced to make him take the pill to rid himself of his alcoholism in order to accomplish that."

"Annette is a patient person, Dani. She has the time and resources to wait until they come through this. And I believe they *will* come through, eventually."

"But what about us?" asked Dani. "I mean, we're ready to leave now. Are we going to desert our best friend?"

"It's not a problem," said Aideen. "We'll live nearby, and visit every day, and we'll help them to help themselves."

Aideen seemed confident, but Dani couldn't rid herself of doubt.

"I don't know," she said. "It seems like they're going to need something to shock them out of this. Some kind of… something."

"A challenge," said Aideen, firmly. "What we all need is a challenge. It's part of why we became time links to begin with."

Chapter 23

The challenge came in a completely unexpected and otherworldly way. Dani and Aideen had moved into the same residential area where all the other people from the past, except Orla and Liam, had gone to begin their lives in the new time era. Dani was pleased that her parents' adjustment was going so well. They had friends in the building, which had a great common area with many things to do, including card games and sports and restaurants. They had also volunteered at a local youth center, helping to guide young people to a better life than they might have thought possible without a nudge in the right direction. Dani and Aideen had yet to decide if they would seek employment or not, although they were beginning to get restless. Then, early one morning while they were still in bed, a telepathic message came to Dani from Annette.

I need you and Aideen to come to the Time Management building immediately.

Dani's heart jumped. *Is it Orla and Liam?* she asked.

No, they're fine, said Annette. *It's something else entirely. Please, come quickly!*

Dani and Aideen rushed over to the Time Management building and went straight to Annette's office on the 73rd floor.

Annette was behind her desk and waved them toward the two chairs that sat in front of it.

"Coffee?" she asked. "Tea?"

"Coffee would be great for me," said Aideen.

"Me as well," said Dani. "It's early."

"Two coffees," said Annette, and the side of her desk closest to the two visitors produced two steaming cups, one black and one with milk. The AI knew from experience what each of them preferred.

Aideen picked up the black coffee. "Must be somethin' big for you to call us over here before daylight, Annette."

"It is. So big I don't even know where to begin." Annette was more flustered than Dani had ever seen her and she felt the need to help.

"Whatever it is, Annette, we'll face it together," she said. "We've faced bigger challenges than whatever this is, I'm sure."

Annette raised her eyebrows in a skeptical expression. "Probably not," she said, but her voice sounded smoother, more like her old self. Dani tried not to pat herself on the back, but it seemed that her presence had become a calming force for Annette. It was like Annette believed her best chance to solve any seemingly unsolvable problem would ultimately involve Dani. But in this case, Annette was in a very big hurry, for a reason yet to be revealed. "But we need to get on with it," Annette continued. "Time is of the essence. Are you ready to hear about the latest trouble we've gotten ourselves into because of time travel?"

"I thought time travel had been abandoned completely?" asked Aideen.

"Not exactly. You may recall that when I visited you to encourage you to come to this era, I mentioned that time travel would be more 'highly restricted' than before."

"Ah yes, I do remember that," said Aideen. "But then it sounded like all forward and backward travel would be ended."

"And it has," said Annette. "But time travel has been the foundation of our space program for quite some time. It makes it very easy to send probes to places that couldn't otherwise be reached."

"I remember you telling me about this the first time we met," said Dani. "You send AI to star systems that are light years away by sending them back in time, even if only a little ways back. The time travel itself eliminates the barrier that the long distances present, as long as the programming of the location is done correctly."

Annette smiled. "It's funny, but I don't remember telling you that, because I have no memory at all of our first meeting. You erased that reality for me when you sent the team in to try to capture Charles the first time. You remember it because you were the time link that initiated the entire thing."

"Ah yes," said Dani. "But it doesn't matter. Please proceed, Annette. I'm sorry to interrupt."

"Very well," said Annette. "As I said, time travel has been the foundation of our space program for some time. It has allowed us to search for intelligent life in far off places without the need of risking human life, since we send AI units instead."

"Are you the head of the space program too, Annette?" asked Aideen.

"Of the program searching for intelligent life, yes. The rest of space exploration is handled by the commercial sector. The mining of the asteroids, the settlements on Mars and the moon. The things that our current propulsion technology allows us to reach in a reasonable amount of time, which basically limits that sector to our own solar system. Nevertheless, it's a big business and one of the world's largest employers overall."

"So what's the problem, Annette?" asked Dani. "While you don't remember, last time you told me that no intelligent life had been discovered, but you'd keep trying. And it sounds like the new law allows that."

"The new law does indeed allow that, Dani. And in answer to your first question, the problem is that our efforts have recently yielded fruit. Intelligent life has been discovered."

"Where?" asked Dani.

"In a star system that's 737 light years from Earth. The sun is an orange dwarf, which is the kind of star most compatible with the development of life, because they are very stable and have very long lives—tens of billions of years. This star, known as K296, is about half the size of our sun, but has several planets in the Habitable Zone."

"What's the Habitable Zone?" asked Aideen.

"It's the area of a star system where the temperatures will allow for liquid water to be present, which is an essential building block for life. The planet where intelligent life was discovered, known by us as K296e, is in the Habitable Zone of this star system, although it was not one we prioritized, because the average temperatures there are significantly lower than on Earth, but we did ultimately send a probe to that system. K296e is a big planet, 1.75 times the volume of Earth and with a mass 1.5 times greater, and while the poles are large and frozen, the central area of the planet reaches temperatures where life could develop. What's even more significant is that the solar flux on the planet is identical to that of Earth, meaning that conditions on the planet are stable enough to foster the development of intelligent life. And it appears that is what happened."

"How do you know that?" asked Aideen.

"Because the beings from that planet are now circling Earth in a ship the size of a small moon, threatening to destroy all human life if we don't cooperate."

Chapter 24

How did they get here?" asked Dani.

"They simply appeared, yesterday, just as we do when we use time travel to go somewhere."

"So they have time travel too," said Dani.

"I don't think so," said Annette.

"Why?" asked Dani.

"Because they've demanded we supply them with *our* time travel technology."

"How do they know we have time travel technology?" asked Aideen.

"First, I want to make it clear that they didn't find out from my department. The AI probes we send out to these faraway star systems are loaded with a basic history of Earth. Nothing more. We would never disclose any of our most advanced technologies, especially time travel, because we wouldn't want to encourage an alien species that didn't have the technology to covet it. But that's exactly what seems to have happened here."

"How did they find out?" asked Aideen.

"You're not going to believe this," said Annette.

Aideen shook her head, already reaching the answer before Annette revealed it.

"Charles," she said.

Annette nodded.

"How did he do it?" asked Dani.

"In short, OIM," said Annette.

"How do you mean?" asked Dani.

"I think Charles mentioned to you during your meeting with him that we're trying to learn all he knows about OIM. His experiments aimed at making the human body immortal, by blending it with OIM, went much further than we had expected. He was nearly there when we finally captured him."

"But what does that have to do with the aliens knowing about time travel?" asked Dani.

"It seems Charles's experiments on himself have changed him in ways that enable him to communicate subliminally with OIM, in a language other than the basic programming languages we typically infuse it with."

Dani was beginning to get nervous. "So OIM has its own language? Is that what I'm hearing?"

"It would appear so," said Annette. "And I'm ashamed to say, we had no idea."

"Charles used the OIM, the OIM in this very building, to send a message to the aliens," said Aideen, always the first to figure out a mystery.

"He did," said Annette.

"What languages do these aliens understand?" asked Aideen.

"Certainly English," said Annette. "All the messages we've received from them have been in English. By the way, the English translation of what they call themselves is the 'Land People.'"

"That's an odd name for people in a huge space ship to have," said Dani.

"Maybe the translation's off," said Annette. "Although land could be what they want. Our land!"

"What?" asked Aideen.

"The Land People have threatened to kill all human life on Earth if we don't provide the time travel technology to them within twenty-four hours. And three of those hours have already elapsed."

Dani pressed her lips together. "Another world crisis then. That's just great! Do we know how they intend to do that? You know, kill us all?"

"We have no idea," said Annette. "But it's a threat we take seriously. After all, they traveled seven hundred thirty-seven light years to get here, and apparently didn't use time travel to do it. Who knows what weapons they might have."

"But why are we here?" asked Aideen. "I would think you have more impressive and credentialed advisors than us, Annette. Truth be told, we shouldn't even know about this."

"All true, except the last point," she responded. "The whole world knows. You don't need a telescope to see that big ball in the sky."

"Okay fine," said Aideen. "But that still doesn't explain why Dani and I are here. What do you want from us, Annette?'

"It's not so much what we want from you, Aideen. It's what Charles wants."

"Feckin' Charles," said Aideen, shaking her head from side to side in disgust.

Chapter 25

Further discussions with Annette revealed that Charles had been negotiating with the Land People, unbeknownst to the leaders of EarthGov—including Annette. He had effectively coopted EarthGov's authority by directing the OIM to block the outgoing signals being sent by EarthGov to the alien ship. Both EarthGov's and his signals had been originating from the Time Management building itself and with his blocking of the EarthGov signal, Charles had been in direct contact with them, posing as a crisis negotiator for the government. Luckily, his ruse had been quickly discovered and his communication with the Land People had been terminated, but not without its desired effect. The aliens wanted Charles on their ship. Annette, however, had drawn the line on that. Charles would not be going to the Land People's ship, and if that meant the end of the world, so be it. In her mind, having him on that ship would have the same result as if the twenty-four-hour time limit elapsed with the aliens' demands unmet.

Knowing that Annette wouldn't budge, and realizing that his fate would be the same as everyone else on Earth if a solution wasn't found, Charles proposed to Annette that

Aideen and Dani be brought on board as replacement "negotiators," emphasizing that he could easily sell this to the aliens. And while Annette's superiors found this proposal ludicrous, Annette had seen these two in action before and actually had more confidence in them than virtually anyone she knew. Moreover, Charles had spiced up his offer, making it too potentially lucrative to ignore. He promised he would arm Dani and Aideen with the ability to destroy the alien ship and escape unharmed. However, his secret would be revealed only to those two, and only if a written agreement was drawn up to provide him early release. He further agreed to a memory adjustment, which would remove his knowledge of OIM and time travel from his brain prior to his release, meaning he would no longer pose a threat to humanity. The deal was struck. Now a deal needed to be made with Aideen and Dani.

"I mean, we've already saved your world once," said Dani. "Isn't that enough, Annette?"

"I know, Dani," she replied. "And of course, if you two are unwilling to go, then we'll try to come up with something else. Frankly, I don't know what that is, but it will have to happen soon."

"It's obvious," said Aideen. "You'll have to use time travel to end this thing."

"We're prepared to do that," said Annette. "In fact, we're prepared to do anything that's necessary to end this threat. But we don't know if we can penetrate that ship's forcefield, even with time travel. It has a very powerful one. And there are too many unknowns regarding the Land People's planet to have any idea what the strategy for a time travel mission to prevent this situation would be."

"How are we supposed to get off the ship before it's destroyed?" asked Aideen. "Without time travel."

"First," said Annette, "why don't you speak with Charles? He seems to have answers that we don't have. Hear him out, then make your decision about what you want to do. Can that work?"

"All right," said Aideen.

"Okay," said Dani.

The two were escorted to an AI-free holding cell that Charles had demanded for the meeting. He wanted no eavesdropping and swore he would know if they tried. Based on what he'd accomplished so far, from a high security cell monitored by powerful AI, they believed him. Dani and Aideen entered the room. Charles stood toward the back, his arms folded behind his back and his head held high, as if he were proud of his latest disruption to EarthGov's management of the planet. Both women were armed with shooting weapons—guns—since the Ticklers didn't work on Charles. Charles seemed hurt.

"You think I would harm you two?" he whined. "I'm devastated." It was hard to tell if he really meant it, but you never knew with Charles. It could very well be true.

"It doesn't matter," said Aideen. "Tell us what you need to and we'll be on our way. Seems you've got yourself in the middle of yet another crisis, Charles. Now how do you propose to save the world?"

"It's a simple matter, actually," he said.

"Let me guess," said Dani. "OIM."

"Of course," said Charles.

Aideen was unimpressed. "We won't be swallowing any OIM pills, Charles, if that's what you're thinkin'."

"Hmmm," said Charles. "That does complicate things. But I have a workaround."

"Tell us," said Dani.

"The idea is for you to infect the ship with OIM while you're there. Then you leave."

"Won't the aliens notice if we bring an OIM nugget on board with us?" asked Dani.

"Of course," said Charles. "That's why I wanted your skin to be made of OIM, but still look like skin. But you won't take the pill, so we'll have to do it the old-fashioned way. We'll make your clothing out of OIM."

"And just where are you keeping all of these goodies that we need before the world comes to an end?" asked Aideen.

"Somewhere close," he said. "No need for me to tell you where. I have a means of bringing it here." Charles became quiet, concentrating it seemed. Within a few seconds, some garments sprouted from the floor of the holding cell.

"I hope I got your sizes right," he said.

Dani reached down and picked up the two pieces of clothing. They were one-pieces, similar in the appearance to the skinsuits they were wearing, just not made from their own skin.

"Will these things infect us?" she asked.

"No, Dani. I wouldn't harm you."

"I can't say you have a lot of credibility on that subject, Charles," she responded.

"People change," he said. "I want my freedom, yes, but not at the expense of your lives. The suits are designed to leave microscopic particles on any non-living surface they touch. Just brush against some equipment, or walls, or whatever. The OIM will begin working immediately, but the full effect will be delayed for an hour or so, and by then you should be off the ship."

"I have another question for you, Charles," said Aideen.

"What's that, dear?"

"Can you escape from here whenever you want?"

"I'm not sure, to be honest," he said. "The OIM lets me do some things and not others. It's as if it knows what's good for the Earth, and what's not."

"It let you talk to the aliens," said Dani.

"It did."

"And it let you bring us those clothes," said Aideen.

"Indeed."

"It seems you think the OIM wants Dani and me to do this," said Aideen.

"Perhaps the OIM understands how limited our options really are."

"Okay, but I have one more question, Charles," said Dani. "Why Aideen and me? Why are you insisting it must be the two of us that board the alien ship?"

"That's an easy one," he said. "You two will do the right thing. You won't be thinking about what's best for yourselves, like I would. You'll be thinking about the rest of us."

"Fine," said Aideen. "But there's plenty of others, better trained than us, who would do the same thing."

"I disagree," said Charles. "You two have been backward and forward in time, on numerous occasions, and your ability to adapt to unfamiliar circumstances is beyond reproach. There's no one else in this time era, other than me, with that kind of experience. And you're the people I know, and I trust you. I want to make it through this too, ladies."

"Well, thank you Charles, I guess," said Dani. "Anything else we need to know?"

"Yes. I need to be in the control room with Annette and her team during your mission. I might be able to help in case something doesn't go as planned."

Chapter 26

They gathered in the control room above the time station auditorium to begin the mission. Charles was there, along with Annette, Dani, Aideen, and a complement of control room and military personal. Annette had refused to let Dani and Aideen say goodbye to their loved ones, for security reasons, and they weren't happy about it. As a compromise, Annette allowed them to record voice messages, which she promised to play for the people they cared about should they fail to return, yet the world somehow survive and continue on.

Charles was connected to the Land People's ship and quickly arranged for Aideen and Dani to take his place, emphasizing that they were the most experienced time travelers on Earth, other than him. The alien obsession with time travel was satiated by this request. The Land People beamed a canister full of their air down to the control room for analysis. This beaming technology was of great interest to Annette, and she asked Dani and Aideen to find out what they could about it while they were on the ship. The air sample was analyzed and found to have a 27 percent concentration of oxygen, which was higher than the 21 percent of Earth's. The balance of the alien atmosphere was virtually all nitrogen, as it was on Earth, so the air onboard the ship would be completely breathable, as verified by experts who worked for Annette. Dani and Aideen were told they very likely wouldn't even notice a difference in the air, especially since the higher gravity, expected to be 50 percent greater than Earth's gravity, would cause greater exertion on their part and require more oxygen.

The Land People next beamed down two devices that would identify which of the humans in the room were Dani and Aideen. They indicated they could "see" all of them, and wanted to make sure to bring the correct individuals on board. Dani and Aideen were instructed to simply hold the devices in their hands when the time for beaming to the Land People's ship arrived.

The two had been fully briefed on the negotiation. While no one expected them to be successful, their goal was to buy time. They were to invite the Land People to come directly to the time station in the Time Management building after informing them it was the only one in existence on Earth. The story was that the Land People would be allowed to commandeer the station to ensure that it was not used against them, and training on the use of the technology could begin. The expected outcome, however, based on Charles's plan, was that the alien ship would be destroyed, Dani and Aideen would be returned to Earth safely using time travel technology, and the aliens who had transported down to the time station would be captured and imprisoned, for further interrogation.

The Land People initiated a countdown, which appeared on the screens in the control room, suggesting the aliens could also take control of the Earth's computer networks. This exacerbated the feeling of helplessness shared by all in the room, save Charles, who seemed downright jovial, experiencing the high of yet another moment in the center of a worldwide crisis.

The countdown reached "zero," and Dani and Aideen disappeared. Dani didn't lose consciousness in the way it happened with time travel. The feeling was like being in one room, blinking, then being in a completely different room. She and Aideen arrived in a vast, circular chamber, several hundred feet in diameter and with a ceiling at least fifty feet high. It was some kind of auditorium, with seats that circled the central floor on which they stood, rising up toward the ceiling around them.

Dani estimated the auditorium held well over 1,000 seats, and they were all full of aliens. One of them on the bottom row stood and approached them. It was slender, almost frail-looking, and had two legs and two arms, but was even shorter than Orla. She couldn't tell if the being was wearing clothes or not, but there was no sign of sexual organs, and the color of the skin/clothing was nearly pure white. The hands had five fingers, but two of them were thumbs, both on the outside and opposable. All the fingers were around six inches long and seemed to be jointed in five or six places. The alien's head wasn't overly large, but it was bald. It had two large round eyes, a sharp nose and a mouth filled with small teeth, which were easy to see because the creature had virtually no lips, the skin and flesh of the face surrounding the mouth turning in a 90-degree angle and ending at the teeth. And while the creature had eyes, a nose, mouth and teeth, it had no ears, and it soon became apparent why. A voice entered Dani's head.

Welcome to our home, said the voice, and it sounded female. *This station is called "Diaspora One," in your language.*

Dani was alarmed at the name of the ship; she knew what diaspora meant and found the name unsettling because it brought the intentions of the aliens into focus. But she needed to concentrate on the mission and keep things moving forward, while the OIM did its work.

"Thank you. We are honored to be here. I am known as Dani and this is Aideen."

Dani held her arm out and waved it toward Aideen. She wasn't feeling the tug of extra gravity she'd been told to expect. On the contrary, she felt very light, as if the gravity here was actually less than on Earth. She also felt cold on her face and hands, which weren't covered by the protective suit, and she remembered that Annette had mentioned the Land People's planet was colder than Earth.

My name is Clarion, came the voice in her head. *Please, let us sit and talk.*

The being named Clarion approached the table and sat and Dani and Aideen settled into the chairs. The fit was a little tight and their knees brushed against the bottom of the table, which Dani figured would be a good thing, to help the OIM spread.

May I offer you food or drink? asked Clarion.

"Not for me, thank you," said Dani, wondering what she might have been offered if she'd said yes.

"No thank you, Clarion," said Aideen.

Very well, she said. *Perhaps I can tell you something about our history, so that you may better understand our need for time travel technology.*

Clarion explained to Dani and Aideen that the Land People no longer lived on the planet K296e, which they called "Terrene." The land surface of the planet had been rendered uninhabitable by another intelligent race that lived in its oceans—whose name was unsurprisingly translated to them as "Water People"—over 600 years previously. The Water People had melted a large portion of the vast ice-covered poles, covering all the land with water. When it had become clear to the Land People they would not be able to curtail the flooding, they dispersed ten ships, each like the one they were on now, to the far reaches of the galaxy, to look for other habitable planets. Diaspora One was assigned to explore worlds zero to 1,000 light years from Terrene, meaning it also had the responsibility of continuing to observe the home planet, in the event it became habitable again. Each of the other ships was assigned a 1,000 light year segment of space, with Diaspora Ten sent the farthest away, to explore the segment of space 9,000 to 10,000 light years from their planet, with additional permission to go further if circumstances presented themselves that showed promise.

Clarion also pointed out that she was translating their own measurement systems to the ones used by Earth, to make it easier for them to understand the guidelines of their Diaspora Mission. She explained that each ship was equipped with a limited number of message probes, which were to be sent back to orbit Terrene and to be picked up and reviewed by Diaspora One, so updates on the various diaspora missions could be received by the vessel closest to home. The probes came through for several dozen years, informing the crew of Diaspora One that habitable planets discovered by the other ships were inevitably occupied by other intelligent life, and they had never been welcomed. Several ships had been attacked, their last messages in some cases indicating they did not expect to survive. Eventually, the message drones stopped coming and the diaspora ships lost touch with each other, and the fate of their race faded into mystery, except for their own circumstances on Diaspora One.

The Land People of Diaspora One had lived in space for over 600 years, staying close to Terrene most of the time, hoping to one day return. They sometimes ventured away from the planet to explore other potentially habitable worlds, but experienced the same kind of rejection that had been reported by the other diaspora vessels. They were forced to remain in space, and because creating artificial gravity took a vast amount of energy, the gravity levels on the ship were set to only half the gravity on Terrene, explaining why Dani felt lighter on this ship. The lower gravity had changed the Land People's bodies to the point where returning to Terrene would be virtually impossible, even if the land reappeared, unless therapies were developed to rebuild their bodies to something comparable to what they'd had while living on the surface. The original Land People were shorter than the ones on the ship, and built like tanks, to withstand the higher gravity of Terrene, but those physiques had long since disappeared as new generations were born and raised in space, taller and more frail than their ancestors.

The probe from Earth had intrigued them in terms of the possibilities of inhabiting the planet, especially since the recording the probe brought with it had claimed the Earth was a peaceful planet. But when they arrived and heard of the time travel technology (from Charles) they realized they might now be able to turn back the clock and undo the devastation the Water People had inflicted upon their home. The current race of Land People could never live on Terrene, but if they could manipulate time, their ancestors might never have to leave the planet at all.

Dani found it odd that this Clarion was so polite and informative. It was as if she was looking for a way around destroying all human life by providing the reasons why they needed time travel. It didn't really make sense to her because these people seemed peaceful and quite civilized. But the threat to her species by the Land People had been made, and she and Aideen were the emissaries of Earth assigned to stop them, so she carried on with the plan, albeit with trepidation.

"I'm very sorry to hear of your fate," said Dani. "But perhaps when we explain how time travel works, you may reconsider your options. Sometimes changing the past doesn't work out the way it was expected to. By the way, we were wondering how your travel technology works, if I may ask? Frankly, it seems quite similar to time travel."

It is based on the principal of Molecular Reconstruction, said Clarion. *The key to it working is our scope technology, which isn't based on light at all, so it's not restricted by the speed of light. The scope tech is a highly guarded secret, and there is a small guild among our people, whose sole responsibility is to pass down the knowledge of the scopes to the next generation. Our scopes are very powerful, and if the scopes can locate a spot, no matter how far away, we can program a trip to go there. It is the same as the beaming technology we used to send the air sample to you and to bring you to us.*

Dani was intrigued, suspecting that the missing element in the Land People's technology was the ability to program in a time destination, but any follow-up questions she might have raised were abruptly cut off by Clarion.

What news do you bring then, regarding our request to learn about your time travel technology? she asked.

Dani found it paradoxical that Clarion had referred to their demand regarding time travel as a "request," but she was undeterred.

"We have good news, Clarion," she said. "We invite you to send a team to our time station, which is the only one in existence on Earth. We will train you in the technology, and tell you what we have learned from our experience with time travel."

Very well, she said. *We will go now.* As Clarion spoke, three other Land People in the front row stood and approached the table. The four aliens stood together, as if ready to travel. Dani and Aideen tried to join them, but some unseen force caused them to sit back in the chairs, and held them there.

You will wait here until we return, said Clarion, and then the four Land People disappeared.

Chapter 27

W ell, that didn't quite go as planned," whispered Aideen. "Agreed," said Dani. "I'd say we have about thirty minutes before it gets really bad, for us!"

While Dani and Aideen were assessing their options, which were basically nonexistent, three other Land People approached. They all looked similar to Clarion, in both height and stature, but each of them had individual features in their faces that made them unique—a wider nose, a different shape to the eyes, mouths and teeth, slightly varying heights. In this way, it became clear that just as humans had unique individual features, so did the Land People. But they all seemed to communicate telepathically, as Clarion had, and when a thought entered her mind, she had no idea which of the three had sent it.

My name is Zephyr, said a voice different from Clarion's, but still of a female nature.

"Which one are you?" asked Aideen, obviously having received the same message.

The being standing on the left raised its hand.

"How can we help you, Zephyr?" asked Aideen.

Something is happening to our ship, she said. *Do you know what it is?*

Dani realized that even if she told the Land People what was happening, they wouldn't be able to stop it. But she needed more information in order to decide what to do next.

"Zephyr," she said, "would you truly have destroyed all the humans living on Earth if we did not comply with your request to supply the time travel technology?"

Zephyr took a moment before responding, as if she were communicating with others. Then she answered.

The truth is that we have no offensive weapons, she said. *The answer is no.*

"So you were bluffing?" asked Dani.

Yes, I am ashamed to say.

Dani turned to Aideen. "Do you know what I'm thinking?"

"I think I do," said Aideen. "It's not a bad idea. Would likely save our lives, and theirs. Let's go for it."

Dani turned back to the aliens. "Zephyr, your ship will be destroyed within a matter of minutes. We offer you sanctuary on our planet. How many of you are there on this ship?"

Around one thousand five hundred.

"Are they all in this room?"

Yes.

"Will your beaming technology allow us all to be beamed at once?"

This entire room has transporter functionality. As long as we all go to the same location, yes, we can all go. It will take a lot of power, but our ship's fusion engine can produce what is needed, if we go quickly.

"Okay," said Dani. "The place where your four colleagues went is large enough to hold all of us."

Suddenly, a tremor passed through the room, causing it to shake.

The ship is breaking apart, said Zephyr. *We accept your offer of sanctuary. The beaming will take place in thirty seconds, after all power is diverted to the transfer station. I've instructed one of our people to bring the backup file of our database, which will contain essential information for later use.*

"Okay," said Dani.

The next thirty seconds were the longest of Dani's life. As they waited for the power to build and facilitate the transfer, the shaking within the ship became more predominant. The walls of the room started cracking and air hissed out, exiting directly into the vacuum of space. But the walls seemed to heal themselves and the hissing stopped.

This room is strong, said Zephyr. *We will make it.*

A few seconds after the words from Zephyr entered her mind, the transfer took place. Dani and Aideen were now on the floor of the time station on Earth, standing next to Zephyr and her two colleagues, looking up at 1,500 aliens sitting in the seats of the station's auditorium.

Chapter 28

Annette's voice came into Dani's mind. *What just happened?* Dani responded. *These people are not hostile, Annette. They were bluffing about destroying all human life on Earth. So we offered them sanctuary, and saved ourselves in the process.*

We were just about to initiate a time travel transfer of you two according to instructions from Charles. The shields went down, just as he'd predicted. You would have been okay.

But these beings would all be dead, said Dani. *Annette, can you come down here, or can you send someone down here? Also, can you link me into the public address system for the auditorium. I need to address these people.*

I'll come down. Patching you in now.

Dani waited a few seconds then began speaking.

"Testing," she said, and heard her voice come over the auditorium speakers. "Hello, Land People," she began. "Welcome… to Earth. I've spoken with the leadership of the planet and one of them will join us soon. They were not expecting you to be here, but as long as your intentions remain peaceful, you will not be harmed."

Zephyr approached Dani and took her hand in both of her own. Her touch felt cold, but the gesture was meant to be a kind one. *We thank you,* said Zephyr. *It is our own foolishness and impetuous nature which caused this, and we apologize. We are a peaceful people and should never have tried to pretend otherwise. May I ask you, Dani, where our four colleagues are?*

"They are here," said Annette, entering the room, accompanied by the four Land People who had come first to the time station, as well as a complement of military personnel. Annette's voice switched over to the broadcast speakers. "My name is Annette Li. I am the Minister of Time Management here on Earth. You are currently sitting in the only time station on this planet." Annette gestured toward Clarion and her three companions. "Your colleagues have already told us that your nourishment is completely plant-based, and we are working to prepare that now. They have also explained how your clothing recycles all your waste, either as water for your body or as an inert, odorless gas released into the air, so the need for facilities such as the ones humans use is not required. This simplifies things. What we would like to do now is to begin creating a database, which will include each of your identities. We will then provide you with an identification token that will allow us to keep track of you. We are taking steps to create lodging for you here in this building. It won't take long because the material this building is constructed of can be reprogrammed and repurposed quite easily. Please be patient. Our staff will set up stations here on the floor and you will be called down. Please remain seated until you are called."

Aideen addressed Annette. "Do you believe these people are no threat to us?"

"Yes," said Annette. "As soon as we told Clarion's group what was happening to their ship, they were quick to spill the beans about their ruse. We were about to put them in touch with the ship when you and your group appeared."

"Well then," said Aideen, smiling and taking Dani's hand. "The world is saved, again."

Annette smiled back. "Yes, and thank you two, again. You are braves souls and the world of 2254 is lucky to have you."

"What can we tell our friends and family, about the Land People?" asked Dani.

"You can tell them they're here," said Annette. "We aren't going to be able to keep such a big secret from the world. But we'd prefer that the circumstances which led to the Land People coming here are restricted to saying they had a problem with their ship and asked for asylum here on Earth. It would be unwise to reveal their threat of annihilation, wouldn't you agree?"

"Yes," said Dani. "Especially since they didn't really mean it!" The three shared a laugh, and relief cascaded throughout the room.

"Where's Charles?" asked Aideen.

"He's back in his cell, temporarily," said Annette. "But based on the agreement we made with him, he'll be released soon, after his memory is cleared of all his knowledge of OIM and time travel. It's such a waste, really. His knowledge of OIM is so far beyond what any of us know that it could be very beneficial to all the people of Earth, if he would only share it. But that wasn't part of the deal."

"What's the hurry?" asked Aideen. "After all, there's no certainty the world is out of danger. What if these aliens infect us with something, or have some other unknown means of hurting us?" Aideen winked and Annette caught on.

"Yes, that's absolutely correct," she said, nodding her head vigorously, a feigned expression of concern on her face. "I'm sure

Charles and his legal counsel will understand that some time will be needed to further assess the threat these aliens pose."

"Indeed," said Aideen. "Would you like us to break the news to him that his release will be delayed? Perhaps we can encourage him to be more cooperative in his sharing of OIM knowledge as well."

"That's a great idea!" said Annette. "He actually asked to see you two anyway, before his memory is wiped. Go ahead and speak with him and let me know his frame of mind. I remind you, however, that while you are both true heroes, you are not representatives of EarthGov in the negotiation with Charles. If you make any headway with him, please inform him you have to seek my approval. Understood?"

"Of course, Annette," said Aideen. "You've got your hands full here, anyway. Let us worry about Charles, for now."

Chapter 29

Dani and Aideen went to see Charles. He was sitting at his table, drinking wine.

"Ah, my friends," he said. "Please come in. And I hope you don't mind me calling you friends, because these days I don't have many."

"Not a problem," said Aideen, as they joined Charles at his table. "Dani and I are forgiving people, and we both also believe that everyone can change. What about you, Charles? Do you believe that?"

"I do," said Charles. "But I've got further to go than most to become a model citizen. May I offer you some wine?"

"Sure," said Aideen.

"Why not?" said Dani.

"Pinot Noir for my guests," said Charles, and the wine sprouted from the tabletop. Charles raised his glass. "A toast then, to old friends." Dani and Aideen clinked glasses with Charles. "I wanted to see you one more time," he continued, "before they wipe my memory. Since they'll be eliminating my memories of time travel, I don't think I'll know you after that."

"That's quite sad, Charles, don't you think?" asked Dani.

"It is," he said. "But it's the cost of my freedom."

"And that's just a small part of it," Dani continued. "You'll also be losing the knowledge it took a lifetime to build."

"I know," said Charles, pensive. "I know."

"What if there were a different way to go about this?" asked Aideen.

Charles raised his head and looked directly at Aideen. "How do you mean?"

"There've been whispers that your release might be delayed," said Aideen. "Until it becomes clear the aliens are no longer a threat."

"Those wimps?" he asked in a loud voice. "Why, they caved as soon as we told them their ship would be going down. You weren't here but the one called Clarion almost broke down in tears! They're no danger to us."

"That's very likely the case," said Dani. "And I'm sure it won't delay your release for long. But what Aideen is saying is that it might give you time to pursue an alternative plan, where you can keep your memories and still have your freedom."

"How?" he asked, incredulous.

"Make us an offer," said Aideen. "If it's reasonable we'll take it to Annette and try to get her to agree to it."

Charles took a long draft from his wine, nearly emptying the glass. He placed the glass on the table and leaned back in his chair. The two women waited, giving his devious mind time to think things through. Then he asked a question. "Did you learn anything about the aliens when you were on board their ship?"

"As a matter of fact we did," said Dani.

Dani recounted the brief history of the Land People as told to them by Clarion. How the Water People had flooded their land and forced them off their planet. How they yearned to return, but having lived in space for over 600 years, their bodies could no longer take the high gravity even if the land were returned to them. They were hoping to use time travel to turn back the clock and regain their homeland, not for themselves, but for their ancestors. Charles took all of this in, clearly intrigued.

"Fascinating," he said, "and quite tragic." He told the table to give him more wine and as he drank, it was obvious his powerful mind was churning. Then he spoke. "What is Annette going to do with these aliens?" he asked.

"An interesting question," said Aideen. "We have no idea. Would you care to speculate?"

Charles didn't hesitate. "I can't imagine her releasing them into society as she's done with you people from the past. Does that mean she'll simply keep them here in the Time Management building, forever? How long do these things live? Do they breed?"

"We don't know the answers to any of these questions," said Dani. "Where are you going with this, Charles?"

"Tell Annette I would like to present her with a plan on how to handle the aliens," he said.

"Can you give us any specifics?" asked Aideen. "To help us sway her to your cause."

"Tell her I have devised a plan to return the Land People to their planet of origin."

"But there's no land there anymore," said Dani.

"We'll make the land," said Charles.

"How?" asked Dani.

"OIM, of course."

132

Chapter 30

A meeting was arranged between Annette and Charles, with Dani and Aideen present. Charles explained that OIM was capable of using sea water as a raw material for building structures, when programmed correctly, and could also go deep underwater, to the bottom of the ocean if necessary, to access rock and soil needed for building and to bind the new island to solid bedrock at its foundation. Therefore, it would be possible to create as much land as they wanted on Terrene, using OIM, and to build it high enough above the water's surface to protect the land from any further sea level rises initiated by the Water People. The underside of the OIM could be made hard enough to be impervious to all but nuclear explosions, so the assessment of that issue would depend to some degree on the knowledge of the Land People regarding the Water People's technology. The OIM could also make soil for growing crops, and buildings for shelter and any other use the Land People desired.

"What about the gravity?" asked Anette. "It's twice as high as what they've been living in for six hundred years."

"But only fifty percent higher than the gravity on Earth," said Charles. "Spending time here will help them prepare themselves for life back on Terrene. We can also get them on an exercise regimen and begin drug therapy to build them up."

Annette added credibility to Charles's assertion. "We have drugs to help people returning from the moon and Mars colonies to adjust to Earth's higher gravity when they return," she said.

"Developed by the Community of Minds, no doubt," said Charles.

Annette nodded. "Yes, they can study the Land People and make some adaptations, assuming we go forward with the relocation project you're proposing."

"Why wouldn't we?" asked Charles.

"That depends on what you want, Charles. What is it?"

"I want to keep my memories," he said. "And to be free."

Annette paused, her trademark method of buying time while she thought something through. Then she resumed the negotiation. "I don't see how that would work, Charles. You've already told us your plan for the Land People, and while it's a good one, we don't need you to implement it. And you've proven time and time again that you can't be trusted. The knowledge you have is too dangerous to allow you to be free while still possessing it."

"I suppose that depends on where I go, doesn't it? After all, Annette, have you considered that an OIM specialist will be needed on site to implement the land creation project?"

"Of course," she said. "You may recall that OIM was once my primary area of expertise." Annette had worked for Charles in the early days of time travel, building the first time station with him, the one that he stole and began using clandestinely to build the Time Chain. "Anyway, OIM projects don't last forever, Charles. What would you do when it's completed?"

"I'd stay, of course. Help build a human colony on a planet 737 light years away. It would be quite a coup for your space program, wouldn't you say?"

"We need more than one person to establish a colony, Charles."

"Just as you needed more than one to establish the colonies on the moon and on Mars," he countered. "There would be more volunteers than you could accommodate. That's my belief."

Annette fell silent, but Aideen kept the conversation going.

"And there's also the matter of your OIM knowledge, Charles. Are you willing to share that, before you leave, as part of this deal?"

"Yes," he said. "I'm prepared to do that."

As Dani reflected on Charles's proposal, she felt it was too good of a deal for Annette to pass up. First, the issue of what to do with the Land People would be handled. Yes, they would have to agree to allow for an Earth settlement on their planet, but there were some positives in that, especially the potential of combining the strength of the two species' technologies to advance both. Second, the settlement would be the first on an Earth-like world, where the air was breathable, and where many different alien species could be studied. The Water People were an unknown, and more would have to be discussed regarding their capabilities and intentions. In fact, if anything could derail the project before it got off the ground, it would be the potential threat of the Water People to the well-being of the Land People and the settlers from Earth. And the final leg of the stool was Charles. Not only had he agreed to provide his knowledge of OIM, he would be gone from Earth. But because Charles was Charles, and the risk of him causing problems on Terrene was always present, any volunteers would have to be briefed on such risks, and perhaps some of them would be assigned to "manage" Charles as well. Overall, however, there was tremendous potential in what Charles had proposed. But it would be up to Annette to decide what happened next.

"Charles, thank you for your offer. I must admit, it's worth serious consideration. I'll form an exploratory committee, of which you will be a member, and we'll begin to compile the information we will need to make a more informed decision."

"Thank you, Annette," said Charles. "I'm at your service."

Chapter 31

The Land People were overjoyed about the possibility of resettling Terrene, and were actually comforted by the thought of being joined by settlers from Earth. They admitted to being a very passive people, and while they believed humans were a peaceful species, they had also witnessed human bravery in the face of adversity. The Land People explained that their natural tendency was to run from problems rather than stand and fight, just as they had run when faced with the aggression of the Water People.

The question arose regarding how the Land People had learned English so quickly. After all, they had arrived in orbit around Earth and immediately began transmitting in English. The Land People explained that their computers had learned the language based on data provided by their scopes of human activity on Earth. In fact, they had learned many Earth languages, but when they received signals in English, the computers responded in kind. However, the Land People themselves did not speak English, or any other language, and actually had no language of their own. They'd begun communicating telepathically tens of thousands of years in the past, and the way their telepathy worked completely circumvented language.

They explained that most living things, including themselves, and also humans, don't think in languages. Thinking is a process whereby the brain fires neurons, creating waves of electrical signals that are then organized into thoughts. When the Land People sent thoughts to others, including themselves and humans, they were picked up by the receiving brain and then translated by the receiver into their own language, if they had one.

The Land People thought in a pure and simple way, and it seemed the translation of their thoughts was also being translated in a pure and simple way. *Hence the name Land People,* thought Dani. *A very basic name.* For communication in the other direction, when humans spoke English out loud to them, the Land People already knew what was going to be said because they received the thoughts directly from the human's mind before they spoke. They further explained that they were not at all inconvenienced by the human act of speaking, although it was unnecessary when a human was communicating with one of them.

The Land People's knowledge of the Water People was actually more up to date than expected. They hadn't lived on Terrene for over 600 years but their technology for detailed observation enabled them to look beneath the surface of Terrene's oceans to keep track of what the Water People were up to. The Water People were a warlike species, but the Land People admitted their adversaries really had no choice. There were many hostile forms of life in the oceans of Terrene, none as intelligent and advanced as the Water People, but they were often large and fierce predators.

The Water People themselves were described as humanoid fish, and the drawing software being used to simulate them produced images of beings that vaguely resembled mermaids from the fables of old, but without the hair and beauty of the mythical creatures, and significantly more terrifying. The Water People were over two meters long, with a tailfin where humans had legs, two strong arms, each with dexterous hands that very closely resembled the hands of the Land People—five total fingers, two of which were opposable thumbs—but they had no necks, and their heads were more an extension of the torso than heads, with large mouths full of sharp teeth, resembling the head of a shark. They had no scales and their skin was more like that of a dolphin, although somewhat cream-colored, and they breathed through gills on the upper torso, just below the head. The hands seemed to be the key to advancement of the Water People, along with their advanced brain, because the hands could make things that other creatures of the deep could not.

The Water People built homes in the undersea mountains that rose from the ocean bottom. These mountains were taller than any on Earth, rising tens of thousands of meters from the floor of the sea. Several of these vast rises were the foundations of the land that once dotted the planet, particularly south of the equator, but now their tops were nearly a thousand meters below the surface of the water. The depth of the oceans on Terrene was far greater than the oceans of Earth, reaching down as far as 80,000 meters, and was no less than 15,000 meters deep anywhere on the planet.

The technology of the Water People was primarily chemical-based. They had learned how to combine certain substances to produce heat, and this led to underwater smelting of metals, and welding to make steel doors that could not be breached by the terrible beasts that they shared the ocean with.

They had developed vehicles that could propel them at great speeds, faster than any creature lurking in the depths of the vast oceans. To expel the Land People from the planet, the Water People created massive heating factories under the poles, which they maintained to this day, raising the water level of the oceans high above the plateaus that used to be the land of the planet. They had yet to discover atomic or nuclear power, but could make explosions that would test the durability of the OIM that would supply the new land. This suggested further testing and development of the OIM to enhance its ability to resist explosive forces and heat. The Land People were not yet ready to live on Terrene anyway because of their need for conditioning to withstand its gravity. It was estimated that it would take at least two years for all the equipment needed for the mission to be prepared, so there was plenty of time for them to adapt.

The Land People also had a better idea than time travel for returning to Terrene. They would share their travel technology with Earth, as a trade for Earth sharing the OIM technology that would allow them to rebuild Terrene. They no longer seemed to have any interest in time travel, especially after learning of all the troubles it had caused on Earth, and after being briefed on the minerals and other raw materials available, the Land People were confident they could create the metals most compatible with their form of space travel, and were also happy to hear that fusion power existed on Earth, as it was the primary source of power on the Diaspora vessels.

After the offer of a technology trade, it was virtually impossible for Annette and the Executive Committee to turn down Charles's proposal, and it was approved with little dissension and great anticipation. There was much work to be completed, however, and the Community of Minds was brought to bear on a variety of projects, including the gravity drugs, the OIM resistance to heat and explosive forces, and the creation of new metals and new space vessels that used the travel tech of the Land People. A team of settlers would also be recruited and selected, which would include Charles. He came through with his promise to disclose all of his knowledge of OIM immediately following the execution of newly signed agreements, which would grant him his freedom (on Terrene only) while allowing him to keep all of his memories. The biggest surprise, however, was who wanted to be part of the team of settlers, and who did not.

Chapter 32

C harles's knowledge of OIM was far ahead of the rest of world, in two areas. The first was the creation of OIM formulas that could be ingested by humans, without killing them, and with the primary purpose of extending the human life span to mimic that of OIM, which was thought to be nearly infinite. Charles had been successfully imbibing OIM for five years by the time he was caught, and while he claimed it caused him to go insane, it had also enabled him to discover an entirely unknown aspect of OIM—specifically, that it had a consciousness of its own, separate from and unrelated to the AI it was infused with.

"One day," he said, "I was working on something in the time station that had nothing to do with OIM, when a thought entered my mind. It was a message from the OIM."

"What was it?" asked Annette.

"It was a message that said 'We don't want to die,'" said Charles. "The message was from the OIM which composed the station. You will remember that my unstable mental state, admittedly from the ingestion of OIM, had led me to convince myself that I should destroy the worlds' entire network of OIM."

"Yes, we remember that very clearly, Charles," said Annette, seemingly annoyed to be discussing the subject of Charles's criminality, even as he had once again finagled his own freedom, albeit for a good cause.

"But we stopped you," said Dani. Dani and Aideen had joined the meeting at Annette's request. While neither of them had an official post at the Department of Time Management, Annette had become quite dependent on them, especially when it came to Charles. They knew how to read him, how to manage him, and frequently asked questions that others might not consider. "What I'm wondering," Dani continued, "is why the OIM didn't stop you?"

"That's a good question," said Charles. "What I have theorized is that the OIM was just beginning to form a collective consciousness at that time, and was still completely controlled by the AI it had been infused with. Over time, the OIM has developed a means of circumventing the AI in certain situations, like when I took over the communications with the aliens. And I will point out, that at this moment in history, I am the only human that can communicate directly with the OIM, because I am now, part OIM."

"Do you know if you'll live longer?" asked Aideen.

"To be honest, I think I would need to resume my ingestion of the OIM in order to ensure that," said Charles.

"Would you really want to do that, Charles?" asked Aideen. "Knowin' it made you crazy."

"Of course not," said Charles. "Not without some major reformulating."

"Which you will not be allowed to pursue," said Annette. "Either here, or on Terrene."

"That goes without saying," said Charles, appearing put off by Annette's reminder of one of the things he had agreed to in writing. He had also agreed to undergo periodic interviews and testing from a Monitoring team that would be assigned to him on Terrene.

"We can give the project to the Community of Minds, at the appropriate time," said Annette.

"You mean, after I'm gone," he said.

"Yes, that's what I mean. You can share the details of your formulas with us later. What we need to focus on now is this collective consciousness the OIM has developed. We must consider two things: One, is it a potential threat to humanity? And two, how can we begin to communicate with the OIM, without the necessity of imbibing it, as you did?"

Charles had a quick response. "When I said I was the only human that could interact with the OIM consciousness, I should have clarified that I was the only *biological* human that could communicate with it. The Community of Minds, which lives in a vessel constructed entirely of OIM, has been in touch with this consciousness from the beginning. In fact, I think it's one of their projects."

"A project not assigned by us, if it's true," said Annette.

"Yes, but neither was the first time travel technology," said Charles.

"And look where that got us," countered Annette.

"True," said Charles. "But I don't think the Community of Minds is hiding it from you. I suggest you take it up with them. They should be able to get this thing under control for you."

"We'll do that," said Annette.

"Great," said Charles. "I'm happy to continue helping in any way I can. But do you mind switching subjects for a moment?"

"To what?"

"To the settlement team. Where do things stand on that? I'd like to start working with them as soon as possible."

"It's going well," said Annette. "We've got a team of scientists from various disciplines assembled. Now we're moving on to the medical team, the farmers, the food processing technicians, and the final group will be your basic settlers. People who want a new start who can pass the test criteria we've established."

"How many of that last type, the basic settler, are you planning on?" asked Charles.

"At least 100," said Annette. "Maybe more." She turned toward Dani and Aideen. "In fact, I'd like to invite anyone from your group from the past to go."

"I can't speak for Aideen, or for any of the others," said Dani, "but would you consider a few of us going on a temporary basis, and then returning to Earth?"

"I don't like the sound of that," said Aideen, shaking her head.

Chapter 33

Dani's idea led to further discussion on the transit system to and from Terrene. If they were successful recreating the travel technology of the Land People, the link between Earth and Terrene would theoretically be quite solid. The transit would be instantaneous, and while it took a tremendous amount of power to move a ship the size of Diaspora One via molecular transfer, it had been confirmed that smaller ships could be built for ferrying smaller numbers of passengers to and from Terrene. The plan was to build several of the smaller vessels—up to a dozen of them—and this could be done much more efficiently and quickly than building a large ship like Diaspora One. The new fleet could be used not only for travel to and from Terrene, but for shorter trips to the moon and Mars, and for exploration throughout the galaxy.

With that plan as background knowledge, Dani's inquiry regarding temporary placement on Terrene was easy to answer in the affirmative, but Annette wanted more information. "What's your logic, Dani? Why go at all. There'll be some risks, some unknowns, after all."

"And that answers your question," replied Dani. "The unknown. After all, I'm an anthropologist, and we're always trying to learn more about human behavior. Now I can do that in the context of colonizing a new world, and also have the opportunity to study at least two new intelligent species."

Dani had submitted her dissertation and successfully defended it the previous fall, after she and Aideen had brought Orla from 1801 to live with them permanently in 2022. She'd written Orla out of the document to preserve the secret of time travel, but it was still rich with context and wisdom that Orla had provided. Dani was now a PhD in Anthropology, and while she hadn't practiced her craft since obtaining her degree, she still wanted to. In her mind, studying the people of Terrene, including the Water People, if it could be done safely, was intriguing, and she said as much to Annette.

"But you can study the Land People here," said Annette. "In fact, you can join the team I've assigned to do that."

"I'd like that, Annette, especially since the project development plan is two years in duration. But the planning should include the necessary preparation for return trips to Earth, if you're willing to consider that."

"Certainly," said Annette. "It makes sense."

"I'm not yet on board with this idea," blurted Aideen. "I hope Dani and I can discuss it further, privately."

"Of course," said Dani.

***

Aideen and Dani returned to their apartment in the early afternoon. A dinner with the people from the past had been scheduled for that evening, but it gave them time to talk things through.

Dani tried to elaborate on her thinking for Aideen. "We've come here to a future time to live, and there's still much for both of us to learn here."

Aideen interrupted. "Agreed. But why go seven hundred thirty-seven light years away to find it? There's plenty of learning and new experiences for us to enjoy right here."

"And we will! We already are, right?"

"Not really," said Aideen. "Most of our time is spent at the Time Management building, and while I'll admit, it's been exciting, we still haven't made any friends from this time outside of the people we're working with on the inside of that building."

"True, but since when did you develop the need to have friends, Aideen? I mean, until I came along you were living alone, with no friends I'm aware of. Now we have Orla, although she's tied at the hip to Liam now, and we have my parents."

"Who we rarely see, I'll admit," said Aideen.

"Because they've adjusted so well! Far better than us, for sure. They have plenty of friends from this era and are thriving here. It's a beautiful thing. But as far as the trip to Terrene, we don't have to be on the first ship out, although we could be useful if we were, because of…"

"Charles," said Aideen. "It's always you and me managing Charles, and now you want to manage him on a planet full of known terrorists that's hundreds of light years away."

"Well, I worry about Charles. Who knows what kind of trouble he can cause for the settlers on Terrene, and even for the people back here on Earth. And the Water People aren't terrorists, necessarily. We need to spend more time with the Land People finding out what motivated the Water People to do what they did. I'm not even sure the two species can communicate. Maybe the Water People don't even know the Land People exist."

"Who knows," said Aideen. "And more to the point, who cares."

"Well, that's my point, actually. I care."

That comment hit Aideen's soft spot. She loved Dani and wanted her to be happy and fulfilled by her life. Up to this point, their interests had always aligned, but here was the first challenge in their relationship, when the alignment wasn't there. But the love was, and Aideen seemed to rely on that when she made her next comment. "Why don't we see what the others are thinking, before we make a decision on this. Can we do that, Dani?"

"Good idea."

Chapter 34

The dinner for the group from the past was held at the Time Management building, primarily because Liam and Orla still had not been released into society. Liam continued wearing clothes from his era and drinking ale from a pint mug. Orla was wearing a skinsuit, which did little to hide her voluptuous physique, although Dani was glad she hadn't completely retrenched into the old ways. But she was glued to Liam as a newborn calf was to its mother, holding his free hand and whispering in his ear, almost as if she were translating what was being said. Dani knew Liam had spoken rudimentary English when he arrived, and wondered if he'd made much progress improving his mastery of the language since he'd been here. She decided to spend some time speaking with him directly to learn more, if the opportunity presented itself.

Everyone from the past was there. Pat and Don Peterson, Sadiki, Eahba, Aoife, Roisin, Ciara, Orla, Liam, and of course, Aideen and Dani. Annette had also joined them, as she would be announcing the Terrene Expedition to the group and inviting any of them that had been released to society to join the expedition as settlers. Everyone already knew about the expedition, but this would make it official. After the group settled into their seats, she stood up, raising her glass of wine for a toast.

"I'd like to make a toast to all of the people from the past who've been released into society here in 2254. And also express my confidence they will soon be joined by Liam and Orla, the two who remain in training." Everyone raised a glass and toasted, even Liam, who didn't seem bothered by anything, as long as he had his ale, and Orla by his side. Annette remained standing. "I'd also like to inform you of a new and extremely exciting project that has been authorized by the EarthGov Executive Committee. By now, you've all been thoroughly briefed on the First Contact breakthrough that occurred recently, and that we are currently housing the beings who call themselves the Land People, here in the Time Management building. Dani and Aideen were actually the first people on Earth to ever interact with an intelligent alien species, and are part of the exploratory committee that's been working with the Land People to plan an expedition to their planet, known as Terrene."

Out of the blue, Liam Murphy stood up.

"I'd like to volunteer to go," he said, then sat back down, but then Orla stood up.

"I would also like to volunteer," she said.

The room was silent. Most were confused, since Annette had not yet announced that the people from the past would be given the opportunity to become settlers on the expedition. Dani, on the other hand, was stunned, and she assumed Aideen was as well. Neither had expected any of the group to volunteer, and Liam Murphy was perhaps last on the list of possible participants. People started whispering to one another, and to regain control of the room, Annette continued along the line she had planned from the beginning.

"That's good news!" she said. "Because I am here to announce that all the people of your group are invited to join the expedition. The one requirement is that you have passed all of the training courses that are required for you to be released into society. And since our first two volunteers are the only ones who have not yet passed through all of the classes, we hope their desire to join the expedition encourages them to accelerate their learning."

"Twill indeed," said Liam, raising his mug and then disposing of its contents down his throat.

Orla raised her glass of wine and emptied it. Not to be outdone, Aoife, Roisin and Ciara all raised their glasses and chugged down the wine they held. The Peterson's didn't really know what to do, so they raised their glasses and took healthy sips. Sadiki and Eabha did the same, but Dani and Aideen did not. They were still in a state of shock.

Annette took over. "It had not been my intent to actually solicit volunteers at this dinner," she said. "I merely want to inform you of the project's existence, to let you know that you may join if you like, but not without first having attended a briefing for potential volunteers, to be held in a few days' time. With that, I will leave you to your friends, as I have another meeting to attend. And if I might ask Dani and Aideen to join me briefly outside, I promise they will return soon to enjoy the wonderful upcoming meal with your group."

Annette skirted around the table toward an opening that had appeared in the wall of the room and gestured with her head for Dani and Aideen to follow her. The two got up, both still trying to shake off the implications of what had just happened.

"I hadn't expected that," said Annette, as the three of them stood in the hallway. "I'm sorry. I realize it must have been a shock to you both."

"That's an understatement," said Dani.

Aideen remained silent, but Dani knew from experience this meant she was profoundly affected by what had transpired. Orla was like a daughter to Dani, because they had bonded when Orla was only twelve years old, but to Aideen she was a daughter, and a sister. Their true ages were similar, and with that came an understanding of life that Dani had yet to attain. But she could tell Aideen was taking this hard, and it was unclear at that moment where this would lead.

Annette seemed to understand the emotions both Dani and Aideen were experiencing, and tried to help. "First, remember that they both have to get serious about their classes now if they want to qualify for the expedition. Second, once they hear the details, they may have second thoughts and not want to go. And third, if your judgement is that this is a mistake, I'm willing to rescind the offer allowing your group to volunteer."

"Thank you, Annette," said Dani. "It was just a complete surprise to us. Why don't we go back in and speak with Liam and Orla, to find out more of their thinking on this?"

"The others will likely have a lot of questions for you as well," said Annette. "Can you handle that right now? If not, I can go back in. I'm supposed to attend a meeting with a group of Land People, but we can postpone that, if necessary."

"We'll be fine," said Aideen, who had gathered herself. "Thank you for your help on this, Annette. We'll speak more with you about it tomorrow."

Chapter 35

2256

The two years it took to prepare for the expedition to Terrene passed quickly. The Community of Minds was instrumental in formulating gravity tolerance medicine for the Land People, and their bodies looked much stronger and able than they had when they'd arrived on Earth. The Community had also helped to engineer new metals for the spacecraft, and quickly prepared the schematics from which the vessels would be built. The AI would then create programs from the schematics which would instruct the OIM on how to build the ships, including the chemical composition of the new metals that would compose the hull, as well the intricacies of the new travel technology and all other components of the vessels.

The uploaded Minds were also the first to fully understand the concept of Molecular Reconstruction, because it was virtually identical to the time travel technology they had developed themselves. Both technologies worked with four dimensions—the three dimensions of space plus time—but the travel technology of the Land People focused on locating the present moment of the location they wanted to go, whereas time travel had the additional capability of locating moments in the past and future. The Land People had never been able to fully describe the past and future with equations, although they were very, very close.

The key with Molecular Reconstruction was pinpointing the target location with great accuracy. The scopes which the Land People had developed to do this were far more advanced than anything comparable on Earth, and in their own way, were a form of time travel unto themselves. The light reaching Earth from Terrene was 737 years old, and that was why the telescopes of Earth had observed land masses on the planet, because the land had not been flooded until 600 years ago. It would be a long wait before people on Earth could see the planet in its current form, but not for those who would soon use the travel technology of the Land People.

It wasn't sight technology, which relied on light; it was a form of time travel technology, and all that was missing before it became pure time travel was the ability to locate times in the past and future. But by pinpointing the present moment of a location in space, the need to travel there in a traditional way was circumvented. A burst of energy dispersed through the equipment of the Land People pierced the veil of space-time, and with highly detailed programming, any three-dimensional object—whether alive or inanimate—could be reconstructed in the new location. The molecular reconstruction technology was the same as what happened in time travel, although the scientists and Minds on Earth had never understood how that worked in time travel—it just happened—until the science of the Land People was revealed to them.

The living beings for the Terrene Expedition had been selected and trained over the past two years. Ten ships, each holding twelve people, had been constructed. The first ship would hold six of the Land People and six humans. The six humans would be Charles, three military personnel with combat and medical training, and Dani and Aideen. The nine ships that would follow when the settlement was ready would each carry two Land People and ten humans. Counting Charles, Dani and Aideen, there were ninety-six humans— including scientific, military, medical and tradespeople who would help build the settlement and set up farming. The human professionals took priority over the Land People because the tech being used to build the settlement was Earth's. Subsequent waves, which would launch after the infrastructure of the settlement was nearly completed, would include ten Land People and two human settlers per ship. Liam and Orla would be part of the 104 settlers who intended to live permanently on Terrene, and would be part of the final waves venturing forth to the Terrene settlement.

Dani and Aideen had spoken many times with Liam and Orla about why the two had chosen to go, and during each conversation, Liam's steadfast logic held strong.

"I want to live in a world that's like the one I come from," he said. "I want a pub, and to go fishin', and to raise crops. I can't have that here."

Dani and Aideen countered this argument, arguing that Liam *could* have that on Earth, that there was still plenty of unsettled land in Ireland itself, where he could build these things, and that Aideen, being one of the wealthiest people in the world due to her investment in Bitcoin in 2023, could pay for all of it. They also pointed out that fishing in the oceans of Terrene would be forbidden, due to the threat of the Water People and other treacherous creatures. But Liam always had a counter point.

"We'll build a freshwater lake," he said. "Like Fahey Lough on Omey Island, only bigger, and we'll do our fishin' there. And I've seen the people livin' in Ireland these days. Orla and I went there for that very purpose—to see if we could make a life there—after we were granted our release. They all wear the new fancy clothes and the pubs are all modern and don't even have staff behind the bar or in the kitchen, like the old days. We'll make the old ways real again, on Terrene. And I'll guarantee that the people livin' there will choose our pub over any other place on the planet to spend their free time. I'm bettin' even the Land People will come in for a pint now and again."

For her part, Orla agreed with Liam entirely. She wanted the old ways again, but both Dani and Aideen knew she was deeply in love with the fisherman from Omey Island. She confessed that she had fallen in love with him the first time she'd met him, when she was twelve and Charles was recruiting young Liam to be a time link. They also knew how much Orla loved the pubs of Ireland, and even in 2023, the pubs retained the friendly atmosphere of old Ireland.

"I could live in 2023 because in many ways, it still resembled when I come from," she said. "But this time era, 2256, is like livin' on a different planet anyway, so why not just go to another planet and build a world like the one we love?"

Orla and Liam were both resolute, and while Annette had promised to rescind the offer if asked to by Dani and Aideen, neither could bring themselves to deny Orla and Liam what they truly desired. Dani had once said that what Liam needed was a challenge, and it had proven to be so very true, even though it would mean them losing their best friend.

Aideen had agreed to become part of the first wave based on Dani's commitment to return to Earth as soon as she was sure that Orla would be safe on Terrene, and Aideen couldn't resist the need to make her own assessment of the very same thing. They loved Orla, and they hoped they could visit her often, and vice versa. Of course, the need to take the gravity pills would always be present when they were traveling to Terrene, but as with all the pills of the future, they had virtually no side effects. For humans, they simply made the bones and tendons and muscles stronger, with no substantial change in physical appearance. The Land People were a different matter. They were not only stronger than they'd been when they arrived, they were thicker and heavier and claimed they were much closer now in appearance to their ancestors than before, albeit taller, but it made them very happy since they would soon reclaim their planet in nearly the same physical form as when they'd left.

The day of the launch of Return One—another simple name coined by the Land People, of course—arrived. And it wasn't really a launch since all of the vessels would travel from Earth orbit directly to Terrene. The twelve members of Team One would board the ship on one of the many space stations orbiting Earth for various purposes, and had said their goodbyes the previous day, then beamed up to the space station using the molecular relocation technology Earth had obtained from the Land People. Dani's parents had been distraught, not understanding her need to make this trip, but she promised them she would be back in a few months' time, and that one day they might want to take the trip to Terrene with her. Aoife, Aideen's mother, was stoic, as always, knowing her daughter was a grown woman and would make her own decisions, as she always had. And there was also something the two shared, which was the fact that both had already lived full lives and counted their current situation as something akin to bonus time. But however long Aideen lived, it would be with Dani by her side; she would not remain on Earth while Dani was whisked away to some distant world without her.

With all the goodbyes having been said, the six Land People and six humans boarded Return One, the ship was released from its berth into space, and the final countdown began.

Chapter 36

Day One of the Terrene Expedition

Microseconds after it disappeared from Earth's orbit, Return One reappeared above the planet known as Terrene. What Dani saw below was a water world, with blue oceans ringing the center of the sphere and large poles of white ice to the north and south. There were less clouds than on Earth, because the atmosphere was colder overall and therefore absorbed less water vapor, so Dani could see much more of the surface of the planet than an observer in space could see of the Earth's surface. She imagined that if this planet were Earth, the North Pole would stretch all the way to the northern border of the USA and cover most of Europe. And the South Pole would reach all the way up above New Zealand and the southern part of Australia, and blanket half the continent of South America. The Land People said the poles used to be even larger, before the Water People began melting them to drive the Land People from the planet.

Further discussions revealed that the Water People communicated telepathically, just as the Land People did, and the two species could communicate with one other, although they rarely did. According to the Land People, the Water People were a warring species, and treated anyone or anything that inhabited their planet as the enemy. The Land People claimed ignorance regarding why the Water People had wanted them gone, other than the assertion that the Water People wanted everything gone that wasn't them. Dani had made it her personal goal for the mission to try to establish communication with the Water People, and eventually reach some kind of accord with them that would lead to peace. It was an ambitious goal, and one that seemed very unlikely to ever be fulfilled. But Dani was undeterred. She had some ideas she felt might motivate the Water People to cooperate.

The moment they arrived in orbit above Terrene, Charles became the most important member of the crew. Clarion was the captain of the ship, but most of the decisions going forward would be made by Charles. He directed the navigator of the ship, Zephyr, to use their powerful scopes to measure the temperature of the atmosphere and the depth of the water at various locations on the planet, to give them an idea of where to begin making land. Zephyr reminded Charles that their database already contained that information, but said she would verify that it remained accurate.

As with the Earth, the temperature at the equator of the planet was highest. This was because the rays from the sun—named Energy One by the Land People—hit more directly at the equator. Additionally, the tilt of the planet was similar to Earth's and this meant the poles received much less light during the year than the equator. Thirdly, the atmosphere above the poles was thicker and contained more particles to deflect the sunlight than the atmosphere above the equator. Finally, the fact that the snow and ice of the poles was white caused it to reflect a much greater amount of sunlight than was deflected at the equator.

All of this led to a mean temperature at the equator of around 21 Celsius (70 degrees Fahrenheit) during the day and around 13 Celsius (55 Fahrenheit) at night. This was significantly lower than the mean temperature at the equator on Earth, but from the perspective of the humans on this mission, the weather conditions at the equator of Terrene were ideal. The Land People were less enthusiastic, explaining that most of the land masses their people had inhabited were south of the equator, where the average daily temperatures were much lower.

The challenge of building on the equator was the water depth. The oceans of Terrene tended to be deepest around the equator and shallowest toward the poles. There were massive plateaus that rose from the ocean depths all over the planet, and the ones where the Land People had once lived, further to the south, still rose to within 600 meters of the water's surface, and would have been the easiest place to build land using OIM. The OIM could effortlessly anchor to the submerged land and quickly build the plateau up above the water surface in only a matter of days, but Charles had argued that the temperatures in the south, while bearable for human beings, would not be pleasant for them. He promised to build land there under any circumstances, whether or not the OIM was successful near the equator, and this land could be settled by the Land People if that was their desire. For now, however, they would see what they could accomplish at the equator. The Land People did not object, their passive nature leading them to feel more comfortable having the humans with them, at least in the early phases of resettlement.

The scopes had identified several large land masses at the equator which were around 12,000 meters below the water's surface. This was further down than the deepest water on Earth, the Mariana trench in the Pacific ocean, which was around 11,000 meters deep, but Charles was undeterred.

"There are a few peaks near the equator that come relatively close to the surface, but the bedrock we need for a strong foundation is twelve thousand meters down. It will take a little longer, but it can be done. We may want to deploy some guard drones to keep the Water People from interfering with the process, but even large explosions won't stop the OIM from doing its work. If anything, the energy from the explosions might even be absorbed and speed up the process."

"How long will it take to build a twelve thousand meter mountain?" asked Dani.

"Actually, I was thinking of building a mountain thirteen thousand meters tall," said Charles. "The Land People have reported waves nearly five hundred meters high, which isn't surprising considering the wind patterns and the vast distances waves can travel on this world, which is nearly twice the size of Earth. But to answer your question, I'm thinking thirty days."

"Longer than I would have hoped," said Dani. "But you have to live here, Charles, so it's your call."

"Indeed," he said.

"I think the guard drones are good idea," said Aideen. "If nothing else it might give us a chance to have a look at these Water People, and some of the other monsters living down there."

Yes, Clarion interjected. *The scopes of the guard drones are very powerful and will show us all that is going on under the water.*

It turned out that it wasn't technically correct to refer to Clarion as "she" or "he." The Land People were an interesting kind of androgynous beings. They were neither male nor female and all were basically the same. The only thing that gave them a gender identity, as perceived by humans, was their use of either a male or a female voice. But the more accurate pronoun would have been "it," since the Land People didn't breed as humans do. They once did, many eons in the past, but their technology had allowed them to breed using cloning for tens of thousands of years, and over this long span their sexual organs disappeared and they ceased to engage in conjugal mating activities.

The Land People did not produce new beings as a means of increasing their population. They simply replaced those who died, and with lifespans exceeding 300 years, it wasn't a daily activity. But the most interesting part of the cloning technology was that the newly cloned individual retained the memories of its "parent," and thus, with cloning, the Land People had come very close to achieving the immortality that Charles had been pursuing through OIM ingestion. On the other hand, there were no children in the society of the Land People, and while this had its advantages, most of the humans who were exposed to this concept didn't react favorably. Advancing the species was the most deeply imbued genetic desire of all animals on Earth, including humans, and even though children in 2256 were sometimes created by cloning, the vast majority of people on Earth still preferred to reproduce the old fashioned way.

There had been some discussion during the planning phase of the mission as to whether the presence of human children on the settlement would disrupt the relations with the Land People, but the humans were pleasantly surprised when the Land People expressed excitement about having children in their lives, after so many eons without them. At the moment, however, the mission had hardly begun, and thoughts of children living on Terrene were far from the minds of the twelve crew members of Return One. The first task at hand was to make land, and that meant Charles was in charge, and he was not known to procrastinate when he set his mind to something.

"Very well," he said. "I'll deploy the land-building OIM sample and four guard drone OIM samples now."

Chapter 37

The OIM samples were deployed using the molecular relocation technology and all appeared to have arrived safely at the bottom of the dark ocean. Even though no light penetrated that far down, the scopes on the guard drones could read with such great detail, that light enhancement software on board the ship could reproduce the scene on video screens as if it were happening in broad daylight rather than near perfect darkness. It took only about twenty minutes for the guard drones to build themselves, the result being four spherical units about three meters in diameter that were as black as the water surrounding them. What the screens on board the ship showed now were bubbles, lots of bubbles. The OIM land-building sample was sucking the minerals from the seawater while at the same time boring down vertically into the earth of the vast, rolling plateau on which it had landed, creating deep shafts of OIM into the rock that would ultimately extend below the ocean bottom, and then spread horizontally. The result would be a vast network of OIM tunnels that would transport rock and soil up to where it was needed, then convert it into the OIM which would grow a 13,000 meter mountain on top of the plateau. Once it reached a height of

1000 meters above sea level, it would build the island out horizontally, eventually creating a continent-sized land mass.

Perhaps even more intriguing than the OIM building process was the attention it had garnered from the outside world at this great depth. The Land People had informed the humans that the Water People could not survive at depths below 1,500 meters, where the pressure would be over 150 times the pressure of the Earth's atmosphere at sea level. Likewise, the propulsion vehicles they used were of no use in the deeper waters because they were open, like a convertible, designed only for higher speeds than the Water People could achieve on their own. The Water People also possessed rudimentary missile technology, but these could not withstand the pressure of the deep below 3,000 meters. At a depth of 12,000 meters the pressure was equal to well over 1,000 atmospheres, so they wouldn't be seeing any Water People down there. But according to the Land People, other creatures lurked in the great depths of the Terrene oceans, some of them living on the deepest ocean floor, 80,000 meters below the surface. These beasts were larger than a high rise building and far stronger, with exterior shells three meters thick that could withstand the pressure of over 8,000 atmospheres at such tremendous depth. Such creatures wouldn't venture far from the bottom, however, and weren't a threat at the current depth of the OIM project. The organisms living at 12,000 meters were more of the massive predator type, and a few such species had already made an appearance.

The first was a gigantic, phosphorescent blowfish of some kind, that resembled a bloated Zeppelin airship from the first half of twentieth century Earth, easily 100 meters long but with a diameter of at least fifty meters, making it much wider than a Zeppelin. The fish was larger, by far, than any living creature that had ever existed on Earth.

Charles was the first to comment.

"The drones will hit it with a stun blast to drive it back," he said.

Not necessary, said Zephyr. *I am overriding the programming of the drones in this case.*

"Why?" asked Charles, appearing disappointed.

This fish is just looking for food, said Zephyr. *When it smells that none is present it will move on. However, another more virulent species has just arrived.*

The video screen now showed the approach of an animal resembling a giant squid, except it had only four appendages and they appeared to be more rigid than the tentacles of the Earth-based variety. It was also significantly larger. The creature was currently in a horizontal position and was easily 150 meters long. The legs made up about 80 percent of this length and when the squid turned to a vertical position, they came to rest on the land as would the legs of a four-legged stool. This monster could apparently see, and didn't seem to care much for what it was witnessing, because it raised one leg and pointed it toward the land-building OIM's center and fired a projectile of some sort at it. This all happened very quickly, before Zephyr could end her override of the drones' blast programming. The projectile exploded in the center of the churning mass of bubbles and earth, releasing a red liquid that dispersed in all directions.

It's poison, said Zephyr. *Will kill any living thing on this planet. That's how this one hunts.*

It was about to be determined if the poison would kill the OIM, which wouldn't have been disastrous, since they had many other land-building OIM samples on board Return

One. It would have been a setback, however, requiring the relocation of the project to more shallow waters, where this creature would not venture. But that potential problem soon became moot as the poison cloud disappeared, becoming nothing more than food for the OIM's voracious appetite to make land using anything it could find. About that time, the drones blasted the squid-like creature and it simply rose up from the surface of the land, leaned into a horizontal position, and propelled itself away using a stream of water that exited from the center of its body, at the apex of the legs.

"Take that, you foul beast!" said Charles, bringing chuckles from the other humans on board and confusion from the Land People, apparently because they didn't understand the human need to celebrate victory. Charles's euphoria stemmed not so much from the fact that the drones had driven away the predator, but because his precious OIM had stood its ground when confronted with the most poisonous animal on Terrene.

Day One of the land-building continued without further engagements with the beasts of the deep, but more treacherous encounters would follow as the elevation of the land rose inexorably toward the water's surface.

Chapter 38

Day 31 of the Terrene Expedition

W e've got land!" yelled Charles. "Wine for everyone!"
The OIM console in the center of the control room
produced twelve glasses of wine. Even the Land People took
a glass and raised it to celebrate the OIM bringing the land
above the surface of the water. It hadn't been completely
without incident, but they'd gotten there.

"To Land!" toasted Charles.

"To Land!" yelled the voices of the five other humans on
board Return One.

To Land! came the voices of the six Land People, resonat-
ing in the minds of all on board.

Things had gone relatively smoothly until they reached a
depth of around 3,000 meters below the surface. Yes, they'd
encountered other creatures of the deep on the way up, some
large, some small, and they actually had more difficulty with
the smaller ones. One tiny species of shrimp-like creatures had
proven to be undigestible by the OIM. The problem was that
this species traveled in swarms numbering in the millions, and
from time to time a swarm would envelope the area, blinding
the drones—whose stun capability seemed ineffective against
the swarm—and literally shutting down OIM production and

rendering the OIM unable to resume its task. This ultimately forced the crew to send down another land-building sample to get things going again, and after that, the original OIM regained its competency and kept living, which would be its primary task once all production was finished.

When they reached 3,000 meters below the water's surface, the missile attacks from the Water People began. Charles was confident the OIM could withstand these strikes once it was done building and had received its final programming, but while building, it was more vulnerable, and the missiles that penetrated the drone defense did some damage that needed to be repaired, costing them time. To help minimize the damage, four more guard drones were dispatched and together, the eight drones were able to repel 95 percent of the missiles before they reached their target, which was the OIM itself.

Upon reaching a depth of 1,500 meters the Water People themselves appeared, some in transport vehicles mounted with missile launchers, others swimming on their own, at speeds far greater than any fish or mammal in the seas of Earth could attain. The Water People looked very much like the visual representations the crew had seen on Earth—fierce human sharks whose arms and hands could manipulate controls and build weapons. But the extent and duration of their attacks diminished day by day, and the Land People speculated that the local forces who were fighting them had run low on ammunition and were waiting for additional supplies from other regions of the planet. Observations by the crew confirmed that a massive force of arms and soldiers was heading toward them from literally everywhere in the oceans of Terrene, and Charles was encouraged to create more guard drone samples as fast as he could.

Charles being Charles, he produced dozens more guard drone samples plus an additional supply of land-building OIM samples that could be deployed via molecular transfer to any areas damaged or destroyed by the enemy's weapons. In this way, the relentless drive to break the surface of the water continued, and on Day 31, succeeded. The area of land above water was small at first, but the OIM was moving outward as well as upward, and within a day of breaking the surface, there was a substantial island above the surface. The land would rise until it reached 1,000 meters above sea level and would continue expanding outward for the foreseeable future. The plateau on which the OIM had been placed covered an area as large as Australia, and while the settlement needed far less land than this, the larger the land mass they built, the harder it would be for the Water People to destroy it.

Another defensive measure available to the Water People, which had been speculated upon while the mission was being planned, was expanding their ice melting operations at the poles in order to raise the sea level once again. And while it would be challenging for them to bring the water level up another 1,000 meters, that's exactly what they tried to do, although the impact from this venture would take years to produce meaningful results. When the land above water reached 1,000 meters, the crew of Return One transported down to the surface to begin building the settlement, protected by a force field culled from the portfolio of technology the Land People had supplied them with. Above water missile attacks were repelled with ease.

But the balance of life on Terrene was threatened, not so much from the new arrivals, but from the defensive measures taken by the Water People. The Water People had been smart in one way, not so much in another. The melting operation was fueled by hydrogenated carbon dioxide, which was a carbon neutral fuel that produced no pollution in either the water or the atmosphere. But the melting operation itself was slowly yet relentlessly increasing the temperature of the water and the atmosphere of the planet, and had already destroyed certain species that were an important part of the food chain in the ocean. Doubling the heat, which was what would be needed for another 1,000-meter water level rise, would further threaten life in the sea and have an unpredictable effect on the atmosphere, which could endanger the lives of those who hoped to live on the newly created land.

As a result, Dani's project to make contact with the Water People in search of a peaceful solution was elevated to the highest priority of the Terrene Expedition, alongside making the land habitable. A vessel was prepared to take her into the depths and the day arrived when its launch could be delayed no longer.

Chapter 39

Day 59 of The Terrene Expedition

T ell me once again why you have to go down under the water," said Aideen.

"Zephyr and Clarion both told me it's because the telepathic signals can't travel from one medium into another over a long distance," said Dani.

"Air to air is good, and water to water is good, but not air to water or water to air, is that right?"

"That's what I've been told," said Dani.

"But just in case, since we came down here twenty-eight days ago, all six of the Land People have been sendin' messages of peace to the Water People, with no response?"

"Correct," said Dani. "We have to go under the water in order to make contact with them. We've been over this." Dani was losing patience but Aideen was undeterred.

"I want to go with you," she said.

That cannot be permitted said Clarion, the captain of the ship and the logical authority on Terrene Base One.

"Why?" asked Aideen.

"We cannot spare an additional human for this task. You are needed here on Base One to continue preparing for the arrival of the settlers from Earth."

The current plan for Dani's mission was to send her and Zephyr under the water, and have Zephyr translate Dani's words to them. They could have sent Zephyr by herself, but Dani felt that was unfair. It was also the view of the Land People that the presence of a human, from another world, might create leverage, in the form of fear, among the Water People. The humans were the inventers of OIM, and the OIM could destroy all of the Water People, if they chose to use it for that purpose. Moreover, Dani was quick on her feet when the ground underneath was unsteady, and she believed she was a better negotiator than any of the more passive Land People.

Dani approached Aideen and hugged her tightly, whispering into her ear.

"I love you, and I love Orla, and I want you to make sure Orla is okay if I don't come back. It's a waste for both of us to go."

"I'm coming after you if you don't return soon, so forget about that logic," said Aideen.

"Okay," said Dani. "Let's see what happens."

Aideen reluctantly released her and Dani and Zephyr entered the mission vessel. It was a sphere, about ten meters in diameter, with extra thick walls and any number of defensive and offensive weapons systems on board. It would be hard for the Water People to breach this vessel, but as a precautionary measure it would be surrounded by a complement of ten guard drones, just in case an attack was forthcoming. The vessel was named Peace One, continuing the long line of "Ones" for this mission, again named by the Land People, whose obsession with basic names was in striking contrast to their possession of highly advanced technology. Dani wondered how these seemingly passive and simple people could have achieved such heights of technological prowess, but that question would have to be answered at another time. For now, her only hope was that a vessel named Peace Two would not be needed.

The vessel was beamed to a depth of 1,000 meters, and Zephyr began transmitting. Peace One had been equipped with a unique communication platform, whereby Zephyr's thoughts, while she was inside the vessel, would be transferred to equipment on the outside of the aquatic vehicle which would amplify her thoughts and send them in all directions. The same equipment was designed to pick up thoughts and bring them back inside the vessel.

Water People, said Zephyr. *I am a descendant of the Land People who once inhabited this world. We now return to claim our rightful place on the land of this planet. We have brought with us powerful beings from another world, known as Humans. The Humans have the power to build new land for us, and you have seen that you cannot stop them. The same substance that allows them to do this can destroy all life on Terrene, if necessary. But that is not our intent. Please contact us to begin negotiating a peaceful compromise regarding how to share this world.*

Dani and Zephyr waited, as did their ten colleagues up above, patched in with audio, video and advanced radar of everything that was happening inside and outside of Peace One. They didn't have to wait long.

Dani, said Zephyr, *they are asking to see what you look like. With your permission I will project an image of you to the Water People.*

"How will you do that?" asked Dani.

It is something we can do with one another, and with the Water People. We have never tried to send images to Humans.

But with your permission, you will have the chance to see if it can be done. I will simply look at you, then transmit what I see.

"Sure, go ahead."

Dani waited, and suddenly, an apparition of herself appeared, not in her mind, but in front of her, in the form of a holograph. It was highly detailed, and she was disappointed that the expression on her face at the time Zephyr captured the image was one of confusion, rather than one of stern confidence. But it was too late; the image had been sent.

Dani and Zephyr waited for a response from the Water People but nothing came. About thirty seconds later a transmission from Base One came in. It was Charles.

"There's something approaching at high speed from a westerly direction," he said.

"What is it?" asked Dani.

"We don't know," said Charles. "We're going to bring you out of there."

Just then, Dani felt their vessel lurch to the side, and it seemed to be picking up speed.

"Charles, we're moving. What's going on?"

"We're having trouble locking onto you, Dani, due to your movement."

"What's doing this, Charles?" asked Dani.

"It's some kind of underwater tsunami!" he screamed. "We still can't lock onto you. Can you maneuver the ship up or down? It appears to be a relatively narrow stream of water that is moving you. The guard drones are unaffected and have fallen far behind you."

Zephyr attempted to move the ship up, then down, with no success. The vessel was now beginning to rotate on a horizontal axis as it continued to pick up speed. Essentially, it was rolling forward like a bowling ball. Both Dani and Zephyr were plastered against the wall of the vessel, held in place by centrifugal force. *Controls are not responsive,* said Zephyr.

Suddenly, the underwater wave hit the sphere, pressing Dani and Zephyr against the wall with great force. They were moving at tremendous speed and the rate of the rotation continued to increase. Stuck to the wall, Zephyr had no way of accessing the controls of the ship. The video screens had gone blank so they couldn't see anything outside. They knew only that they were barreling forward, pushed by some exceedingly powerful underwater wave. Suddenly, they abruptly slowed, the force of the change throwing them to the floor. It was like a wave hitting the shore of a beach, its force diminished by the impact with land. Perhaps the underwater wave had hit land under the water, a mountain perhaps, but it was unclear how their bodies could withstand such a sudden impact, unless the ship were somehow taken in by some kind of protective opening. Immediately after coming to a near halt, Peace One begin rolling again, but slowly, like a ball on a hard surface rolling down a very slight incline, pushing them against the walls again. Gradually, the rotation slowed further and the vessel came to a complete stop. Dani and Zephyr lowered themselves to the floor of the cabin, stumbling around, quite disoriented, and then a voice from the Water People came over the speakers.

You are now our prisoners. Open your vessel and you will not be harmed.

Chapter 40

T ell them we can't survive in water without breathing gear," Dani said to Zephyr. "And try to raise Charles on the comms."

I've done as you asked, said Zephyr. *We have no contact with Base One. Something is blocking the signal. The Water People say there is air where we are now, and our instruments confirm that.*

"Are they out there?" asked Dani. "The video screens seem to be off."

Something is out there, said Zephyr.

"How do you know?"

Because they are communicating with me and told me they are out there, and won't harm us.

"I think it's a mistake to go out right now," said Dani. "We need time to get our instruments working again."

Very well. I will tell them we are frightened and do not want to come out at this time.

"No!" yelled Dani. "Don't tell them that. We can't let them know we're afraid."

What should I say?

"Tell them we're consulting with our leaders on what to do and the Water People will pay a terrible price for what they have done."

Very well, I will say that.

"Did they respond?"

Zephyr's face looked defeated. *They laughed,* she said. *They know we cannot communicate with our people from this place.*

"Can you get the video screens working so we can look around?" asked Dani.

I will try.

While Zephyr was working with the equipment, a noise could be heard coming from the outside of the ship. It sounded like being in a carwash, the splash of spraying water hitting the surface of a car.

"Is that water?" asked Dani. "Are we being sprayed with water?"

No, said Zephyr. *It's fire. They probably can't get through the OIM walls with fire, but I'm not sure the OIM can keep the heat out forever.*

As if answering Zephyr's question, the temperature in the cabin began to rise. The OIM was keeping most of the heat out, but the continued presence of the fire outside was pushing the limits of what the OIM could do.

"Do we have any functionality on this ship?" asked Dani, desperate for a solution. "Are any of the weapons systems working?"

Zephyr made some system checks and reported back to Dani. *Negative. Even the air-conditioning system is nonfunctional. The only thing keeping us alive at this point is the OIM itself, and I do not believe it can prevent us from being baked alive over the long term. The Water People are heartless. They will kill us if we don't surrender.*

"But won't they kill us if we do surrender?" asked Dani.

I don't think so. More likely, they will use us for leverage, to negotiate with our colleagues on Base One.

Dani thought about what to do, as the temperature continued its relentless rise. She was sweating now, and knew that Zephyr would be suffering even more since her people were used to living in lower temperatures than most humans. But she had to think. She needed to think clearly in order to make the right decision. The first thing she considered was that their people on Base One very likely knew their general location. This meant that Aideen would form a rescue party and come after them. No matter if it meant the same fate or worse for herself, she would come. And therefore, the answer was now clear to Dani.

"Tell them we'll come out," she told Zephyr.

Chapter 41

The Water People told Zephyr to remain inside their craft until they cooled the chamber in which Peace One was located. Within a few minutes they felt their vessel become buoyant, as if the chamber had been flooded with water. Not long after that, the ship gradually dropped down, and then settled back onto the floor, presumably after the water had been drained. They were given the okay to disembark.

Dani provided some last-minute guidance to Zephyr. "To the degree that you can, Zephyr, let me answer the questions. It's best that we pretend I'm in charge, because I'm the one who's a mystery to them, and is most likely to succeed in a negotiation."

I agree with your logic, Dani, about you being in charge. But I don't think this is really a negotiation, since we are prisoners, and have no leverage.

"Just leave the leverage part to me, okay?" asked Dani.

Certainly.

"All right, let's go out then." Dani reached over and pushed a button and the OIM shell of the craft created an opening.

The two crew members exited the craft and stepped down onto what seemed to be a glass floor. The walls and ceiling of the well-lit rectangular room were also made of glass, except for the end where they had entered, which was made of solid metal. Dani assumed that as soon as the craft had been forced into the chamber by the wave, the metal door had sealed off the outside water and the chamber had been emptied, just as it had been emptied moments ago after the cooling process had been facilitated by the water from outside.

She looked out of through the glass and saw hundreds of Water People floating in the water that surrounded the chamber on all sides. They peered in from all the faces of the rectangular prism, including the top and bottom. The structure was like an aquarium filled with air instead of water, and Dani and Zephyr were the "fish" inside, there for the enjoyment of the Water People, or for whatever other purpose their captors had in mind.

"Are they speaking to you yet?" asked Dani.

Yes, replied Zephyr, raising her arm and pointing at one of the Water People. *That one.*

The individual in question was actually in a vertical position. Its tail fin, shaped like a dolphin's, was resting on a platform, and its hands were placed against the glass wall to steady it. This one was the only Water Person in this position and was obviously the leader.

"Do you have any idea why it isn't including me in its thought communication?" asked Dani, remembering that the way the telepathy of the Land People worked circumvented the need for language and was a direct link between one brain and another. Dani was thinking that the Water People should be able to do the same thing.

I believe he can do it, said Zephyr. *By the way, he is a male. I know for a fact that the Water People communicate with many other underwater species this way, and often work together with them to achieve mutual goals. I will politely ask if he is willing to include you in the communication link in order to eliminate the need for my translating.*

A few seconds passed and Zephyr reported back to Dani. *He says that his people will not risk linking minds with an off-worlder for fear of your use of mind control or mind weapons on them. Trust must be established first.*

"Well, that's actually a good sign," said Dani.

Why?

"Because the implication is that we might live through this, if he's considering giving me time to establish trust. It's a very good sign. A sign that they might be willing to negotiate."

I see your point. What would you like me to say to him now?

"Tell him my name is Dani Peterson. I am a human from the planet Earth in a far off solar system. We come in peace and mean them no harm. We are here only to support the efforts of the Land People to reclaim the land that was taken from them."

Zephyr conveyed what Dani had said to the leader of the Water People.

"What did he say?" asked Dani.

He said that the Water People shared this planet with the Land People for many eons. But when the Land People decided the Ocean could be theirs too, they left the Water People no choice but to defend their home.

"I'm confused, Zephyr. What's he talking about? Nothing like this was mentioned to us by the Land People."

It is true that when we had the power to defend ourselves from the Water People, we would use the ocean from time to time. There were many fish in the sea, and our people had always caught fish from the shores of our land, and we ate the fish, and it gave good energy and excellent taste. But we could not catch enough fish for our needs from the shores of land, so we built boats to harvest more fish, and the Water People attacked our boats, but they could not get through our force fields. So the fishing continued. And we built barriers in the water so our people could swim and enjoy it without fear of being attacked.

"But you are a plant-based people, and land-based people," said Dani. "Why did you need fish, and why did you need to swim in the ocean?"

That is easy to answer, because humans are the same. You are land-based people, but eons ago, you ancestors lived in the water, and you will forever have a deep-seeded need, a genetic pull to be near the water, and to go into it, and to eat the food from it. It is the same with us, because we are descended from the Water People, but for eons they kept us from the water. But no longer could they do that as we advanced beyond them with our technology. When we lost the war, we were forced to resume a plant-based diet, to live efficiently in space.

"It would have been better if we'd known this before we came," said Dani.

And would you still have come?

"I don't know," said Dani. "I suppose that would depend on your intentions upon your return. Do you intend to use the sea as you were doing before the war was lost with the Water People?"

It has not been discussed.

"But it could be the basis of a new peace between your people and the Water People!" said Dani.

Perhaps. But the genetic desire to be in the water, to eat the food from the water, is still there. How can we be truly free if we are not allowed to exercise these desires, as humans on Earth are allowed to do, and as your settlers here will want to do?

"I don't know," said Dani. "But my gut tells me that we'll solve a lot of problems if we can figure it out."

Chapter 42

Dani came up with a plan. Through Zephyr, she explained to the Water People that the sea was genetically important to both Land People and humans. But she also admitted that it was wrong of the Land People to take from their waters without a full discussion of limits, and of exchanges that could benefit the Water People. Now, in this new age, these discussions would happen, or the humans would force the Land People to leave. She made this promise, and said that no violence from either side would be needed. She explained that humans had the power to completely destroy the polar heating stations of the Water People, allowing all of the land that had disappeared to return. But this was not required. In fact, an agreement could include limits on how much land would be made using the methods that had been started only a short time ago. Dani emphasized that a sharing of technology could occur if a formal peace treaty were signed by all parties: Land People, Water People and humans.

"But we need to return to the surface in order for these plans and agreements to be made. It is also critical that we communicate with the surface, immediately, to prevent an attack from above to attempt to rescue us."

The leader of the Water People, whose name was Cabal, thought about this, then told Zephyr they would be allowed to speak to the surface. Equipment would be brought into the chamber that would allow for this. Cabal told Zephyr it should be done urgently because many vessels from above were approaching the underwater mountain they were inside at that moment. Dani and Zephyr were instructed to go back into their ship while the equipment was brought in, which would require the partial filling of the chamber. It all happened quickly, and when the chamber was empty, Dani and Zephyr came out of their ship. Zephyr had no problem using the equipment and quickly established contact and handed the controls to Dani.

"Hold off on any attack! We are fine. Please confirm you are standing down."

Charles came on the line. "What's going on down there?" he asked. "Aideen is leading a fleet to attempt a rescue. She's located the doors to where you disappeared and is about to fire."

"Tell her if she does, Zephyr and I will drown. We are currently being held in an airtight chamber behind those very doors."

"She's standing down," said Charles. "What next, Dani?"

"These Water People are not as vicious as we've been led to believe. There's more to the story than we were told by the Land People. I've established a framework for a potential peace treaty between the three species, but a lot of details have to be worked out. They are still skeptical about us humans, as well as the intentions of the Land People, so I'm not sure they will let us go, immediately. I'd like to propose that a group come down here to participate in the negotiations. That group will need to include you, Charles."

There was silence from the other end of the line.

"Charles? Are you there?"

"Yes, I'm here. But frankly, this is not what I had in mind, Dani."

"You've trusted me, and Aideen, to get you this far, Charles. I'm asking you to trust me now. We'll need you, Clarion, one more of the Land People, and Aideen. That will be three humans, and three Land People. The others are going to have to let the six of us make this deal. Okay?"

More silence.

"Charles?"

"All right," he said. "Give me two hours."

Chapter 43

C harles arrived, accompanied by Aideen, Clarion and another Land Person whose name translated as Dia, who was an expert in the travel technology used by the Land People. They were in a vessel identical to the one Dani and Zephyr had taken, manufactured by Charles after he had agreed to come. Of course, the ship had been named Peace Two, and it was accompanied by a show of force, nearly two dozen guard drones, each with weapons powerful enough to vaporize the steel door that held Peace One inside. But the door opened with no problem, the chamber was flooded, and Peace Two entered, leaving the guard drones behind. When the chamber was emptied of water, the occupants of both vessels emerged and came together on the floor of the chamber. Dani and Aideen embraced.

"I was about to fire everythin' we had at that door," said Aideen. "But then Charles told me what was goin' on, so I returned to the surface and we came here together."

"I'm glad you're here," said Dani. "Let me bring you all up to date so we can begin the negotiations."

Dani explained the missing background information regarding the fishing of the waters by the Land People. She clarified that while on Earth, humans had met little tangible resistance from the creatures of the deep, but she was certain that if it could have, the life under the sea would have tried to stop them, just as the Water People had tried, and succeeded, in stopping the Land People. However, there was no denying the innate desire of both Land People and humans to enjoy the fruits of the sea, and she explained that the negotiation should attempt to provide such use, with limits, and with whatever they could offer the Water People that was commensurate with what they received.

"They'll want all the technology, not only of the Land People, but also ours," said Charles. "Is going for a swim really worth all that?"

"It's more than that and you know it, Charles," said Dani. "We'll be settling a world that will still be 90 percent ocean when we're done. Why would we want to live in a place where we could access only 10 percent of the planet's surface?"

"It's better than living in space, isn't it?" he countered, but then Aideen stepped in.

"You think we're stupid, Charles!" she said. "You think we'll just give everythin' away that creates our advantage over these people? You need to get on board with this process, Charles, and you need ta' do it now. Establishing a lastin' peace with the Water People's what this is all about, while giving the settlement access to the oceans."

"All right," said Charles. "But we agree that no concessions are made until we've all thoroughly discussed it, and voted on it. A majority of us is needed to approve anything. Four votes, all right?" The others nodded. "Okay, let's get on with this," he said.

The group approached the wall where the leader of the Water People, Cabal, was still perched on his pedestal. Now that she was close to him, Dani could see that Cabal had some unique physical features compared to the rest of the Water People and this caused her to wonder if that was the reason he was the leader. He was at least two feet shorter than the rest of them, making him around six feet in height, and his head was less pointed at the top, more rounded, and while his mouth was large and full of sharp teeth, his overall appearance was closer to the Land People than the others. Even his eyes were larger and rounder than the other Water People, whose eyes were more almond-shaped. Closer inspection of his tail fin showed vestiges of toes on the two pointed ends, and while the ends of the fins faced outward, to give him the proper balance, it was clear Cabal was biologically closer to the Land People than the rest of his species. As an anthropologist, it was easy for Dani to conclude that the Water People valued this, as if they considered the Land People a superior species and wanted to be like them. She tucked this away for further use and addressed Cabal.

"Thank you for... having us here to discuss these important matters," said Dani. "The six of us have the power to make agreements for both of our species—the humans and the Land People."

Which of you is the leader? asked Cabal.

Dani was encouraged that for the first time, his message came directly into her head. This was a sign that trust had been established between humans and the Water People, apparently based on her opinion that the Land People were wrong to fish the waters without first discussing it with the Water People.

"Our mission is not set up that way," said Dani. "Each of us has specific responsibilities. Our military leader is currently up on the land surface we created. Our leader of the space vessel is here and is named Clarion." Dani pointed at Clarion. "The second in command of the space vessel is Dia, who is also here." She pointed at Dia. "Zephyr, here, is our navigator. The head of construction is named Charles." She pointed at Charles. "Aideen and myself are observers from Earth, our planet, and will return there soon."

How will you make decisions? he asked.

"We will vote," said Dani. "If four of us agree to something, it will be approved."

This is not our way, he said. *I make the decisions for our people. I have been appointed by God to fulfill this responsibility.*

Dani was surprised. Her understanding of the Land People was they didn't worship a deity, and they'd provided no indication that the Water People *did*, but this new information suggested that Dani would need to demonstrate respect for their faith if it continued to come up as the negotiations continued, but for now she would steer clear of it.

"Our experience is that different species often manage their affairs differently," she said. "It is the way of the universe."

Very well, said Cabal. *Do you require nourishment before we begin the discussions?*

Dani and Zephyr had been able to restore the food production capability inside Peace One, and had eaten while they waited for Charles and the others to arrive. But she appreciated that the Water People had manners, yet another small sign that these beings were not as barbaric as had been suggested by the Land People. She checked with the others and they all declined the offer of food.

"No thank you," said Dani. "We took nourishment on our ships. Shall we begin?"

Very well. You have said the Land People and Humans want to share the oceans with us, and with the many other creatures who live here. We ask only two things in return for this. First, you must abide by the laws of the sea, which we will share with you during these discussions.

"We must learn about these laws, of course, and hopefully we can abide by them," said Dani. "And your other request?"

We want to share the land and space with Humans and the Land People.

Chapter 44

T he laws of the sea were relatively straightforward, although somewhat ironic, considering they'd been developed by a predatory species—the Water People—who lived by hunting other inhabitants of the deep. The first law was that no one should take more from the sea than they needed. Any species that did this, for example, a species that killed for sport, would be deemed to be an enemy of the sea. The Water People believed they'd been appointed by their God to be judge, jury and executioner, and they readily admitted to have brought more than one species to extinction for violating the first law. They further clarified that their banishment of the Land People from the planet was based on their belief that the Land People did not actually need the fish they caught.

Dani reiterated that the *need* of both Land People and humans to be near the sea and to eat from its waters was a deep, genetic one, similar to what the Water People experienced when they ate the fish of the sea. And since the Land People were known to be descended from the Water People, she hoped they could now understand this more clearly. Cabal acknowledged that he could. Dani then secured a promise from the Land People to abide by this law, which they found reasonable, now that the Water People better understood their need to eat fish. And while some of the Land People had been able to rid themselves of their desire to eat seafood, after years living in space, all Land People loved the water, and wanted to enjoy it recreationally without fear of being attacked by the Water People or their allies. This was also acceptable to the Water People, as long as the details of such recreational activities were clarified before final clearance was given.

The second law of the sea forbid polluting the ocean and the sky. The Water People's use of non-polluting power sources— primarily based on the same hydrogenated carbon dioxide fuel source that was melting the poles—was a perfect fit with the second law of the sea, and since humans and the Land People already lived by this law, it was readily agreed to and accepted.

The third and final law of the sea was the most problematic. This law stated that the creatures of the deep would be left in peace, never to be disturbed. It turned out that the 3,000 meter depth limitation of the Water People was not a physical limitation. They claimed to have equipment that would go far deeper, but it was a known fact that the creatures of the deep never came higher than this depth, and the Water People believed this was a boundary their God did not want them to cross. The members of the Terrene Expedition had seen several of these creatures when the OIM and the guard drones were deployed at a depth of 12,000 meters to begin the building of their land, but the Water People warned them this could never happen again, and it appeared this might be the straw that broke the camel's back in the negotiations. Charles wanted to live near the equator, and while it wasn't the preferred location for the Land People, they respected Charles enough—almost to the point of reverence due to his status as the greatest time traveler and the greatest OIM expert of all time—to hold the line, and would not agree to the Water People's demand to cease land building from the great depths.

But Aideen had an idea. She suggested that as part of the final agreement, the Water People should terminate their pole heating projects, which would ultimately restore all the land that had been present on Terrene 600 years ago. This was an acceptable solution to the Water People, and knowing the restoration of land would take many years to come to fruition, they agreed to allow the OIM island that was currently being built to remain, but they requested that the OIM expansion be halted, as soon as the agreement was finalized. This was completely acceptable to the Land People and humans because the OIM island was already nearly as large as the island country of Madagascar off the coast of East Africa—the fourth largest island on Earth.

Having reached an agreement on the three laws of the sea, the negotiations turned to the larger subject: the sharing of the land and space with the Water People. The details were generally acceptable to all parties, although quite a bit of work would need to take place, back on Earth and on Terrene, for the Water People's wish to become reality.

They weren't asking to be given the technology of the humans or the Land People, they simply wanted to benefit from it. They believed their God wanted them to come upon the land and to travel into space, and using the technology of the Land People and the humans could achieve this. They asked for salt water canals to be built throughout the lands of Terrene, so they could swim to any location they chose. And they asked for the humans and Land People to devise a means for them to come out of the water and to socialize with all the residents, learning and living beside them. They also wanted space vehicles they could live and travel in, so they could participate in the exploration of the galaxy that the Land People had been doing for thousands of years.

Charles had some ideas about pills that would enable the gills of the Water People to function as lungs, drawing oxygen from the air just as they did from water. And he had ideas about mobile devices that could move them around on land, and even envisioned surgeries that might convert their tail fin areas to legs and feet, for those who wanted to stay on the land on a more permanent basis. All of these ideas would be best suited for the Community of Minds back on Earth to tackle, and promises were made to make that happen. The Land People felt space vessels could easily be built that held water rather than air, or a combination of the two, for joint missions, and so the talents of the Land People in piloting space vehicles could be used for the benefit of the Water People.

All in all, the discussions were productive, and documents were drawn up, and ultimately signed by both parties, memorializing these historic negotiations, forever to be known as the Terrene and Earth Peace Accords. All parties set out to fulfill their commitments, the first act being the extinguishing of the fires that had burned under the poles for over 600 years. The settlement process continued, and the Land People and human settlers still on Earth were ferried to Terrene, while key information for the Mind Upload projects was transited back and forth.

Dani was proud of her role in the peace accords, and messages from Earth indicated that Annette and the Executive Committee were also pleased with her contributions, and looking forward to her and Aideen returning to Earth, where they would forever be remembered as pioneers of the first human settlement outside of the solar system. The future seemed bright for both Earth and Terrene, and no one would have guessed that the challenges faced thus far would pale in comparison to what lay ahead.

Chapter 45

L iam Murphy stood behind the bar of the pub he'd named Murphy's and served up pints of ale for his first three guests—Orla, Dani and Aideen—back together again, if only for a while. Liam was dressed as he always was, in clothing from his era, and Orla had also gone back to the long skirts and linen undergarments of her original life on Earth. In the spirit of celebrating Murphy's grand opening, Dani and Aideen wore the jeans and flannel shirts from their own era on Earth, and felt good doing it, nostalgia washing through all of them.

Next to enter the pub were Clarion and Zephyr, the two Land People who had done the most to bring their people home. Zephyr and Dani were fast friends, and Dani would miss her dearly when the day to return to Earth arrived. They'd been on Terrene for six months, and so much had happened it was hard to believe this place had been pure ocean such a short time ago. Next to arrive was Charles, and Liam came out from behind the bar and gave him a bear hug. The two were surprisingly good friends, and had been since they'd schemed together back in 1801, when Liam was sixty-six years old and Charles was intending to take over the world. But all of that was in the past. Liam would build the world he wanted here on Terrene, and Charles... would be Charles. As far as Dani was concerned, it was only a matter of time until Charles got himself, and the rest of them, into trouble again.

After a few pints, Dani and Aideen stepped outside into the sunshine. The light wasn't as bright here on Terrene, since the sun was half the size of Sol and didn't burn as hot. But Terrene itself was much closer to its sun than Earth was, and traveled much faster, making a year on Terrene only thirty-four Earth days, but no one really noticed. The planet's orbit was circular rather than elliptical, and this meant the weather conditions didn't change as Terrene circled its sun. It was these exceptionally stable weather conditions—from a long-living sun and a circular orbit on a planet with liquid water—that had allowed life to develop on Terrene. The days were a little longer—thirty hours—because the planet's rotation was slower than Earth's, but everyone easily adjusted to that as well. Dani and Aideen had grown fond of the place, and had actually spoken about living there permanently, but they missed Earth too and were glad that transit between the two planets had become fairly regular, because this meant they could visit often after they departed.

Dani was pleased that the Land People and humans had decided to live together, rather than building separate towns for each species. Other than Murphy's pub, which Liam had insisted on building with a white stucco exterior and a slate roof, and with wide plank floors, an oaken bar and wooden chairs on the inside, the rest of the town was composed of the same black stone, OIM architecture which covered most of the Earth at that time. The Land People loved black, claiming that all of their buildings in the southerly regions of Terrene, before their diaspora, had been black, to gather as much of the sun's energy as possible.

While there were currently 1,500 Land People compared to only 200 humans living on Base One, Dani expected that would change quickly when word spread back to Earth of what a wonderful place the world of Terrene had become. The weather was perfect, year round, it didn't rain that often, and the huge waves that sometimes came through, crashed harmlessly against the cliffs 500 meters below. The crops were already growing and producing food, and the OIM could make anything people wanted if the natural produce from the island wasn't enough for them. Grass fields and forests had sprung up, blanketing the island in green, and streams meandered peacefully and randomly throughout the countryside. Charles kept the OIM busy making his wine, and who knows what else. He had built his home on the outskirts of town, and kept to himself more than Dani liked, causing her to wonder if he was up to no good again. She wanted him to be happy, but wondered if happiness was something a person like Charles could ever find.

While Dani was reminiscing, Aideen took her hand. "What say we take a boat ride out to see our old friend, Cabal?" she asked "Would you like to do that, my love?"

"A fabulous idea!" said Dani. "We haven't seen Cabal for a while now."

"I was thinkin' it might be time for us to say our goodbyes to Cabal, and the others here on Terrene, soon."

Hearing this, Dani lowered her head and choked up, her thoughts moving to Orla. Aideen squeezed her hand.

"She'll be fine, Dani. She's in love. She's happy. And you and I have to do what all parents must do at some point. We have to let go."

"I know," said Dani, as tears rolled down her cheeks. "It's just so far away."

"Just a blink of an eye away, is all it is, my dear. Just a blink of an eye."

Dani wiped her tears away and the two boarded a lift that would take them down to the water's edge, 1,000 meters below. They signed out a small boat and charted a course to the area where Cabal and his team had based themselves to provide easy access to those from the land. A true spirit of cooperation existed between the three species now, and Dani took some pride in being an important part of making that happen.

When they arrived, they pulled the boat up alongside one of the floating pontoon docks that had been assembled there. In the clear water all around them they could see Water People swimming here and there, busy with tasks surrounding the joint project to get them on land. And as they looked further, they saw Cabal, lounging in a specially-designed chair on the dock, looking as if he were trying to get a suntan. They approached him with smiles on their faces, amazed that he wasn't wearing any breathing gear. He looked up at them and a smile formed on his huge mouth, full of spiked teeth that sparkled in the sun.

I've been up here for over an hour and haven't died yet, he said. *These pills from Earth seem to be working well.*

"That's great news," said Dani. "Any side effects?"

Nothing yet.

"Awesome."

What brings you two out this way? he asked.

"We wanted to see you," said Aideen. "To say hello."

And to say goodbye, he said, and Dani thought she detected sadness in him. Cabal obviously hadn't been distracted from the truth of their visit by Aideen's small talk. *I will be sad to see you two leave this world, with so much left to be done.*

"Terrene is in the hands of many who are better equipped than us to succeed," said Dani.

Cabal reflected on this for a moment. *I'm not so sure,* he said. *Will you return soon?*

"That is our intent," said Aideen.

You're hedging your bets then, he said, smiling, and Aideen and Dani smiled back.

While Dani was reflecting on how marvelous it was to be friends with an alien being who lived in the sea, and who happened to be the leader of what they'd learned were nearly a billion Water People. Amazing. But as her euphoria bubbled inside her, she noticed that Cabal's expression had changed. A serous look came onto his face.

"What's the matter, Cabal?" she asked.

I've just received a message from Clarion.

"What is it?" asked Aideen.

He said he has received a message, the details of which have not been disclosed to him. It is a locked recording that came with the latest vessel from Earth. It can only be opened by you two.

"Who is it from?" asked Aideen.

Minister Li. And the disk is marked "Urgent!"

"Oh my," said Dani. "We need to get back to Base One ASAP. I'm sorry, Cabal, we'd intended to spend more time with you."

I understand, he said. *It is always so nice to see you both. And please, let me know if the Water People can help, in any way, once you determine what the problem is, if indeed it is a problem.*

"Oh, it's a problem all right," said Aideen. "Just a matter of finding out what it is. Goodbye for now, Cabal."

Chapter 46

Dani and Aideen rushed back to Base One. When they reached Clarion's office, she stood up, handed them the disk and told them to make themselves comfortable. The disk was about the size of a quarter and was the kind that would transmit whatever it contained telepathically. There was no risk of anyone but Dani and Aideen receiving the information on the disk, so all that was needed was for one of them to touch it. The disk would recognize their DNA and begin playing. Dani reached out and touched the disk, and the message began transmitting, directly to their brains.

Dani and Aideen, I'm sorry for all this secrecy, but I thought it was best to send this message to the two people I trust the most on Terrene. Once you hear what I have to say, I request that you share it with those on Terrene who might be able to help us. The bottom line is that the Earth is under attack, and this one is real. It appears that another one of our space-time travel probes was found, by yet another intelligent alien species. We don't know which one, however, so we have no idea where these creatures are from. What we do know is that they are hostile, and seem to have only one intention: To destroy all life on this planet, very likely so they can occupy it themselves. We really don't know what their aim is because there has been no communication with them whatsoever. Not that we haven't tried.

They do not appear to have the same travel technology as the Land People. They arrived at the edge of the solar system and began decelerating, slowing themselves from some kind of faster-than-light travel. They came in a fleet of over 100 warships, encircled the Earth, forming a spherical shape around us, then deployed some kind of energy field that displayed itself as a white sphere, casting the Earth into darkness and blocking out nearly all the light and heat from our sun. The temperature on Earth is dropping rapidly and the energy demands will soon be far too great for us to remain alive for more than a week, unless a solution is found.

We can send space vehicles through the energy field, which seems designed to block only one thing—the light of our sun— but as you know, the Earth of 2256 is a peaceful planet, with no weapons to destroy the alien fleet. I write primarily to tell you not to return here, but also with some hope that you can share this information with the Land People, the Water People, and God help me for asking this, with Charles. There are additional files on this disk which show pictures of the white blanket that surrounds us, the ships that created it, and technical details we've been able to gather regarding the nature of the blanket and of the ships. You can release this data and this file by pressing the disk three times. If we do not find a way out of this, I take some solace in knowing that the human race will continue on, on the very planet you have settled. Thank you for this. You both are my dear friends, and I'm so glad I met you.

Dani looked up at Aideen.

"Here we go again," she said. "Shall we proceed?"

"Absolutely," said Aideen.

Dani gave the instructions. "Clarion, can you please send a message to Charles, and to Cabal, that they are needed here at Base One headquarters immediately. Send a hovercraft equipped with the gear that provides Cabal mobility while here on land. I'd also like Zephyr to be here for the meeting."

Within thirty minutes, all parties were present, sitting around the conference table in Clarion's office. Cabal sat comfortably in a chair designed for his form, and had removed the mobility equipment from his tailfin. Dani pushed the disk three times, then played Annette's message. Charles was the first to speak.

"Get a message to Annette to program OIM to drill to the core of the Earth and tap into its heat. The OIM can transfer heat into the atmosphere, but what will be coming up from the core will be extremely hot, so they have to do this from as many remote locations as possible. Dozens to start, but hundreds, if possible."

Clarion responded. *Your words have been recorded and uploaded to one of our space vessels. It will be dispatched to Earth within thirty seconds.*

"Thank you," said Charles.

Next, the pictures and technical files were displayed. Zephyr immediately commented.

We know these beings, she said. *We visited their planet, tried to make contact, and they sent vessels such as this to destroy us. We transported out of that system immediately and they could not follow us.*

"Where is their planet?" asked Dani.

It's in a star system which is about forty light years from Earth, said Zephyr. *Your naming database calls the planet "TRAPPIS 1d." It is about the same size and temperature as Earth, but its gravity is thirty percent less than Earth's. It would have been a nice planet for my people to live on, but the inhabitants are very aggressive.*

"So you had no contact with them?" asked Aideen.

They did not communicate with us, but we had enough time to scour their databases before we were attacked. We can search the database we brought from Diaspora One, but I'm sure Clarion remembers quite a lot of it because she was always the first to see the information when it was received.

Clarion filled them in. *These creatures are not humanoid. They call themselves, the Fury, and the name is well deserved; they are a violent race. They are cold blooded, so they need the heat of the sun or other heating sources to be comfortable. In their original form, they used to go into a state of hibernation on a periodic basis, but were able to genetically engineer that feature out of their biology when it no longer served a purpose. They have highly advanced brains and six appendages with functional hands and fingers, so they can build things. Their spacecraft are powered by fusion engines, and they have hyper-drive capabilities that can propel them at up to ten times the speed of light, so it probably took them four years to reach Earth. There is no doubt they will want to colonize the planet if they succeed in destroying life there. They will grow plants from their own planet to replenish the oxygen and to make the planet more familiar to them, although there will be enough oxygen on Earth to last 1000 years, even with all the plant life destroyed. They will be able to take possession of the planet as soon as it warms back up, which won't take long when their light-blocking veil is turned off.*

"Do you have any information that could help us defeat them in battle?" asked Charles.

Clarion did not speak immediately. She was thinking. *I believe we might*, she said.

Chapter 47

Only thirty-six hours after the meeting, nine small, spherical space vessels—the ones that had ferried Land People and human settlers from Earth to Terrene—popped into high orbit around Earth, not far outside of the white sphere that surrounded the planet, and the 108 ships that had built the veil that was freezing Earth. The small vessels had placed themselves far from each other, and each of the nine was assigned to neutralize twelve of the enemy ships. But they started taking fire almost immediately, as lasers tried and failed to break through their shields. The shield technology of the Land People was three separate layers, separated from one another by about 100 meters. The outer layer was a light diffuser and was very effective against any light-based weapon, including lasers. The second layer was a powerful force field designed to repel anything that hit it, be it light-based or any kind of explosive projectile. The third layer, closest to the ship, was a cooling field, designed to moderate any heat build-up experienced by the second layer. In this case, the outer layer did the job, leaving very little for the second layer to repel, and minimal heat for the inner field to dissipate. The lasers were ineffective against the much smaller crafts, proving, as had happened many times in history, that size did not always overcome wits.

The next phase began, and each of the nine ships used their powerful scopes to map the interior of each enemy vessel, followed by the transporting of pre-programmed OIM samples into rarely occupied areas in those ships. Upon arrival, each OIM sample started eating whatever it could find, growing into a rectangular shape about the size of a large freezer. And that's exactly what it was, but it was the most powerful freezer unit known to man, designed by the Land People hundreds of years previously to attempt to refreeze the poles of their world. The technology had failed in its first application, because the blazing infernos placed underneath the poles by the Water People were producing too much heat to overcome. But the newly designed units, using OIM technology, were expected to easily outpace the heating systems on the enemy vessels.

Within twenty minutes, the units were full size and the AI program told the OIM to begin producing cold air and to deploy a force field to render attempts to destroy the units inert. The cold in the room dropped to -75 degrees Celsius (-100 Fahrenheit) within five minutes, and continued falling. The metal walls of the vessel conducted the cold to other parts of the ship and the cold-blooded crew began to fall asleep. When the cold reached the fusion reactors, they shut down, and at that point, systems on board began to fail, then came back on when battery backup kicked in. But the batteries were emergency systems and the white veil required a tremendous amount of energy to be sustained, so it blinked out of existence, forever. And then the batteries themselves froze and all the ships' systems shut down, including the atmospheric production and distribution systems. All the Fury on board every one of the 108 ships either froze to death or suffocated, while the sun's rays once again washed over the Earth, bringing it back from the brink of death.

The nine ships from Terrene were directed by authorities on Earth to dock at a nearby space station for an important meeting. The crews from each ship had been Land People, and included Clarion and Zephyr, but there had been three humans on board as well—Dani, Aideen and Charles. Charles was needed to supervise and monitor the OIM deployment, and Aideen and Dani were present at the request of Clarion and Zephyr, who had seen both in crisis mode before, and had wanted them in charge of the mission in the event something went wrong. Luckily, everything had gone smoothly, but the Land People had risked their lives on behalf of humanity, and would do it again, if necessary. They would be forever grateful to the people of Earth for enabling them to reclaim their homeland, and to Dani in particular for negotiating the peace with the Water People.

Soon after their arrival on the space station, Annette Li beamed up from Earth, and they all gathered together for cocktails and dinner. Annette stood and raised her glass. "I would like to say to all of you brave people, on behalf of all the living species of Earth, thank you. We've known the Land People for less than three years, but the things we've accomplished together are the most amazing things I have ever been part of. And that includes time travel, which I must tell you, is a technology that I wish we'd never discovered. After the attack by the Fury, which was germinated by a time travel probe we sent to their star system around five years ago, the last vestige of time travel, the exploration of space, has been officially mothballed. But that is not why I am here. I am here to thank you, and to honor you. So I raise a toast to the Land

People of Terrene, and to the brave humans who were at their side during this decisive battle."

Everyone raised their glass, and the toast was consummated. A wonderful dinner ensued, and then people were shown to their cabins for a good sleep. But before Dani, Aideen, Charles, Clarion and Zephyr could leave, Annette approached them.

"Do you five have enough strength left for another meeting?" she asked.

The five nodded and Annette showed them into a smaller, luxurious private lounge. They sat in comfortable chairs and looked out at the stars through a floor-to-ceiling window. Drinks were served and Annette began.

"The galaxy has proven to be a bit more than we bargained for," she said. "In retrospect, we were quite naïve. We thought other advanced, intelligent species would share our philosophy of peace."

Yes, said Clarion. *We have encountered many other species in our travels, and I am sad to say that virtually all are warriors.*

"Speaking of warriors," said Aideen. "What will you do with the thousands of dead and their 108 warships?"

"It will be a long cleanup process," said Annette. "A few of the bodies will be preserved for further study, and we thought we'd move most of the ships to the moon. But if we can get one of them down to Earth, that would be nice. A motion has been raised to upgrade our defenses and some of the Fury tech might be useful in that regard."

"I'd put my money on the tech of the Land People if defense is what you're looking for," said Charles.

"Indeed," said Aideen. "And to that point, I'm wondering, Clarion, what it would take to create a shield like the ones you surround your vessels with, around the entire Earth."

Clarion did not hesitate. *Energy,* she said. *Lots of energy. But with fusion technology, the required energy can be produced. We are happy to help. And it's probably a good idea we do the same thing for Terrene.*

"Will you help us?" asked Annette.

Of course, replied Clarion.

"Thank you," said Annette. "Now I have one more topic to discuss. And I feel it should be put on the table in front of all of you."

"What is it?" asked Dani.

"It's another reason why time travel will be banished forever," said Annette. "I'm sorry to tell you that another Dani was found wandering around the time station in our building, confused and disoriented."

Chapter 48

A nnette, Dani and Aideen stood at the glass wall of the time station control room, peering down at the seats of the auditorium and the floor which held the massive monolith that was the home of the Community of Minds. Clarion, Zephyr, Charles and the rest of the crews of the successful mission to defeat the Fury had all returned to Terrene. Annette had briefly considered keeping Charles on Earth to help with the "Dani Issue," as it was being called, but decided he might be more trouble than help, so she sent him back to the one place where he was legally allowed to be.

"She comes about this time, every day now," said Annette. "You may remember that it was just this time, around two p.m., when Charles sent himself back to 1801 to avoid being captured by the team Dani sent to his time station. It was at that moment that the future was changed. The Dani who sat down below in the time station and functioned as the time link for that mission, ceased to live in this reality. The Dani from her recent past, who was still in Charles's time station when the mission took place, became the Dani living in this reality, the reality we created by keeping Charles from destroying all the OIM in the world. The Dani who is here with us now was the one who remained in this reality."

"Is this other Dani, the one you say will appear below at any moment, a ghost?" asked Aideen.

"Yes and no," said Annette. "Yes, in the sense that she doesn't belong here and cannot seem to stay in this reality for long. No, in the sense that she is flesh and blood, and unfortunately, very confused. Our theory is that time simply stopped in her reality at the moment the mission succeeded, and since Dani was the time link who had made it all happen, she has the ability to share in both realities. But since there is no future for her in the reality which ended, she had nowhere to go but here, to the primary reality of all life on Earth. I told you some time ago that our scientists believe these alternate realities have been created exclusively by the indiscretions of time travel participants, i.e., Charles, and unwittingly, the time links who joined his cause and later fought to stop him. But there is only supposed to be one reality, at least that's what our scientists, and the Community of Minds believe. For some time, actually, the Community of Minds has been strongly recommending an end to all time travel. They say that Dani's appearing and disappearing is evidence that time itself is out of balance, and is attempting to correct itself by purging the false reality from existence. Dani is in the unique position of being the one person, so far, who has been exempted from this purging and is unknowingly attempting to move herself from a reality that was dead-ended by time travel, to the primary reality we all live in now. Her role as a time link in the mission that changed reality seems to be central to this happening."

"What about the jungle?" asked Aideen. "The one that Ciara and I were in that we don't remember, because reality was changed once again when your team captured Charles in 1801, eliminating the need for Dani, Ciara, Orla and me to escape from Charles. And we came here in that other reality, to get your help in stopping Charles. You made notes on it, remember, so you would know that it had happened after reality changed."

"Yes, I remember," said Annette. "And if you're asking whether there will be more doppelgangers appearing, such as you, Ciara, Orla and yet another Dani, I don't know. I'm hoping the second Dani is the only one, and that it has something to do with the old Time Chain tech that we used for that mission, but I have no way of knowing."

As Annette was speaking, the second Dani appeared down below, sitting in the exact seat she had used as a time link in the mission to capture Charles one day in the past, while he held her, Aideen and Orla prisoner in his time station in the year 2253.

"There she is," said Annette, lowering her voice as if the second Dani might hear her.

The Dani standing beside Annette, the "real Dani," gasped. It was as if she could feel the confusion and turmoil of the second Dani, just as an identical twin could sometimes feel the emotions of their sibling. Dani was deeply moved by the tragic figure down below, another version of herself, who had come from a reality that had once happened, but had been relegated to the sidelines of existence by time travel. Aideen took her hand.

"It will be all right," she said. "It will be all right." But just as Annette had no answers, neither did Aideen.

"Each time she comes," said Annette, "she stays in this reality a little bit longer, then disappears and returns to the reality she came from."

"Have you had time to talk to her?" asked Dani.

"Yes, I have," said Annette. "We've stationed a guard just off the floor of the time station to intercept Dani and bring her to a conference room down there when she starts to wander."

"Did she remember you?" asked Aideen.

"Yes, but only the time we spent together in the reality which we changed, and you'll remember, I had forgotten about that one and had to be briefed on it by the real Dani here, who remembers both realities. There! You see, she's getting up."

A female guard dressed in the familiar light blue skinsuit entered the room and approached the Dani down below and spoke to her, then led her off the floor. Dani in the control room was torn about what to do. She closed her eyes and searched her heart, then made a decision.

"I want to speak with her," she said.

Chapter 49

The three women went down to the conference room, but only Annette and Dani entered. Aideen remained outside because it was felt seeing her would further confuse the second Dani, but she was told to remain nearby in the event an opportunity presented itself to bring her in. When second Dani saw real Dani, she started crying, then screamed at Annette.

"So it's true!" she said. "What you told me?"

Annette remained calm, putting on a reassuring smile on. "Yes, it's true. This is you a little over three years after what you remember. I've been trying to figure out a way to address you two while you're together, and here's my idea. I'll call you Danielle, and this one here Dani. I've had more time with Dani, and I'm just getting to know you, Danielle. Is that approach all right with you two?"

Dani nodded and Danielle grimaced.

"It's fine," she spat. "But what are you going to do with me? After all, I'm not living a real life anymore. Why don't you just kill me and put me out of my misery!" She put her elbows on the table and lowered her face into her hands.

Dani walked around the table and sat beside Danielle, taking one of her hands in her own. She felt the confusion and agony

217

so strongly in her own being that she had to dig very deeply to find words that might help… herself. "That's not gonna happen, Danielle. You're like my kid sister now, after all, I'm more than three years older than you!" Dani's effort to lighten the mood in the room seemed to help a little, and she felt the turmoil inside herself begin to dissipate. Danielle looked up at her.

"I'm just so confused!" she said, leaning into Dani.

"Tell me what it's like for you," said Dani.

"It's like I'm in a time loop," said Danielle. "I'm sitting in that chair in the time station here in this building, observing what's going on in Charles's time station, through you, then you guys find Charles using Orla to send himself back in time, and I don't know if Aideen and Orla are okay, because then I blank out, and whenever I wake up, I'm back in that damn chair! It happens over and over again."

"But Annette told you that Aideen and Orla are just fine, right?"

"Yes, she did, but I want to see them! I want to be with them again! But I keep popping back to that stupid seat in the auditorium of the time station. It's really a living hell, I'm telling you!" Danielle shook her head from side to side, but Dani held on tightly and she didn't start crying again.

Dani looked over at Annette, gesturing toward the wall of the room with a movement of her head, and Annette nodded. Dani held up one finger, telling Annette to wait, for just a moment. "Aideen is doing well, and she'd like to see you too, Danielle. Did you know she took that pill that makes you look younger?"

"So she looks thirty years old now?"

"She does, and she feels it too! More energy than ever."

"Can I see her?"

Dani nodded her head and Annette caused an opening to appear in the wall of the conference room, and Aideen peeked in. Danielle's eyes widened, and so did Aideen's, seeing the two of them side by side. The Dani she had come here with had longer hair than the one who had just arrived from the false reality, but other than that, they were identical. Aideen moved briskly around the table and did just what Dani had hoped she would do. She dragged Danielle up out the chair and hugged her tightly. Danielle melted into Aideen like she wanted to become part of her.

"Now I've got two of you!" said Aideen. "What a lucky girl I am!"

"I'm afraid I'll be leaving soon," fretted Danielle, but Dani knew Danielle was feeling better because she herself was feeling a surge of relief, brought on by the entrance of Aideen.

Dani looked at Annette, wondering how much longer they would have with Danielle. Annette seemed to understand what she wanted to know.

"Last time Danielle visited, she was here for a little over an hour," said Annette. "I'd guess we have about twenty more minutes."

"Good," said Dani. "If I could just get these two to unclench, perhaps we can talk a little." When Aideen and Danielle had hugged, in addition to relief she'd felt, Danielle's relief, she also experienced a pang of jealousy that was her own. She wondered if it would always be like that. She also tried to imagine what Aideen was feeling, having two of them to worry about now. But she needed to make something clear to Danielle, right away, before she disappeared. "Before we tell you how Orla's doing, and where she is right now, I want to promise you that after you leave, we'll make a plan, okay, Danielle?"

"Okay," she responded, somewhat despondently. But then she raised her head up, a look of hope on her face. "Are you saying there's actually something that can be done to help me?"

"There's always something that can be done," said Dani. "We'll figure this out and we'll be waiting for you next time." Dani noticed Annette showing signs of doubt on her face, but that quickly disappeared and she brought the calm smile back which was most appropriate for the meeting.

Dani told Danielle that Charles had finally been captured, and that he was now living on the first settlement outside of the solar system, with Orla and Liam and their new friends, the Land People. She also conveyed that time travel had continued to create problems for Earth, and they had narrowly escaped annihilation at the hands of the aliens known as the Fury. Danielle was amazed that so much could happen in just three years, and expressed a deep yearning to be part of life in this reality, and Dani promised her they would try to figure something out. And then, without warning, Danielle simply disappeared, going back to what she had described as a "living hell," and causing Dani to feel great anxiety.

She looked directly at Annette. "I have an idea. But I want to discuss it first with Aideen, and a few other people, and if everyone's okay with it, we'll come to you."

Annette's eyes widened, as if she knew that whatever plan Dani had concocted would end up being a headache for her. But she nodded, always willing to listen to one of her most trusted friends and confidants.

Chapter 50

S he's not your sister," said Aideen, her tone serious. "She's you, and I love her the same way I love you. And that, my dearest, is the heart of the issue, for both of us."

"It is," said Dani. "I know I'd be jealous if you spent more time with her than with me."

"And at night? If I spent time in the bedroom with her?"

"That would be difficult."

"For both of us!" said Aideen, exasperated.

Dani had asked Annette what she thought would happen with Danielle, if they did nothing, and Annette had said it was the opinion of the experts that the time of Danielle's stays in this reality would continue to increase, until she was more anchored here than in the false reality, and then she would no longer be pulled back into the time loop. The issue was, would she lose her sanity and end her life before that happened? It was a real possibility, in everyone's minds.

Dani had waited until she and Aideen were alone in their apartment before sharing her idea, which was to go back in time and physically bring Danielle to this time, and this reality.

Aideen had questions. "You mean, during the time when you were sittin' in the time station, performin' your role as a time link for the mission to capture Charles?"

"Yes," said Dani.

"The timin' is goin' to be tricky," said Aideen, and Dani nodded.

"For sure. We can't jeopardize the original mission, which means we have to let Charles transport himself out of his station, back to 1801. At that instant, we need to move Danielle here, before she disappears into the time loop."

Dani suggested they might have plenty of time, because whatever time loop Danielle was caught in hadn't started bringing her to the present day until recently. Aideen countered that Danielle could have been appearing here for some time, but just for microseconds, and she hadn't been seen until her visits started lasting long enough for someone to notice her. She also pointed out that the time station wasn't even being used anymore, and hadn't been for some time, so no one was even there most of the time, meaning Danielle may have been there but not been seen. In the end, they concluded this approach could only be proven viable, or not, by trying it. But Aideen was not yet ready to commit to coexisting with two Dani's in her life.

"I think it would be every bit as hard for you as it would be for me, Dani, very likely harder," she said. "If you think about it, if all I was thinking about was myself, I'd want as many Dani's as I could get."

Dani laughed at that, assuming Aideen was simply joking.

"What, you don't believe me?" asked Aideen, a sly smile on her face.

"I admit it would be difficult, for all of three of us," said Dani. "But Aideen, she's a living being, and she's living in agony as we speak, confused and alone. We have to figure something out! And letting her, letting me, kill myself is not an option."

"Do you think if Danielle died that you would also die?" asked Aideen. "I mean, she's you at a younger age than you are now."

"But living in a different reality," said Dani. "I think I'd be fine, but letting Danielle die is just not an option. Is it an option for you?"

"When you put it that way, no, it isn't," said Aideen. "So we have no choice. Too bad there's not two of me."

Dani paused, thinking. "What if there *were* two of you?" she asked, and then she shared her next idea with Aideen.

"That might work," said Aideen. "I'm willing to try that, so who's next on your list to talk to?"

"My mom and dad," said Dani. "We have to see how they'd feel about having two of me in their lives."

Dani and Aideen went to visit Pat and Don, and eventually found them down at the community center, playing tennis with another couple. When they saw Dani and Aideen, they rushed off the court and embraced them, not having seen them for over six months since the two had been on Terrene. After things settled down, Dani asked them if they could speak privately, then she and Aideen explained the entire saga to them. It seemed to Dani that neither of them understood fully how this had happened, but it was abundantly clear that they loved the idea of Dani having an identical twin.

Annette was the next person on Dani's short list of people who needed to agree to pursue her ideas. She realized Annette would have to seek approval from the Executive Committee regarding the entire plan, and while Annette felt it wasn't without risk, in a few areas, it was still very likely the least bad of all solutions. The Executive Committee agreed.

The next day, Dani and Aideen shared the good news with Danielle when she transited through 2256 on her way to nowhere, and she was so excited that all she wanted to know was how soon it could happen. Dani told her there was only one more group that needed to approve the plan: the Land People of Terrene. She and Aideen would travel to Terrene immediately, and Annette would keep meeting with Danielle until they returned.

Chapter 51

I t had been less than a week since they'd left Terrene. The battle with the Fury hadn't taken long, thankfully, although the cleanup of that mess would take months. The detour to Earth had not been part of the plan for Dani and Aideen, and they had promised Orla they would return for a proper goodbye. But the appearances and disappearances of Danielle had caused them to change their plans, and after arriving at a potential solution, they spent a few days with Dani's parents and Aoife, who were always happy to spend time with their children. They had sent word on a shuttle to Terrene of their expected arrival date, and Orla was waiting for them at Murphy's pub when they beamed down from orbit. In fact, it seemed half the town was there, eager to have yet another celebration of Terrene's victory over the Fury on behalf of Earth, and to greet the two remaining heroes from that mission.

Orla rushed up to them when they came through the door to Murphy's, while Liam remained behind the bar raising his mug to them, a big smile on his handsome face. He was the bartender, but part of Liam's charm was his insistence on getting drunk right along with his patrons, and while this might have been construed as unsavory behavior back on Earth, it seemed completely appropriate here on Base One of Terrene. After all, Liam had come here to build a life based on who he was, and having a pint or two, or ten, in a friendly pub was a big part of it.

Orla hugged them both tightly and didn't seem to want to let go, but was anxious to hear more about the strange happenings back on Earth. "Charles told us about the other Dani," she said. "He was a bit miffed not bein' invited to help with the problem, but I told him you two and Annette were more than enough to handle it. So was I right about that?"

Dani nodded. "We have a plan, but we need one more approval to make it work."

"Who do you need that from?" asked Orla. "Annette seems to have her way with the Executive Committee when she wants something."

"Annette and the Executive Committee are on board, as are all the other related parties on Earth. We need to meet with Clarion and Zephyr about it."

"What for?" asked Orla, confused.

Dani had considered not telling Orla about the plan, because it hadn't been finalized and hadn't been successfully executed, but when confronted with her face to face, there was no doubt she was going to spill all the beans to her friend. While Dani described the plan to Orla, she watched her friend's beautiful green eyes widen and her pretty mouth fall open, absolute shock on her face, but soon, after it had all sunk in, the smile that had been there upon their arrival returned, bigger than ever.

"Oh my god!" she exclaimed. "I can't believe it! Goodness me, I hope it works."

"We do too," said Aideen. "But now lass, we must go and see if that last piece of the puzzle can be put into place. And

I see the two we need are here, making their way over to us through this wonderfully crowded pub."

The pub was indeed packed, and nearly half of the crowd were Land People, who seemed to enjoy Liam's ale and stout, which were still made by OIM, but which he planned to begin making himself as soon as he could. The Land People had no problem holding their drink, as their systems seemed to process alcohol better than most humans. They said they really didn't feel it, but they liked the taste of ale, and most of all, they enjoyed the company of their newly found friends, and the joyful atmosphere of Murphy's pub.

After greeting each other, Dani asked Clarion and Zephyr if they could speak privately, as soon as possible. It was 13 p.m., but still daylight. Since they'd had the opportunity to decide how to schedule the thirty-hour days on Terrene when they settled there, the inhabitants of Base One had decided to make the daylight hours end at 15 a.m., the equivalent of midnight on Earth, and begin at 15 p.m., the equivalent of noon. The farmers and fisherman were the first to begin working, and started around daybreak, which was 15 p.m. The number of hours they worked varied, but the Land People tended to work twelve to fourteen hour days, while the humans normally worked eight to ten hours. No one cared. People all did the best they could, and that was the philosophy upon which the colony was founded, and would ultimately prosper.

Clarion suggested they go down the street to the Base One administrative offices where both she and Zephyr worked. They entered Clarion's office and sat in the comfortable chairs there, around a coffee table, but everyone leaned forward, knowing something momentous was about to be discussed. Dani jumped right into it.

"We have a plan regarding the other Dani," she said. "But the plan won't work unless you can help us with something. And it's no small request."

What is it? asked Clarion.

"We need your help creating a clone of Aideen."

Chapter 52

T he idea," Dani continued, "is for one couple to live on Earth and the other couple to live on Terrene."

Hmmm, pondered Clarion. *That might be enough to overcome a major hurdle. Cloning has been part of our culture for thousands of years, and in the early years, it is said that more than one of the same person were allowed to live at the same time. But these people inevitably ended up killing themselves.*

"I can guess why," said Dani, "because I have some experience with that issue myself. I've found that when I'm in the presence of Danielle, I feel what she is feeling. It's very disconcerting because I end up trying to make her feel the way I'm feeling, in the hope of helping her, but I can see how that whole back and forth processing of emotions could get very old, very quickly."

And in the case of two clones of the same person, at least for us Land People, said Zephyr, *it's more than a sharing of emotions. It's a sharing of experiences. The blending of experiences is very disorienting, and causes the two clones to want to be together at all times, so they both experience the same things. Of course, that is no way to live, and it is not a long-term solution to the issue.*

"Do you think your technology could be adapted to work with humans?" asked Aideen.

We assume you need our cloning technology because the cloning technology of Earth does not capture the memories of the person being cloned, but ours does.

"I must admit, I'm not up to date on the cloning technology in 2256 on Earth," said Aideen, "but I'll take your word for it. Dani may know more."

And Dani did know more. "I've spoken at length with Annette about it, and of course, borrowing the cloning technology of the Land People is on the 'To Do List' of Earth, but the more important priority right now is how to move an uploaded mind into a biological body. The humans of 2256 are quite skilled at transferring the contents of a human mind to a computer, and even though they can make a clone that looks exactly like the person whose mind now lives in a computer, they have not successfully made the transfer in the opposite direction. Interestingly, most Minds that have been uploaded want to stay where they are. They find the world inside the computer to be stimulating beyond anything they ever experienced as biological humans—for example the binding with other Minds to work together on a project—and would never want to give that up. But around thirty percent of the Minds have stated they would prefer to become biological humans again, if given the chance. That's about thirty million Minds that are pushing for, and working on, the project to achieve the transfer back into biological form."

Interesting, said Clarion. *But that's a different issue than what you're proposing we do with Aideen. In this case, you want the body and mind of a human to be duplicated in another human.*

"How does it work?" asked Aideen.

Our technology is able to capture the memories and grow them into the clone, said Clarion. *We do it using scopes that map the brain in such detail that literally everything that's in there, including the memories, is captured.*

"Amazing," said Aideen. "What are the chances you could do this with a human."

Very high, said Clarion.

"And the risks?" asked Dani.

I'm not a specialist in cloning, nor is Zephyr, but my guess is that the risks would be minimal. Zephyr nodded in agreement. *Why don't we bring in our cloning experts to discuss this further?*

"Do we have to wait until tomorrow for that?" asked Dani, anxious to move as quickly as possible.

I have sent two of them a message just now, said Zephyr. *They're down at Murphy's pub and will join us in a few moments.*

The two cloning experts arrived. There were more than two of these experts in the Land People population, but these two happened to socialize with humans more than the others. Their names were Latif, who spoke in a male voice, and Sharell, who spoke in a female voice. Dani wondered how the Land People came up with their names. They supposedly had no language other than thought itself, so it wasn't clear to her how that manifested itself into names that a human could understand. Perhaps they had obtained assistance from their computers in choosing names for themselves, much as the Chinese people of centuries past had chosen "English names" so Westerners could remember them.

Clarion explained to Latif and Sharell what was being proposed, without unnecessary background information, which Dani appreciated. The task was to use Land People cloning tech to make another Aideen, who would be living 737 light years away from the Aideen currently in the room. The two experts agreed that the sheer distance should render the issues associated with shared feelings and experiences moot, although they couldn't guarantee it, since it had never been tried before. They further cautioned that the clone and the original would have to be immediately separated under any circumstances, which Dani and Aideen had already assumed.

"How long does it take to grow the clone?" asked Dani.

It takes around one month, said Latif.

"Can Aideen leave as soon as the full scans are complete?" asked Dani.

Yes, and this would provide further assurance that the brain linkage between the two would never occur, said Latif.

"And what about me being human rather than Land People," said Aideen. "Will it make a difference in whether or not your tech will work?"

As far as the cloning process itself, said Sharell, *from what we know about the human brain, it is no more complex than the brain of the Land People, so full duplication should be easily accomplished. However, we would like to take a closer look at the subject's brain to have full confidence in this assertion.*

"I am at your service," said Aideen.

"And time is of the essence," said Dani.

We can go over to the medical center now and have a look, said Latif.

"Are you sober?" asked Aideen, joking.

I'm sorry to say the answer is yes, for both of us, said Sharell. *We need to come up with a higher alcohol content ale than what Liam serves to have any chance of ever getting drunk. We are interested to find out what it feels like, actually, as the humans seems to enjoy it so much.*

"I'm sure you'll get no complaints from Liam about a high-alcohol ale!" said Aideen. "Shall we go?"

Chapter 53

The cloning experts put their scopes on Aideen's brain and found nothing that would lead them to believe the memory transfer would be unsuccessful. Their level of certainty was 99 percent for the memory transfer, and 100 percent for perfect duplication of the body itself. Armed with that information, Dani and Aideen said some hasty goodbyes, promising to return if they were successful in the next phase of the project, which was to bring Danielle permanently to what had been named "Primary Reality" by the experts on Earth.

Dani and Aideen returned to Earth and met with Annette to update her on their successful trip to Terrene and to put together the mission plan to bring Danielle to Primary Reality, using time travel. According to Annette, it would be easy to send a traveler to Danielle's time, carrying a time location device that would bring the traveler and Danielle to the present. Everyone understood how critical it was that Danielle not be moved until the exact moment when Charles sent himself back to 1801, which cancelled the reality Danielle had been living in. The records of the exact time of Charles's travel had been obtained from his time station before it was decommissioned and destroyed, so the correct time could be programmed into the mission.

The next question was who would go on the mission. Annette argued it should be a volunteer from the dedicated Time Management military force and suggested they introduce the volunteer to Danielle during her next visit, to make certain she was comfortable with them.

"I suppose we could try the volunteer," said Dani, "if Aideen and I can be part of the selection process. Are you okay with that Aideen?"

"I'd prefer to be the one to go," said Aideen. "But if Annette is going to insist on doing it this way, at the very least you and I should be comfortable with the person."

"Why don't I get five volunteers and you two interview all of them," suggested Annette. "You can rank them, and your number one choice will be the one to meet Danielle first. If Danielle gets comfortable with this volunteer, and I believe she will, then the mission will proceed. If not, we'll move down the list."

"You're probably right, Annette," said Dani. "But the Dani I saw was a very different Dani than anything I remember being. Highly unstable would be my description. So we can't assume anything. Let's just get the five volunteers and go through the process you've described."

The five volunteers were gathered and interviewed. Dani and Aideen agreed on the volunteer they felt Danielle would be most comfortable with. She was a soldier named Sergeant Cheryl Blackwell, a petite woman, about the same height as Orla. She had short blonde hair and a friendly, empathetic personality, and was a specialist in hostage negotiations. Although they rarely happened in 2256, the unique living circumstances of the Time Management complex—where all people were required to stay in the building for a minimum of a two-year tour—sometimes created dramatic circumstances involving hostages. The sole aim of the perpetrator was often to simply be released from the building. Cheryl was therefore an ideal candidate to deal with a highly agitated, unstable personality such as Danielle.

Cheryl was introduced to Danielle, who showed no reluctance about Cheryl being the one who would bring her to 2256 via time travel. On the contrary, she seemed to bond with her almost immediately. The mission unfolded the next day, at noon, well before the time when Danielle regularly appeared. Cheryl took a seat on the upper rows of the time station. She would be sent to one of the viewing areas that circled the entire station, where she wouldn't be seen by anyone involved in the mission to capture Charles. Cheryl would be carrying a watch that was synched to alert her at the exact moment of Charles's transfer from 2253 to 1801. The watch would also give her a running countdown, letting her know when to approach Danielle and initiate the transfer.

Dani and Aideen joined Annette and the time travel technicians in the control room. Cheryl was just below them, dressed in one of the light blue skinsuits, and they could see her clearly. At noon, they sent her back in time. As expected, four hours later, Cheryl reappeared in the seat from which she had left, but Danielle wasn't with her.

"I made it smoothly to the correct time and place," she explained, calm, as always. "Danielle was down below. I saw you walking out of the time station, Minister Li, and the four soldiers that Danielle sent to capture Charles Burke were sitting around her. You left the room and the mission proceeded. With thirty minutes left on the watch until Zero Moment, I approached Danielle, who was in a deep sleep since the mission was still underway. When Zero Moment arrived, Danielle woke up and

I handed her the time location device. As rehearsed, I counted to three and we both pushed the buttons on our devices. I don't know why Danielle didn't come through with me."

"I don't know why either," said Dani. "But I know where she is right now."

Dani was looking down on the floor of the time station, and a scene that had repeated itself dozens of times was playing out once more. A confused and disoriented Danielle was wandering aimlessly around the floor, wondering, like everyone else, why the transfer hadn't worked.

Chapter 54

Annette, Dani, Aideen and Cheryl had joined Danielle in the conference room. The assumption was that since Danielle hadn't arrived in the upper seats, which is where Cheryl had arrived and where Danielle's time location device had been programmed to bring her, then the attempt to pull her out of the time loop and ground her from that point forward in Primary Reality, had failed. The confirming data would be if and when Danielle disappeared, which would be in about forty-five minutes, according to Annette.

During the time they had together, the first moments were spent calming Danielle down, and Dani suffered right along with her as this process unfolded. Eventually, the joint effort was successful and the team was able to assure Danielle this was only the first attempt, and that other alternatives would surface, be approved, and tried, until a successful outcome was achieved.

Prior to entering the conference room, the four team members agreed that ideas would not be put on the table until Danielle disappeared back into the time loop, for fear that their utter confusion became clear to Danielle, throwing her into an even deeper canyon of despair. Instead, a series of questions would be put to Danielle that would, hopefully, help the team achieve a greater understanding of what was going on. It was agreed that Cheryl would ask the questions because of her experience as a hostage negotiator, and in a very real way Danielle *was* a hostage, trapped and helpless, in an endless time loop which would inevitably cause her to take her own life to make the pain stop.

Cheryl opened with a relatively simple question. "Danielle, what is the last thing you remember, in your time link observer role, during the mission to capture Charles and his station? Please try to be as specific as possible."

Danielle responded quickly. "So through Dani's eyes, I rushed into Charles's time chamber through the hole the soldiers had blasted in the wall, and I saw Aideen tied to one time cradle, and Orla tied to the other, and Charles was holding Orla's hand."

"What happened next?"

"I watched Charles push the button on the time cradle to initiate the trip."

"And then?"

"Charles disappeared."

"Did you see anything else in Charles's time chamber after that?"

"No, I lost the connection at that point."

Cheryl paused, giving Danielle time to regroup, then continued with her calm and deliberate questioning. "So what happened next for you, after you lost the connection?"

"I woke up here, I mean over there in the time station, sitting in my seat. The place was empty, I mean no one was here at all, not in the station, not in the control room. No one."

"What did you do next?"

"I wandered around, and then I blanked out, and I was in the chair again."

"And then?"

"I blanked out again, and then I was in the chair again."

Just then, Aideen interrupted. "Annette, I think we got this backwards," she said.

"How so?" asked Annette, raising her eyebrows repeatedly, warning Aideen not to get off script and upset Danielle.

"The time loop didn't begin in the past," said Aideen. "It began in the present."

"Please elaborate," said Annette, intrigued by Aideens logic.

"It means that to get Danielle out of the time loop, we have to do it in the present, where it began. We have to do it here! Now! How much time before Danielle is expected to leave again?"

"About twenty minutes," said Annette. "What are you proposing?"

"Take her somewhere, out of the present. To the past or to the future. Future is probably best, because it's somewhere she hasn't been yet. We have to get her out of the present to get her out of the time loop. Because it began in the present. She is continually chasing the present because her reality wants to end. And it can't end until she is gone, for good. But for her to be gone, she has to be anchored in this reality, in the present moment, which is a moving target."

"Your logic makes sense," said Annette. "We did indeed appear to have it backwards. But we need time to assess this. To have our experts weigh in. We need time to evaluate the risks."

"I'm willing to do it, Minister Li," said Cheryl. "Right now. I believe it can work."

"But we might lose Danielle, or you," said Annette.

"Not likely," said Aideen. "We all know where we can find Danielle if we don't get her out of the time loop. Take her to the future, well outside of the time loop. Leave her there for a day or so, then bring her back."

"I think it will work," said Dani, feeling the excitement of a viable solution in her bones.

"So do I," said Danielle.

"So do I, ma'am," Cheryl added.

Annette took a deep breath and forced herself to take a chance. "Okay, let's do it."

The five rushed back to the time station and, when they arrived there, she told the techs to set the time station for the year 2588, here in the building, and to give two new time locators to Cheryl and Danielle. She then sent the two time travelers back into the station, with instructions that they sit anywhere but the seat where Danielle had been sitting originally. If they were going to break the time loop, they might as well start with taking the seat that started it all out of the equation. The two took their seats. Annette announced there were only an estimated five minutes left before the time loop pulled Danielle out of the present, taking her to one of an infinite number of moments between the present and the end time of her reality.

Annette gave the order, the control room technicians initiated the command to go, and the two women in the station disappeared. The people in the control room would know in twenty-four hours if they were successful or not.

Chapter 55

D ani and Aideen spent the night alone in their apartment, anxious, unable to sleep, waiting for word to come in from Annette, one way or the other. Cheryl and Danielle had been sent to a time in the future that Annette had been to many times, the Utopia which she had helped to found in the year 2585. They were being sent to 2588 to see how things were progressing in that era. The Utopia of 2585 had originally been planned as the failsafe to save humanity in the event Charles's plan to infect all the world's OIM with a virus could not be altered. But Dani's plan had succeeded, and now she was Danielle, the only remaining inhabitant of a reality that no longer was reality.

Annette had given Cheryl additional instructions to do a quick assessment of the state of the world in 2588, well aware that this was only a twenty-four-hour mission, but she was emotionally invested in that era. Over two million travelers had been sent from her time to populate and enrich a post-apocalyptic world that had been shrunk to ten million survivors from the plague Charles had unleashed. But when Charles's evil act had been reversed, the world of 2585 became a world of six billion people, thriving the last time

Annette had been there, before time travel to the future had been banned by her government. Her most urgent request of Cheryl, other than ensuring the well-being of Danielle, was to meet with government officials to see if any reports of separate reality incidents, such as the one they were experiencing now, had occurred in the former Utopia.

The night passed slowly, and finally the sun rose in the east. Dani and Aideen were sitting out on their deck, which faced that direction, and they watched a glorious sunrise from the floor of the high rise they lived in. But nature's beauty did little to assuage their anxiety, and they had another ten hours of nervous waiting remaining, with nothing to occupy their minds.

"Why don't we go see your parents," suggested Aideen. "Maybe take them to breakfast. Talk about this. After all, it will affect them too if it comes to pass, and I believe in my heart that it will."

Dani had been trying to avoid seeing her parents, to shield them from the worry she was feeling, but Aideen's logic made sense. They should assume the best outcome and begin planning for it. The sooner everyone adjusted to the presence of Danielle, the sooner Aideen and Dani could leave for Terrene to have Aideen cloned.

"Okay," she said. "Let's go."

At breakfast, Aideen brought the Petersons up to date on where things stood. They couldn't seem to grasp why the original effort to bring Danielle permanently to this time had failed, and having never truly understood the whole separate reality concept, they were confused about why this trip to the future stood a better chance of succeeding than the trip to the past. But Aideen got them to focus on their role, should the mission succeed, which would soon be known.

"The plan, Pat and Don, is that Dani and I will do a one-year tour on Terrene, while Danielle and new Aideen do a one-year tour here. To be honest, we haven't really decided who will do what first, because there are some logistical issues that have to be worked out."

Aideen was referring to the fact that she couldn't be on the same planet as new Aideen, so the official plan was for her to leave after the cloning process was underway. It took thirty days for the clone to grow fully into an adult, and Aideen was supposed to be long gone before that happened. It was also believed that Danielle would adjust much more smoothly by spending her first year on Earth, having no experience whatsoever with the Land People, the Water People, space travel, or Terrene itself. If she stayed on Earth for the first one-year tour, she could be around her parents, Annette, all of the other time links except Orla and Liam, and she could also be near Cheryl, who seemed to have bonded with her during the short time they'd known each other, and would very likely be bonding further, as they spent twenty-four hours together in the year 2588.

The dilemma is that the most simple logistical plan would cause original Aideen to be coming back to Earth, while the Dani she had been with during the three years since Danielle had changed the future—a period of time Danielle had not experienced—would remain on Terrene and be matched with new Aideen, the clone. Original Aideen would be matched with Danielle, the time loop victim. And while both Danielle and the clone of Aideen would be the same people they'd always been, it just didn't feel right, to either Dani or Aideen, for the two of them to be separated, forever. They simply couldn't get over the fact that even though their new match would be the person they loved, it wouldn't be the person they loved the most.

Aideen had mentioned to Dani that she had an idea that might enable them to remain together, but she hadn't wanted to discuss it until they got to Terrene. She said it wasn't worth Dani getting her hopes up if it was a non-starter, and she needed to speak to Clarion and Zephyr first, to determine if it had any chance of working. Aideen further stated that all of the planning and thinking about how to manage two versions of themselves would be moot if they couldn't get Danielle into this reality permanently.

"How will we know the differences between Dani One and Dani Two, and Aideen One and Aideen Two?" asked Pat.

"Theoretically, there'll be no difference at the start in the two Aideens, but as time goes by and we live separate lives, our experiences will be different. Same with the two Dani's, plus the Dani we're trying to bring here, as we speak, did not experience the past three years that Dani and I experienced together."

"And what an action-packed three years it was!" said Dani. "We fought for our lives to get Orla to 2022, you and Ciara ended up in a jungle being attacked by crocodiles and chimpanzees, and that reality was then canceled. Then we brought my parents to the future, made peace with an alien invader and helped them resettle their original world, where we made peace with their mortal enemy, the Water People. We then fought off an alien horde from another planet that was very close to freezing all living things on Earth. It's safe to say, Danielle missed a lot, so I think you'll be able to tell which Dani she is, from the start."

"Agreed," said Aideen.

The breakfast with Dani's parents killed a few hours, and helped Don and Pat understand more fully how things would work going forward, and they remained enthusiastic about having two daughters and two Aideens in their lives. All that remained was to see if the mission succeeded. Dani was amazed at how calm her parents were about all of it, so much so that they begged off to keep a tennis date they had with friends later that morning.

That left Dani and Aideen alone again. To kill some time, they took the one-hour AirRail ride over to Omey Island, then walked the entire island, finding most of the beaches were still there, although packed with tourists. Electric boats whizzed around Fahey Lough, people water skiing and fishing and having a good time. By the time they arrived back in Brussels it was nearly 4 p.m., the moment of truth. Luckily, they didn't have to wait any longer because the thought message came in from Annette.

They're both here! And both fine. Get over here as soon as you can.

Chapter 56

D anielle updated them on what they had learned in 2588 while guests at the Space Exploration building in Brussels, the same complex they were in now, only no longer named the Time Management building. Time travel remained a dead technology in 2588, but space exploration was booming. There were now colonies in twenty-seven different solar systems, and Earth was peacefully coexisting in a galaxy full of alien species, many of whom were highly militaristic. Earth had built a triple shield around itself, modeled after the ones used by the Land People, the same kind that had protected the nine small vessels from the powerful lasers of the Fury, another species now at peace with Earth. And while Earth remained a peaceful planet, powerful defensive weapons had also been developed as a result of those first contacts in 2254 with the Land People and then in 2256 with the Fury.

The other news from 2588 was there had been no appearance of doppelgangers in that time, and in fact, none, other than Danielle, had been seen during the 332 years that separated the two eras. There had been reports of dreams among the ten million survivors of the OIM plague and the two million colonists from 2253, dreams of the world in 2585 as it had been before reality was changed and life returned to the peaceful and fruitful existence that was now enjoyed by six billion people. But overall, life was good in the future, and this was especially comforting to Annette, one the original architects of the 2585 Utopia.

The time loop appeared to have been broken, and both Dani and Danielle were anxious to get on with life without the presence of the other, as it was a highly chaotic and frustrating to experience two sets of emotions. Annette had agreed that after one week had passed by, if Danielle was still present in the Primary Reality, then Dani and Aideen could travel to Terrene to begin the cloning phase of the project.

A week later, Dani was very emotional when saying goodbye to Danielle, because she very likely would never see her again, but even more poignant was watching Aideen and Danielle say goodbye.

"Will you be coming back to me soon?" asked Danielle.

"The cloning takes thirty days," said Aideen. "Soon after that you'll be seein' me."

"But will it be you, or your clone?"

"I don't know the answer at this moment, Danielle, but I'm thinkin' you won't know the difference."

"I love you," said Danielle, embracing Aideen.

"I love you too," answered Aideen, but Dani could tell from the tears in Aideen's eyes that she was saying goodbye, forever, to Danielle, having made her choice to stay with Dani. It was unclear how she intended to accomplish that, but Aideen had promised to share her plan with Dani upon their arrival on Terrene. What neither expected at that moment was that their arrival on the surface of Terrene would be delayed by entirely unforeseen events.

Having said all of their goodbyes and promising to return in a year for their tour on Earth, Dani and Aideen were beamed up to the space station where the vessel was docked. They boarded, saying hello to the crew—one Land Person and one human pilot. All the shuttles between Earth and Terrene were now staffed this way, and the Land People pilots always held first seat on the craft, making them Captain of the ship, because they were far more experienced with the travel technology. The intent was to one day have humans share equally in first seat assignments, but that day had not yet arrived.

When their ship materialized in orbit around Terrene, their scopes showed them to be sharing orbit with a huge spherical vessel, the same size as the original craft that had brought the Land People to Earth—Diaspora One—now just ashes in space. But this massive spacecraft—a hundred times larger than the one they were on—while in a higher orbit and many thousands of miles from them, appeared as large as a planet itself, a menacing unknown presence. Suddenly, a message beamed into all of their heads.

We are the Land People of Terrene. We have returned to claim sovereignty of our planet. Invaders from Earth are not welcome here.

"What is that ship?" Dani asked the captain.

Diaspora Ten, she said. *It seems they have returned from their long mission in deep space.*

"But why are they being hostile?" asked Dani. "Is it a bluff, like Diaspora One tried when it first came to Earth?"

I don't think so, said the captain. *Their ship is clearly outfitted with weapons systems that it did not have when it left Terrene over 600 years ago. And they are pointed directly at us.*

Chapter 57

*A*ctivate shields, said the captain. *Attempt to contact the hostile ship.*

"No response to all our hails," said the copilot. "Is your mind messaging having any luck?"

Not yet, said the captain. *Keep trying.*

"Will our shields work against those weapons?" asked Dani. "What kind of weapons are they?"

I believe the ones they are about to employ are harmonic-based weapons, said the captain. *They will generate a variety of frequencies until they find one that destabilizes our shields. If they can do that, then virtually any kind of weapon system can destroy us.*

"Should we abandon ship?" asked Aideen.

I think you should, said the captain. *I think all humans should leave the ship.*

"I'm willing to stay and defend our vessel," said the copilot. "I request permission to remain at my post."

Denied, said the captain. *Their scopes are powerful enough to ascertain that we have three humans on board. I believe that if only I remain, they will not kill me. Now go.*

Dani, Aideen and the second seat moved to the transport chamber and beamed down to the planet, leaving the captain alone to her fate. They materialized outside of the administrative building on Base One and ran inside, quickly making their way to Clarion's office.

Clarion, Zephyr and a variety of other Land People were gathered in the room. The only human present was Charles, who looked up as they entered the room.

"You should go to the underground shelters," he said.

"Not happening," said Dani. "What's going on? Why are they doing this?"

"Clarion is communicating with the Captain of Diaspora Ten as we speak. Only those two can hear what is being said."

"That's not right," said Aideen. "We have a right to hear this. Our lives are at stake too."

"The captain of the enemy vessel demanded it," said Charles. "I don't know why. But it was better to have some dialogue than no dialogue."

"Are you ready to beam up there and infect that ship with OIM?" asked Aideen.

"Of course I am," said Charles. "Are you ready to come with me? After all, you've got more experience destroying spaceships than I do."

"Just say when, Charles. I'll be there."

"Please stop this banter!" screamed Dani. "Just wait. Clarion seems to be finishing up."

Clarion broke the connection and made his report.

The Land People of Diaspora Ten are willing to accept the peace agreement we made with the Water People. But they are still refusing to allow humans to live on Terrene.

"Why?" asked Dani.

They've not given a good reason, in my opinion, said Clarion. *They state that they have traveled in the deep space of our galaxy for over 600 years, encountering dozens of habitable planets, all occupied by intelligent life, yet not one of them welcomed them to stay. They say it is the way of the universe. Species from different planets do not intermingle.*

"That's absurd," said Dani. "Where did they get their weapons then, if they don't intermingle?"

It appears a technology trade led to their acquisition of their weapons systems.

"What did they trade?" asked Charles.

That wasn't discussed, said Clarion. *But one would assume it was either our travel technology or our cloning technology, or both.*

"Why do they need weapons?" asked Charles. "With your travel technology you can escape nearly any danger and your shields are very powerful."

Their weapons are for one purpose, said Clarion. *To reclaim our land on Terrene from the Water People or destroy it.*

"Well, we've done their work for them," said Dani. "With no bloodshed."

I understand, said Clarion, bowing his head.

"Let me go to them," said Dani. "Not to destroy them, but to talk to them."

"I'm goin' with you," said Aideen.

"As am I," said Charles. "Three humans for them to evaluate should be enough."

I will attempt to arrange it, said Clarion.

Let me go with them, pleaded Zephyr. *Just as you know many of them, so do I. Just as you have vouched for the humans' integrity and peaceful intentions, so can I. But I will do it face to face with them.*

Clarion nodded and reestablished contact with Diaspora Ten. The meeting was arranged.

Chapter 58

The three humans and Zephyr materialized on the floor of an auditorium that Dani recognized as a duplicate of the one from Diaspora One. The first difference she observed was that most of the 1500 seats were empty. She estimated that less than 100 Land People had come for this meeting, and wondered if the hatred for humans was so profound they couldn't stomach being in the same room with them. But then she noticed that the Land People in attendance looked worn out, their skintight clothing torn in places, their skin more yellow and their stature thinner than their brethren.

One of the Land People in the lower seats stood and approached them. This one seemed angry, and even though it was short in stature, it stood straight and proud, its large, alert eyes boring into the four arrivals from the surface of Terrene. Zephyr sent them a message informing them this was Droden. She knew him.

I am the Captain of this ship, came his voice, which was decidedly male, deep and foreboding.

"I am Dani, this is Aideen, and this is Charles," said Dani. "You will remember Zephyr. Thank you for inviting us to your ship."

I recall that you invited yourselves, said the captain. His eyes remained on the humans, never straying or acknowledging the presence of Zephyr. *Why have you come?*

"We come to convince you that we are friends of the Land People," said Dani.

Droden turned to Zephyr. *And why have you come?*

I come to vouch for the humans, she said. *They are honest, peaceful people, and without them we would not have been able to build land on Terrene, nor would the peace with the Water People have come to pass.*

Clarion told me this, and more. I need not hear it repeated.

I want you to see it, in my face, said Zephyr, her eyes blazing. Her intensity seemed to move Droden, ever so slightly.

Trying to capitalize, Dani bored in. "Why do you reject us humans?" she asked.

Droden bowed his head and did not respond, as if he was deciding what to say. Then he raised his head up. *We are a people that has been ravaged by years of war, disease, and near starvation. All at the hands of uncaring aliens. We've encountered dozens of alien species. They have fought us, sickened us, rejected us. We simply want to return to our planet and live with our own kind, in peace.*

"How many of you are there?" asked Charles.

Just what you see here. There are only eighty-nine of us left. Dani felt the pain in Droden's voice as he said this.

"We will not give you disease," said Aideen. "We have lived with your people for nearly three years now, and neither human nor Land Person has fallen ill."

Charles added to this. "And for two of those years your people were guests on our planet, and were welcome to stay, but we found a way to help them return to Terrene and rebuild your homeland. And now the friendship between our two species is strong. Please, let me show you. The scene in front of me that is about to appear took place just last night, on the base Land People and humans share together, just below us, on your wonderful planet."

A hologram appeared behind Droden, and he turned around to watch it, along with his people in the crowd. It was a portrayal of a scene at Murphy's pub, with Irish music playing and crowd of at least fifty humans and an equal number of Land People talking, smiling, singing and laughing. The hologram seemed to be having its desired effect, based on the smiles showing on the faces of many Land People seated in the auditorium, but Dani was more interested in how Charles could play that hologram without any equipment on his person. They'd been warned not to bring any mechanical devices with them, and had undoubtedly been scanned upon their arrival, yet the hologram played, and Dani wondered just how far from human Charles had migrated as a result of his OIM experiments. But the opportunity to close this deal was so close, and she shirked off her concerns about Charles and poured on the charm.

"Your planet is ready for you now," she said. "Please, come join us there." Dani was aware that the bodies of the crew of Diaspora Ten would not yet be able to withstand the gravity of Terrene, but she wanted to emphasize just how welcome they were there.

Easier to destroy you all and then return, said Droden, seemingly unmoved.

And then the tenor of the party from Terrene changed, beginning with Zephyr.

You will die trying, she said.

Droden laughed. *Ah, the peace-loving humans have weapons that can defeat us? Is that it?*

"Just say the word," said Charles, opening a closed fist and holding an OIM sample in his upturned palm. "If you shoot me where I stand and this small object falls onto this floor, you and your ship are doomed."

Dani wondered, once again, how Charles had smuggled the OIM onto the ship. Surely it would have been detected by the scanners. Had he produced it while they stood in front of their adversaries? But Charles's "Good Guy/Bad Guy" routine was definitely having an effect and she decided to keep the momentum going. Droden was silent, but his eyes burned with anger, so Dani tried to clarify where Charles was coming from.

"The truth, Captain, is that humans will defend themselves when threatened, and you have certainly threatened us. What Charles has said is true. It has happened before. Zephyr, can you tell this story to Droden?"

Zephyr summarized the first encounter between humans and Land People, emphasizing that the humans saved everyone aboard Diaspora One, after the ship was doomed. She testified that the Land People had been treated with respect and friendship by the humans, fostering a bond between the species so strong, that if Droden were to harm the humans, none of the people of Diaspora Ten would be welcome on Terrene, ever.

Put down your sword, Droden, my old friend, and I promise you will find the peace that has alluded you for so long.

Droden lowered his head once more, then slowly turned and raised his face to his people. A vote was obviously being taken. Soon he turned back to the three humans and Zephyr. *It will be as you say, Zephyr, old friend. We will put down our swords and join you, and the humans, on Terrene.*

Chapter 59

Before the party from Terrene departed Diaspora Ten, Dani informed Droden that the humans had developed pills for the Land People of Diaspora One which dramatically accelerated their bodies' adjustment to the higher gravity of Terrene compared to space. Droden mentioned that he had noticed how strong Zephyr looked and said they would very much like to explore this possibility further, and he also humbly requested food be sent from the surface because their hydroponic gardens were barely functioning. Dani asked permission to communicate with Terrene, gave them the good news and asked for immediate emergency aid for the people of Diaspora Ten.

When they returned to Terrene, appearing in front of the administrative building, Dani noticed a huge crowd was formed there, composed of both Land People and humans. They were cheering and clapping, a few holding signs that said "PEACE!" and "WELCOME BACK HEROES!" and other celebratory messages. Dani was humbled, and she realized that all of the accomplishments of hers and Aideen's over the years, on behalf of humanity, and the Land People, had never been acknowledged beyond the inner circles of the Time Management building. And while she'd never craved such praise, it felt good, especially because this public celebration of ordinary citizens was taking place in this new and special community.

Dani, Aideen, Charles and Zephyr joined in the celebration, which gradually migrated down the street to Murphy's pub. Liam brought several kegs out into the street and told everyone to help themselves. The festivities went on well past 15 a.m., midnight on Terrene, and continued on in full force after darkness enshrouded the world. Dani noticed that Charles had stayed, and seemed to be enjoying the attention the success of their mission had bestowed on him. Aideen was nowhere to be seen, probably inside with Orla, so Dani squeezed through the crowd and sidled up to Charles.

"Hey Charles, did you think I wouldn't wonder how you pulled off all those tricks up there on Diaspora Ten?'

Charles turned to face her, a feigned look of confusion on his face. "What on Terrene are you talking about, Dani?" And then a sly smile crept onto his face, inviting her to continue.

"So what gives? Would this have something to do with your OIM experiments, Charles?"

"It might," he said. "I've made some progress."

"And you've started ingesting it again?"

"Why no, actually. The amounts I already have inside me, from my experiments on Earth, seem sufficient for small magic, like I performed on the ship up there. It's the ability to communicate with OIM where I've made progress."

"So you tell it what to do and it does it?"

"Quite so," he said, raising his head up in a gesture of pride.

"Okay, great," said Dani. "But I thought you had probation officers up here who were supposed to be monitoring your activities?'

"Yes, they come to my home once a week, question me, look around, discover nothing, and leave."

"Maybe I should volunteer for that job," said Dani. "I bet I'd find out what you're up to."

"Are you staying?" asked Charles, a hopeful look on his face. "I mean, you are one of my closest friends, Dani, in spite of our history of butting heads from time to time."

Dani grinned, but she had something serious to say. "Use your gifts only for the good of the people of Terrene, and I will be your friend for life, Charles."

"Do you mean that?" he asked.

"As much as I've ever meant anything. Do good, Charles, and you'll have more friends than just me, as you found out tonight."

"Here, here!" he exclaimed, lifting his pint of ale into the air.

Dani clinked and made to move away, but Charles grabbed her lightly by the arm.

"So are you staying?" he asked. "And what's going on with that other Dani, back on Earth?"

"I'll know more tomorrow," said Dani, pulling away, intending to look for Aideen. "I'll update you then, if I see you."

I'll contact you via thought message, came Charles's voice in her mind.

"Did you use a communication device to send that message, Charles, or is that one of your new magic tricks?"

"A new trick! Cheers, Dani!" He raised his mug as she moved away and went to find Aideen.

Chapter 60

Dani and Aideen slept in at the small cottage they'd built previously on the edge of town. When they rose, they showered, took a hangover pill, and went to the administrative building to see Clarion and Zephyr. Aideen had mentioned she needed to ask them something before they went to the medical center for their appointment with Sharell and Latif, the two cloning experts who were working with them. When they arrived at Clarion's office, Zephyr was already there and the two of them were sharing coffee in the comfortable seating area. Dani noticed that both of them seemed a little under the weather.

"I thought Liam's ale didn't have enough alcohol in it to affect you Land People," she said, chiding them and wondering if they understood she was joking.

A narrow-eyed Zephyr turned to her. *But his Irish Whiskey does,* she said, grimacing.

Too much, said Clarion, also with an expression of discomfort on her face.

"Well, you can look at it this way," said Aideen. "You two may be the first of your kind to experience a hangover." Dani and Aideen shared a laugh, and even got a chuckle from their two, compromised friends.

What can we do for you today? asked Clarion. *Our under-standing was that Aideen is scheduled to begin the cloning pro-cess today.*

"Immediately following this meetin," said Aideen. "Assumin' I like what I hear from the two of you."

Aideen still hadn't revealed her plan regarding how she could remain on Terrene, even while her clone was at full maturity, but not yet off the planet. The original plan was for Aideen to leave the planet before the clone was fully grown, and spend the rest of her life with Danielle, but that plan had been thoroughly rejected by both Aideen and Dani. Now Dani would learn how Aideen was going to get around the logistical issues of being on the same planet with her clone, subjecting the two of them to unbearable psychological stress.

What would you like to hear? asked Zephyr.

"I'd like you to refresh my memory on why you have to go underwater to be able to communicate with the Water Peo-ple," said Aideen.

That's an easy one, said Zephyr. *Our telepathic communi-cation signals cannot travel from air to water, or water to air, for long distances. Air to water or water to air communication requires the subjects to be very close to one another in order to work.*

"For example, the air aquarium where we all met with Cabal to negotiate the peace," said Aideen. "In there, we could receive the signals from Cabal, who was right outside, in the water."

Yes, that is a good example said Zephyr. *Was that your only question?*

"No, I'm afraid not. That was the easy question. The more difficult one is for you to speculate on whether or not my clone could receive my thoughts, or if I could receive her thoughts, if I were down there in that aquarium, hidden away a thousand meters below the surface, tucked inside of a rock mountain, and surrounded by more water inside the mountain itself, not to mention the thick glass of the aquarium."

Now Dani understood. Aideen wanted to hide herself away in the Water People's air aquarium until her clone was whisked away to Earth.

Zephyr appeared to be considering the question, but Clarion seemed confident. *I believe it could work,* she said.

"And you, Zeph?" asked Aideen. Dani and Aideen often addressed Zephyr with their own shortened version of her name, and in so doing they conveyed, in a subtle way, the affection they felt for her. Dani believed Zeph knew what this was all about it, and liked it.

I would give that a highly likely, said Zephyr. *Perhaps the cloning experts will have data of some kind that might provide a more conclusive answer.*

"I certainly intend to ask them," said Aideen. "And I'll also have another question for them that might be even more important."

Dani had no idea where this was going, and didn't want to wait until the meeting at the medical center to find out. "What would that be?" she asked. "Perhaps our friends here will have an opinion to share on that as well."

"Can't see why not," said Aideen. "What I'm tryin' to figure out, is just how perfect of a match with me this clone of mine will be, right at the start, mind you, because I know she'll become more and more of a different person than me as she experiences her own life, separate from mine."

The Land People seemed confused by the question, almost as if it was self-evident that a clone was a clone, identical in every way to the original specimen. But Dani knew Aideen well, and she now understood where Aideen was going with this line of questioning.

"Could you be more specific, Aideen?" she asked. "For example, would you by chance want to know if the emotions of your clone would be exactly as yours were at the moment the scans are done?"

"You've always been a smart girl, Dani. PhD and all that. And yes, you're correct. Because if this new Aideen has the same feelin's, exactly, that I have, then she won't be agreein' to go to Earth and live with Danielle, who's missin' three years of the lives we've had together."

"And how are we going to deal with that?" asked Dani.

"No idea."

Chapter 61

I know what to do!" exclaimed Dani. "Theoretically, at least. We need to postpone the cloning," she said.

"Shouldn't we ask the experts the questions we asked Clarion and Zephyr?" asked Aideen. "After all, both of them deferred to the experts, and here we are."

Dani and Aideen were outside the medical center on the way to their appointment, but Dani was adamant.

"I guarantee you, that whatever answers the experts have, are not going to be as perfect as the idea I have," said Dani. "Trust me, Aideen. Let's postpone the meeting, then we'll talk."

The two went into the medical center, which wasn't a large building since neither Land People nor humans became sick on Terrene, at least so far. Most of the space was dedicated to psychological counseling, for humans struggling with the adjustment to a world 737 light years from Earth, and for Land People who missed living in space. In both cases, there were surprisingly few patients. There was also a small trauma center, like an emergency room, to treat wounds from work-related injuries or accidents. The Cloning center was small, but *did* receive patients, albeit not very often, since Land People only needed to be renewed every 300 years. But their renewal dates varied from person to person, so the Cloning center did receive patients from time to time. The person behind the reception counter was a Land Person, of course, and assumed Aideen was there for the procedure, but instead they asked her to postpone it, telling her they'd return soon to speak with the cloning doctors. Then they left the medical center and found a seat at the coffee shop across the street from Murphy's. They ordered coffee, Aideen's anticipation building.

"Tell me, please!" she implored.

"It's time travel, of course!" said Dani, excited.

Aideen caught on quickly. "All we have to do is find the Aideen of three years prior, take the cloning scan of her, then return to this time, and voila, an Aideen who is three years younger and is a perfect match for Danielle."

"Theoretically, yes, that's it."

"It's feckin' brilliant, Dani! In theory, of course, since time travel is now illegal. I know Annette secured an exception for us to pull Danielle out of the time loop, but I can't see the Executive Committee understanding that we need to use time travel, one more time, because poor Aideen just doesn't feel right about spendin' the rest of her life with... none other than the love of her life. It doesn't fly, unless you're me, or you."

"I agree," said Dani. "But let me make a few points. First, time travel is illegal on Earth. What about on Terrene?"

"Who knows?" said Aideen. "But it's probably not covered since this is a settlement with both humans and Land People living on it. I mean, we haven't even written a constitution or anythin' for how we're to live together. Even Clarion and Zephyr were just kind of railroaded into runnin' things. They don't even have titles yet, for feck's sake!"

"Yeah, it's a real frontier town here at Base One, but it works because we all respect one another and have common goals. Survival is number one. Happiness is number two. The laws to help us achieve those things aren't a top priority right now because what we're doing is working."

"And what does all this have to do with time travel, if I may ask? There's no time travel here on Terrene!"

"Not yet," said Dani. "But have you been seeing some of the crazy stuff Charles can do, like his holograms and the magic act with the OIM up on Diaspora Ten?"

"Yes, I was meanin' to ask you what you thought about that."

"Well, I asked Charles himself, last night, and he claimed that his OIM infusions seem to have had a lasting effect, giving him the ability to perform certain 'little tricks,' as he called them."

"Time travel is more than a little trick, Dani."

"Maybe for Charles, it isn't," retorted Dani. "For example, where did that OIM sample he used to build the time station back in 1801 come from. I was there when the four Time Management military popped in on Charles in his conference room. He whooshed himself out of there without a second thought and was on his way to 1801 before we could catch him. He had no warning. No time to pack his things before he left. So where did the time station sample come from. Maybe it came from Charles himself, just like the OIM sample on Diaspora Ten. He couldn't have snuck that thing on board."

Aideen's eyes widened. "Let's go find Charles."

The two jumped up, paid their bill, and rushed out of town to Charles's home. Dani knocked on the door and waited, then Charles opened it, surprised to see them, a big smile forming on his face.

"To what do I owe this pleasure?" he asked. "My two best friends and fellow heroes of the battle with Diaspora Ten! How can I help you?"

"Invite us in and we'll tell ya," said Aideen.

"By all means, please come in. May I offer you coffee? I was just having some."

"That would be great," said Dani.

Charles led them to his kitchen and the two women sat down at the table while Charles got the coffee. He brought three steaming cups over on a tray, which also included pastries and condiments. When all three were seated and had prepared their coffee, Charles surprised them.

"You need time travel, eh?" he asked.

"What leads you to think that?" asked Dani, startled by Charles's revelation.

"I forgot to tell you two. Actually, I forgot to tell anyone. I can read minds now, a little. And since that thought was banging around voraciously in both of your minds, it came through to me."

"Another one of your little tricks?" asked Dani.

"I suppose," said Charles. "I'm just full of surprises, aren't I?"

"Indeed," said Aideen. "But now, because you're an upstanding citizen of Terrene, a hero nonetheless, you will only do good with your special abilities. Am I right?"

"That is my intent," said Charles. "So why are you trying to tempt me into being a bad boy again, with time travel, no less?"

"Can you do it?" asked Dani.

"Of course."

Chapter 62

D ani and Aideen explained the situation to Charles and he
knew exactly what to do.

"We send the cloners, or whatever they're called, to my old
time station in 2253, to the exact time and spot when Aideen
was tied up on the time cradle, alongside Orla, who was on the
other time cradle. They take the scan, then leave. Does that
about sum it up?"

"Well yes," said Dani. "Can it be done from here?"

"Of course," said Charles. "You'll remember that all the
drones Annette sent out to the galaxy, including the one that
came here and was found by the Land People, were sent via
time travel. Otherwise, they'd take years and years to even get
out of the solar system."

"And you can make the time station, here?" asked Aideen.

"I can," said Charles.

"Old tech or new tech?" asked Dani.

"Old tech," he said. "They never let me get close to the new
tech, which isn't an issue because we can use Orla as the time
link. We wouldn't want Aideen to do it because then the
three years since 2253 would go from her to the Aideen in
the station, and that would defeat the purpose of the entire

operation. You want to replicate an Aideen that doesn't know what happened in your lives after that day, the same as Danielle, who you two so brilliantly yanked out of that time loop. Are we all on board with this approach?"

"Yes," said Dani. "Except we've got to talk Orla into it, and then we've got to talk the cloning docs into it."

"Then I shouldn't get started yet?" asked Charles. "It will take a few days for the station to be ready. I'll just make a small one."

"And you'll promise not to make mischief with it?" asked Aideen.

"Absolutely," said Charles. "I'm a new man."

Excited, Dani and Aideen rushed back to the medical center, telling Charles they would be back soon with news as to whether the time station was a go or not. First, they went to the pub and discussed the plan with Orla, who was actually very excited about it. She'd thought she'd be retired from time travel forever, and admitted to missing it, at least the exciting parts, and said she'd be happy to be the time link for the mission.

Next, they met with Latif and Sharell in a small conference room in the medical center, explained the issues to them as best as they could, not really knowing if the emotions of a human would be understood by them in this case, but hoping nonetheless that they would agree to help them.

You say we need to beam to a place on Earth, approximately three years in the past, take the scan of Aideen, and return here, said Latif.

"Uh, yes," said Dani. "That's a good summary."

When do we leave? asked Sharell.

"You'll both be goin' then?" asked Aideen.

Of course, said Latif. *Sharell and I work as a team. And if you're wondering why we don't hesitate, it is because you two spared our lives once, and gave us great happiness by making it possible to return to our home world. If this small trip can bring happiness to you both, we are all in.*

"Well then, thank you!" said Aideen. "You honor us. We'll come back to you with the details. Lookin' forward to workin' with ya."

"I have one more question," said Dani.

Please ask, said Sharell.

"The Aideen you will encounter on this trip to the past, will appear to be older than the Aideen here with us now. How old will the clone appear to be?"

"You may choose the age of the clone. Whatever your choice, she will live for approximately 300 years, and her appearance will be the same for that entire span."

"Now wait just a minute there," said Aideen. "All of us humans from 2256 will live only around 150 years. But now my clone will live twice that long?"

And then be renewed again through another cloning process. Your clone can live forever, if she chooses to. But so can you, Aideen, and Dani, if that is what you choose. There are no restrictions on what the Land People will share with our human brethren.

"That's good to know," said Aideen. "Thank you."

As Latif said, you have earned our eternal gratitude, said Sharell.

Dani was intrigued to hear they had options for the future, but also anxious to bring their present circumstances into balance. "The good news is that we have plenty of time to decide on whether or not we want to live forever. But I'm sure Charles will be happy to hear he can be immortal after all."

"He probably already is, from what you're tellin' me," said Aideen.

"A topic for another day," said Dani. "Let's go tell Charles the good news about cloning!"

***

"Back already, eh? You two do work fast, don't you?"

"Are ya' readin' our minds again, Charles?" asked Aideen.

Charles laughed. "No, I didn't have to. You two don't ever fail when you have your minds set on something. I knew that when you walked out the door, so I've already started! Come, take a look."

Charles led them through the house to his backyard, which had a beautiful view of the ocean and some of the tall cliffs of Base One that jutted out, east of his cottage. Off to one side, apparently so as not to block the view of the ocean, Charles's time station operation was already underway, churning at the thin layer of soil that had been created on top of the OIM bedrock of the island.

"I've instructed the OIM down below to make itself available if contacted by the OIM of the new time station. No problems there!"

"So you've been talkin' to the OIM?" asked Aideen.

"Yes, although the OIM on this planet isn't as smart as the OIM on Earth, yet. How's Annette doing with that project by the way? The one to get her arms around the OIM collective consciousness."

"We haven't spoken to her about it," said Dani. "Should we be worried?"

"I don't think so," said Charles. "The Community of Minds should be able to keep things under control. If not, Annette knows where to find me."

"And you're a new man, are you not Charles?" asked Aideen. "Won't let anythin' bad happen here on Terrene or on Earth, correct?"

"That's right," said Charles. "I much prefer being a hero to being a villain."

"So when should we bring the cloning docs back for the mission?" asked Dani.

"I'll test the station the day after tomorrow. If it's good, we'll make the jump the day after that. I need three days."

Chapter 63

Three days later, Dani and Aideen picked up Orla at the pub, where she lived with Liam up above on the second floor, just as pub owners of old had done. They met Latif and Sharell at the medical center. Each of them had a piece of equipment in their hands, the size and shape of a flashlight from the twenty-first century. The humans walked with the Land People to Charles's house, who was waiting for them on the front porch, grinning, almost maniacally, as a child would before a birthday party. He was obviously thrilled to be back in the time travel game and this bothered Dani immensely. She'd been a victim of the backlash time travel could cause, and while this mission's objective had nothing to do with changing the future, she worried that Charles might one day get back to his old games and become a problem again. On the other hand, he could do this with or without Dani's encouragement, and while the station out back was built to help her and Aideen, she kept reminding herself that Charles had the power to build this station any time he wanted, no matter the reason.

Dani introduced Charles to Latif and Sharell and they all entered the house and went to the kitchen in the back. Charles suggested they sit at the kitchen table for the briefing and brought them all coffee. The Land People seemed to enjoy coffee as much as they did ale and it was inspiring to see them adopt human culture into their lives. Dani wished she could somehow start enjoying the plant-based gruel the Land People ate day after day after day, but that wasn't going to happen.

Charles opened the meeting. "I've pinpointed the exact time we'll send you to. It will be seconds after I sent myself to 1801. You'll appear in the time chamber and complete your work before Dani and the soldiers arrive. And when you get there, please don't hold it against me that Orla and Aideen were tied to the time cradles there. We should all remember, I was fighting for my life."

"So you could destroy the world," added Aideen.

"Well, yes, but I was insane at the time. Thank goodness I've been cured."

"From your mouth to God's ears, Charles," said Aideen.

The Land People seemed utterly lost by the turn in the conversation so Dani brought things back to the task at hand. "How long do the scans take?" she asked, addressing the two cloning experts.

Sharell fielded the question. *We take two scans,* she said. *One is a full body scan, geared toward capturing all the physical characteristics of the subject. The second is a brain scan, focused on copying every single neuron in the brain.*

"So how long do the scans take?" Dani repeated.

The body scan takes less than one minute, said Sharell. *The brain scan takes a little longer, perhaps two minutes.*

Charles asked the question Dani was already trying to answer in her mind. "Dani, how long did it take for you and the soldiers to get into the time chamber after my emergency exit from the conference room?"

"I think it was only about two minutes," she said.

"That could be a problem," said Charles.

"Yes," said Dani. "I'm afraid the soldiers would at the very least stun the Land People if they entered the time chamber and they were still there." Dani noticed the discomfort of the Land People when she said this, and tried to reassure them. "But we'll make sure that doesn't happen. Can the scans be done at the same time?"

It is not the normal procedure, said Latif.

"Would the results be compromised if you did?" Dani asked.

We don't know," said Sharell. *It has never been done.*

Silence ruled the room at that point, as the four humans tried to figure out a way around the problem. Dani had an idea. It wasn't ideal, but it might work.

"I can go with them," she said. "And if the chamber wall is breached, I can delay the soldiers."

"But I can't delay my exit to 1801," Charles pointed out. "When I go, reality changes, and we need that to happen."

"We should have thought this through a bit before we had you build that station," said Aideen, frustrated.

Charles was quick to respond. "Oh no, I'm glad I built it. Who knows when we might need it again."

"We need an alternative plan," said Dani. "There's just not enough time to pull this off. We don't want the soldiers to see us there, even if I can stop them. That's a bad idea, because they would report it to Annette and a whole chain of new information would start circulating in our Primary Reality and who knows what that might lead to."

"Let's get down to basics then," said Aideen. "What we're trying to do is come as close as we can to creating an Aideen clone with exactly the same memories as Danielle. The scene in that time chamber is that moment. It has the additional benefit of exposing no one but me, the me that is here right now, to this episode. Orla would be passed out on the other time cradle, and Charles would be busy trying to escape. But there's no time, so something has to give."

If I may make one correction, said Sharell. *If you had attended the briefing on the cloning procedure you would know this, but for obvious reasons we did not have that meeting yet. But I should point out that the patient must be unconscious while the procedure takes place. Brain activity must be at a minimum for the scan to be perfect.*

This new information put another wrinkle into the mix, but Dani was beginning to piece together a new plan based on what Aideen had said. They wanted to come as close as possible to the right time while exposing as few people as possible from the selected time to the act itself. The new information from Sharell could help them do this. To finalize her idea, Dani needed confirmation of one thing.

"Aideen, I remember you saying that Charles held you in the time chamber the entire time I was gone in Brussels. Is that right?"

"Certainly is," replied Aideen.

"But before I went to Brussels, we were separated and you were taken directly to the time chamber and strapped down on the time cradles, correct?"

"That's right."

"How long were you on the cradles before Charles appeared during his emergency exit?"

"I'd say at least ten minutes," said Aideen.

"Yes, and Charles and I were in the conference room for at least ten minutes before the soldiers arrived. So we have ten minutes, not two minutes!"

"But Orla and I will be awake if the Land People come sooner than Charles does," said Aideen. "I thought we were trying to keep both of us from seeing them?"

"Neither of you will see the Land People," said Dani.

"How so?" asked Aideen.

"Because the first person you're going to see is me. All we need to do is cut my hair to the same length it was back then, and you'll think it's just the same old me from that time."

"But you can't do the scan!" said Aideen, not quite there.

"No, but if I can get ahold of a Tickler, I can knock both you and Orla out, and then the Land People can show up and do their scans. All I need is a Tickler and I think I know a man who might have one."

"At your service," said Charles, bowing to the humans and two very confused Land People. When he rose up from his bow, he had more to say. "You may not realize it Dani, but you'll be solving another problem when you knock Orla out with my Tickler."

"What?" asked Dani.

"By knocking Orla out as soon as you arrive in my time chamber in 2253, you will nullify her ability to absorb the knowledge of her future that would normally come into her mind from the older time link, who of course, is the Orla from this time. The person on the receiving end of a transfer must be conscious for several minutes for the future memories to be lodged permanently in their mind."

"That's great news!" said Dani. "One less thing to worry about."

"Shall we proceed, then?" said Orla. "I'd like to get back to the pub as soon as I can."

Chapter 64

D ani materialized in the time chamber of Charles's time station under the channel between the Irish mainland and Omey Island, in the year 2253, holding Orla's hand. Orla was tied to one time cradle and Aideen to the other. Both were awake.

"How did you get in here, Dani?" asked Aideen.

Dani was dressed in jeans and a flannel shirt, and while she hadn't been able to remember exactly what they looked like, Charles made them up for her based on his memory of that same day, using OIM as the base material and somehow telling it what to become without infusing it with AI, as was the normal procedure. Apparently, her clothing was acceptable, because both Aideen and Orla appeared to believe she was the same Dani who had arrived with them from 2022. The other Dani, however, was still in the conference room on the other side of the station, being instructed by Charles on how to get to Brussels and what to do when she got there.

Dani didn't answer Aideen's question, and it hurt her to do this, but she was on a tight schedule. First, she pointed the Tickler at Orla, who immediately passed out.

"What the feck are you doin', Dani?" screamed Aideen, from the other side of the room. "You need to help us escape, not knock us out!"

Dani pointed the Tickler at Aideen who immediately fell into unconsciousness. The Tickler had been set to inflict only a mild level of grayout, and the hope was that both women would wake up in around ten minutes, before Charles arrived. Now that her two friends were incapacitated, Dani had nothing to do but wait for the arrival of Latif and Sherell, which happened right on schedule. By Dani's watch, they now had nine minutes to perform the cloning scans, which the two Land People pursued immediately.

They approached Aideen, still tied to the time cradle, but completely limp and unresponsive. They checked her heartbeat and nodded to Dani that she was fine. Another minute had passed. Then Sherell stepped back and Latif performed the body scan. It took about one minute and then Latif moved away, his scan completed. Seven minutes to go before Charles arrived. Sherell stepped up and focused her scope on Aideen's head, holding it steady, about one foot in front of Aideen's forehead. She kept checking a digital readout on the scope, which would tell her if a successful scan had been made. After about two minutes, she shook her head from side to side.

The scan was not completed successfully, she said.

"What happened?" asked Dani. "We've only got five minutes left!"

It happens, she said. *I will try again, but it will take a few minutes for me to reset the scanner.*

Sherell reset the device, which took another two minutes, and began again. After two more minutes had passed, she nodded her head. *Successful scan.*

"We've got one minute left," said Dani. "Charles, the one back on Terrene, should be resetting the proximity limit within thirty seconds."

The biggest challenge of the entire project was that the Time Chain method of returning a traveler was based on the proximity of the traveler to the time station that had initiated the trip. Unfortunately, Charles's new time station back on Terrene was 737 light years from where the travelers were now, however, Charles had been able to incorporate vastly expanded proximity limits into his new time station, anticipating this issue. For the initial time jump, he'd set the proximity limit to 1,000 light years, and since the Earth was only 737 light years away, the travelers could get there without being pulled back by the time station on Terrene. But in order to pull the travelers back after they had completed the mission, the proximity limit needed to be set to something less than 737 light years. Charles had a watch that was synched with Dani's, and they'd all agreed that when nine minutes and thirty seconds had passed, he would reset the proximity limit, pulling all three travelers back to Terrene.

While Dani and the two Land People waited, both Orla and Aideen began to stir.

"Get under the time cradles!" hissed Dani. "We don't want them to see you!"

Latif got under Orla's cradle and Sherell slid under Aideen's. Suddenly, Charles appeared from a hole in the floor. He didn't see the Land People, but he did see Dani.

"What the hell are you doing in here?" he screamed, pointing his Tickler at her.

Just then, Dani, Latif and Sherell disappeared, the Land People never having been seen by Charles, Aideen or Orla.

The three reappeared back on Terrene, in Charles's station. Orla, still lying on the time cradle, woke up now that her time link function had been completed. Aideen and Charles came in, having left the chamber so their bodies didn't interfere with the return jump.

"Well?" asked Charles.

"We've got the scans!" said Dani.

Latif and Sherell rushed over to the medical center to begin the cloning process, excited to be the first Land People ever to clone another intelligent species. Dani, Aideen, Orla and Charles went to Murphy's pub to have a pint. Liam was behind the bar, as always, and Orla rushed around and gave him a big hug and kiss on the cheek.

"Things went well then?" he asked.

"Exactly as planned," she said. "As always!" Orla's comment drew a chuckle from Dani and Aideen, since virtually no mission they'd ever been on had gone "exactly as planned". Charles seemed oblivious to the comment, basking in his own internal glory after another successful mission, planned and orchestrated by him.

"Well now, time to get back to work then," Liam said to Orla. "Don't know how we got by without ya'!" Orla was the head barmaid in the pub and took care of customers who didn't make their orders at the bar, but every other free moment she spent near Liam. The lunch hour rush had passed, and the pub was only about half full, and most of these people would come up to the bar to order anyway, so Orla simply went around to the other side of the bar and took a seat with her friends.

"So what happens next?" she asked.

"Soon, we'll go underwater," said Dani. "And then we'll wait to see what the stork brings, around thirty days from now."

"Excitin'!" said Orla. "Let's celebrate!"

"Here's your pints," said Liam, pushing three mugs across the bar. "Drink up! Let's spend some quality time together before you go down under the water, can we now?"

Liam raised his mug. "To Aideen's clone!" he yelled.

And this was followed by a chorus, not just Liam and Orla, but everyone in the pub, human and Land People. "TO AIDEEN'S CLONE!"

"Ya' can't keep a secret in this town," joked Aideen.

"Just like old times on Omey Island!" said Liam. "We all know the Irish love to talk!"

"Certainly, the Irishman who own this pub does!" said Aideen.

"And let's not forget the English," said Charles, raising his mug. "To the English!"

And the chorus came again. "TO THE ENGLISH!"

When things quieted down, Orla leaned over to Dani and Aideen. "Seriously though, are you two really going underwater for thirty days? Is there no other way?"

"It's the easiest way for us to be together," said Dani. "And to spend the next year here with you."

"When will ya' go?" asked Orla.

"We'll give it a few days," said Aideen. "Until we get the thumbs up on baby Aideen."

Chapter 65

Latif and Sherell reported that the cloning process was well underway, all indications being that in just twenty-eight more days a full-grown Aideen would come out of the Cloning baths. This was the green light Dani and Aideen had been waiting for. They went down to the water's edge and found one of the underwater vessels, got a few lessons from Zeph on how to operate it, then dove down under the surface and made their way to the mountain where the aquarium was located. Cabal had been informed of their trip, so the doors were open when they arrived, and they steered the vessel in. The doors closed, the aquarium was drained, and they came out from the ship to look around. Cabal was sitting in a chair that had been bolted to the floor, in front of a table and more chairs that had been secured in the same manner. On the table was a glass sphere full of food, some of which looked like fish, some like plants and some like fruit. The table was set with plates and silverware, held in place by magnetism of some sort.

Outside of the aquarium's glass were about half a dozen other Water People, most of them smaller than normal. *Those are some of my children,* said Cabal. *Come, sit. Let's eat.*

Cabal leaned forward and pushed a button on the sphere and the top half folded open. He reached in with utensils and dished food out onto three plates. Before eating, he asked the two if they would like to share in a prayer. Dani in particular, was anxious to learn more about the culture of the Water People and they were off to a very good start. Instead of bowing his head, Cabal raised his face up, and his arms too, as if he were reaching for the heavens. Self-conscious, but not wanting to offend, Dani did the same. Aideen followed suit and Cabal began the prayer.

Thank you, Watcher from the Sky, for bringing back the Land People, and with them, the Humans from another world. We rejoice in the wisdom you have given us to make peace, at last. And we thank you for the food you bring us from the pure and clean oceans of Terrene. May it always be so.

Cabal lowered his gaze and his arms and the two women did the same.

Please, he said. *Enjoy. The fish is freshly caught and cooked, of course. And yes, we do cook. Our heating technology is not restricted to the melting of the poles or the firing of missiles, or the creation of underwater tsunamis.*

Dani didn't hesitate, picking up a knife and fork and digging in. She hoped the immunity pill she'd taken years ago was smart enough to fight off bacteria from a world 737 light years from Earth and a thousand meters underneath the sea. The fish was white in color, but more moist and rich than cod or sole, more like grouper. Absolutely delicious. The plant was green and tender, also having been cooked, but it didn't taste like seaweed. More like extremely tender asparagus. And the fruit, a yellow color, burst with flavor and sweetness when her teeth pressed down on it. Dani could see Aideen was enjoying the food as well, and it made her happy to be here, with a Sea King who called her friend, and the love of her life.

"So you made that tsunamis you caught us with using heat?" asked Dani.

Heat, and an underwater fan of great power, said Cabal. *But let us not talk of war when we should be enjoying every moment of our great peace.*

"Do you think the peace will last?" asked Aideen.

For the sake of my people and my children, I hope so. And please forgive me for not introducing you to the kids. I placed myself in this chair while the chamber was full of water and do not have my walking device. Plus, I don't really know all of their names.

"Why is that?" asked Dani. "Do you have a lot of children?"

Thousands, I would think.

"How do you make so many?" asked Dani. "We've been told Land People only use cloning to breed, and never increase their population."

Yes, there are some differences between our races. Water People breed in the traditional way of most animals. I'm told Humans are the same, although you also have cloning methods similar to Land People's. But to answer your question, because I am a step closer, biologically, to what our people aspire to be, it is my responsibility to father as many offspring as possible. Other males stay with only one female their entire lives.

"Could be worse fates," said Aideen. Dani got the joke but wasn't sure if Cabal did, and she didn't want to get off this subject yet, anyway. She sensed there was much more beneath the surface of this conversation which would explain the relationship between the Land People and Water People, far more completely than what they had learned so far.

"Why do you want to become Land People?" asked Dani.

Because the Watcher calls for us to come onto the land. The Watcher blesses those who do this with great power, as she did with the Land People.

"What power do you refer to?" asked Dani.

All the technology of the Land People—their cloning, their travel technology, their immortality—was given by the Watcher, when they came onto the land.

"But not to the Water People," said Dani.

That is correct. What we have, we developed ourselves.

"How long ago did this happen?" asked Dani.

Eons. Tens of thousands of your years.

"Do you resent the Land People because of this?" asked Dani.

We are grateful the Watcher has seen fit to send Humans to make the peace so that all of us, Humans, Land People and Water People will soon share the sea, land and space.

"Where does the Watcher live?" asked Aideen.

Somewhere above all things. We say it is the Sky, but to us, the Sky is everything above the sea: the atmosphere, space, the universe. The Watcher is above all of that.

"I wonder why the Land People have not told us this story," said Aideen.

They do not remember the Watcher from the Sky.

"Did any of your people see the Watcher when the gifts were given to the Land People?" asked Dani.

It is our belief the Watcher has never been on the surface of Terrene.

"But how did she give these powers to the Land People?" asked Dani.

She sent an Emmissary to teach them.

"But none of them seem to know about this," said Aideen. "Do you think they would hide this from us?"

They don't remember. It has fallen out of history for them. But not for the Water People. And now we will share in the gifts of the Watcher, so we are happy.

Chapter 66

I *am told you will stay nearly one year below the surface,* said Cabal.

"Nearly one Terrene year," said Dani, remembering that Terrene circled Energy One, its sun, every thirty-four Earth days.

But it will be terribly boring to stay in this cage for so long.

"It will," said Aideen. "But worth it."

Please, let me take you out into the great ocean and show you our world.

"But how?" asked Aideen.

In your vessel, of course. I can go with you.

"We're not very experienced in operating this vessel," said Dani. "I'm afraid it might be risky."

Very well then. We've been working on a vessel of our own, to carry both air and water breathing beings. We will take that. I have called for it. Please go into your ship while we flood the chamber.

Dani and Aideen entered their ship and sealed it shut. The doors to the chamber were opened and it was flooded by the sea from outside, then their video screens showed the vessel Cabal had spoken of entering the chamber. It was shaped like a classic submarine, flat on top, with handholds on it. The bottom and sides of the sub were made from some kind of clear glass material, but the height of the interior was not tall enough for a human to stand in, and Dani wondered how they would fit. The chamber emptied and Dani and Aideen exited their craft. Cabal was already on top, lying on his stomach and holding onto the handrails. His body was about eye level with Dani and Aideen.

Come up, he said. *Use the ladder on the side. The entrance to your compartment is up here.*

They took the three rungs of the ladder and climbed onto the deck. Toward the rear of the sub was a hatch with a circular wheel on it for opening and closing, but Dani was still confused regarding how they would fit down there.

Cabal cleared things up, although what he said wasn't very comforting. *You must lay on your bellies. Then you will see all that is below us as we travel.*

"I'm thinkin' this vessel might need some reengineerin," said Aideen. "Some humans get a little queasy in tight spaces like that."

What about you two humans?

"I think I can do it, for just a short trip," said Dani.

"We're both used to bein' locked away in tight spaces," said Aideen, referencing the time chambers where they once laid on their backs for months at a time. But of course, they were in a state of suspended animation when they were functioning as time links. This was a bit different.

The two opened the hatch and went down a short ladder, one at a time. Dani was the first down and she estimated the height of the ceiling to be about four feet off the floor. She got down on her hands and knees, worked her way into a horizontal position and shimmied forward to make room for Aideen. There was plenty of room to turn her head and watch Aideen go through the same contortions she had.

Ready? asked Cabal.

"Ready," said Dani, using a spoken voice but assuming Cabal was reading their thoughts and didn't really need to hear their voices.

"As ready as I'll ever be, I suppose," said Aideen. "Not too comfortable though, I'll tell ya' that my friend."

It will get better. Trust me.

The chamber flooded and the vessel backed out of the aquarium, then turned and began moving forward. Cabal was obviously riding in the open water, and Dani was surprised at how fast they were going. Then she felt the glass she was lying on beginning to get warmer. It wasn't a burning hot, but it was just on the edge of being uncomfortable. If it kept up, it was going to get very hot in the small cabin.

Relax, said Cabal. *Let your bodies go into a comfortable position.*

Dani did as she was told, relaxing her muscles. The glass, which clearly wasn't glass at all, began to soften, molding itself to their bodies. A protrusion came up and form-fitted itself to her forehead, so as not to strain her neck while allowing plenty of room for her mouth and nose to breath. Dani felt quite comfortable now, but assumed the glass would harden once again now that it had formed itself around them. And it did solidify slightly, but not all the way, and it stayed a little bit warm. It felt like she was lying on a heated yoga mat, except the mat had been molded to the shape of her body. The soft glass now held them in place, not only their fronts, but their sides as well. Dani imagined that now the craft could be rotated to give them views below and to the sides, as soon as they got to a depth where light penetrated.

Is that better for you?

"Much better!" said Dani.

"A nice feature, Cabal!" said Aideen.

The vessel slowed and the endless depths below them were replaced by the bottom of a horizontal lighted tunnel made of stone. As it continued on, the side view Dani had hoped for ensued. The vessel rotated and presented open-mouthed caves, each the home of a Water People family. Lighting in each cave allowed her to see them cooking and cleaning, eating and even drinking, from bottles that fit over their snouts entirely, allowing them to take in the liquid without taking in sea water at the same time. Children played with each other, darting about in the water, scolded by their parents, doing what children do. Dani marveled that there were a billion people, just like these, living below the waters of Terrene, doing their best to make it through life, and seemingly doing a pretty darn good job of it.

"Your people seem happy," Dani commented.

Generally, yes. There is plenty of food, the water is clean, and believe it or not, we are a peaceful people. We fight only to protect what is ours, just as Humans do. Am I right?

"Yes, you are so right," said Dani. "We are more alike than I would have thought at the beginning."

The vessel emerged from the habitation in the mountainside and went higher. This gave Dani and Aideen a better view of the sea above and below them, teeming with life so different yet so much the same as what is found in the oceans of Earth. Billowing shapes like jellyfish propelled themselves along, but they were a bright orange color, much more vibrant than the typical diluted white jellyfish of home. Fish of so many sizes and colors darted here and there, from tiny shrimp-like creatures traveling in vast swarms, to giant shark-like predators, 20 meters long, with jaws meant for only one thing.

"Why don't they attack us?" asked Aideen.

The Water People are the Kings of the Sea. We can communicate with most species, including the large ones you see out there, with the nasty teeth. They know we will destroy them if they attack us, and they also know the rules of the sea. They kill only what they need to survive.

"Fascinating," said Aideen.

I will take you back now, said Cabal. *We will have many more trips like this, and much more to see, if you so desire.*

"Count me in!" said Dani.

"Ditto!" said Aideen. Dani realized Cabal would understand the thought behind Aideen's slang word, so she didn't need to clarify the meaning.

The ship brought them back to the aquarium and the water was emptied. Dani and Aideen thanked Cabal and he told them to return to their vessel so the chamber could be flooded, allowing him to take his craft back out into the sea. He bid them farewell and told them he would return the following day. They thanked him, he departed and the chamber was emptied once again.

"Wow, what a first day!" said Dani.

"A lot to absorb, for certain," said Aideen.

"What do you think about the Watcher? Do you think it's possible she's real?"

"I suppose so," said Aideen. "I just wonder why the Land People know nothin' about it, or at least they haven't told us anythin' about it."

"I'll ask Zeph when we return to the surface," said Dani. "She's always been honest with me."

"She's a good lass, indeed," said Aideen.

"The other thing that really sunk in for me from today, is that the Water People are a lot more like us than we thought, and since there are a billion of them here, we really ought to give it our best to help them achieve their goals."

"Let's make a point of it," said Aideen. "Well, I don't know about you, my love, but I was thinkin' of havin' a glass of wine and goin' to bed."

"Sounds good," said Dani. "We'll need our rest if tomorrow is anything like today."

Chapter 67

The days under the seas of Terrene were full of adventure and learning, and each day, Dani would ask Aideen if she felt anything from her clone up above, and the answer was always the same—nothing. Some days Cabal would take them out to see new sights and new lifeforms under the sea, and on others they would stay in the aquarium and sit and talk all day long. Cabal told them as much as he could about the vast world that was the ocean of Terrene, a planet nearly twice the size of Earth, that was still 99 percent water. When the sea level finally dropped to its former levels, the land from the old days would reappear, but even then, the land of Terrene would only cover around 10 percent of the planet's surface.

The nights, which were the same as the days in the aquarium in which they lived, were times for Dani and Aideen to be alone together, reacquainting themselves with one another. In some ways, this adventure under the sea reminded Dani of their first wonderful journey together, when both of them were twenty-four years old, on the beach of Pelekas on the island of Corfu in Greece, then at the Great Pyramids of Egypt and finally, that wonderful week in Paris, before they had to part and Dani was forced to return to older Aideen. But it was actually the time she'd spent with older Aideen when Dani learned what love truly is, that it had very little to do with age and everything to do with a connection, a special bond with another human being. And now here they were. Dani was nearly twenty-eight years old, and Aideen had the appearance of a thirty-year-old, and a very beautiful one at that, but the wisdom of a seventy-year-old woman. So when word came down that the clone of Aideen had departed the planet, the time came to say "good-bye for now" to the wonderful undersea world of Terrene, and to their dear friend Cabal, had arrived. It was a heartfelt moment, for all three involved.

When she embraced Cabal, Dani felt his strength, knowing he could crush her with his powerful arms if he chose to, but feeling also his tenderness, and she realized that her friendship with him meant as much to him as his did to her.

I'm thinking of having the operation, he said. *To make my tail fin into legs.*

"Will it impair your ability to swim?" asked Dani.

A little, he said. *But I was never a fast swimmer anyway, and of course, we have vessels if I need speed down here. But I want to walk among you under my own power. It belittles me to rely on machines to help me.*

"It's your choice," said Aideen, taking Dani's place in front of Cabal and hugging him tightly. "But just know that we will love you, no matter if you walk on your own or not. Walking is not what makes a person a person."

You are wise, said Cabal. *But I am the leader of my people, and if I am to lead them to the Land and then into Space, I must be the first to conquer these challenges, and show them all the options that are available to them.*

"Understood," said Aideen. "Can't wait to walk beside you."

The two humans boarded their vessel and exited through the steel doors in the side of the mountain and rose up out of the depths, surfacing at the marina at the bottom of the cliffs of Base One. They rode the lift up and were met at the top by Clarion, Zephyr, Orla, Liam, and Charles. Each of them had tears in their eyes, so happy to see their dear friends after their long absence. Dani watched Aideen closely, because she knew what Aideen knew, that each of these people had seen her clone before she left on the voyage to Earth.

Aideen turned her gaze to Orla. "What was she like?" she asked.

"Not quite as pretty as you, lass," Orla joked, and Aideen had to smile. Orla always had a way of softening a difficult moment.

"It's good to be home," said Aideen, and hugs were shared all around.

The seven friends walked to Murphy's pub to celebrate the return of two of Base One's most famous citizens, the two who'd help bring the Land People home and negotiated the peace with both the Water People and the crew of Diaspora Ten. Dani was surprised, but happy, to see a few members of Diaspora Ten in the pub, including Droden, the captain. He looked much healthier than he had when they first met, sturdier from the gravity meds and fatter from the rich food of Terrene. He shook her hand and his grip was firm.

Thank you, he said. *For bringing reason to us in our time of great despair.*

"I am so proud to have been part of that," said Dani.

Drinks were raised and toasts were made, well past 15 o'clock and on into the wee hours of the night. Dani noticed Charles was still there, holding his own with the rest of them, sluggin' down ale and whiskey. Dani kissed Aideen on the cheek and told her she was going to speak with Charles for a while.

"A good idea," said Aideen. "Find out what mischief he's up to these days."

Dani made her way over to Charles, who was standing at the bar, not far from his good friend, Liam, who was behind the bar, serving and drinking, as always, the happiest man in the universe. She held her mug up and clinked it against Charles's.

"Sláinte," she toasted, the Irish word for health.

"Sláinte," he returned. "And frankly, I couldn't feel better. Haven't felt this good in years."

"You're not back on the OIM, are you Charles?" Dani asked.

"Don't need to be," he said. "It seems I took more than enough of that, then broke the habit the hard way when I was captured and imprisoned. The result being, that I am now, officially, immortal."

"Seriously?" asked Dani. "How do you know?"

"I've run some tests and they all lead to the same conclusion. The conclusion I have sought for nearly my entire adult life, which is a lot of years."

"I guess we can all be immortal now, if we want to," said Dani. "With the Land People's cloning technology."

"True," he said. "But I do things in my own way, as you well know Dani."

"What does it all mean, Charles?" asked Dani, her voice philosophical.

"You mean life?" he asked.

"I don't know," she said. "While we were under the water, we learned a lot about the Water People, including their belief in a deity. Some interesting stuff, actually. They said all the tech of the Land People was actually given to them by the 'Watcher from the Sky,' some female goddess that lives beyond the sky and space."

"Really?" said Charles. "I'd like to meet her! After all, I'm a god of sorts now, myself."

"So you say," said Dani. "But just remember Charles, please, that your powers should only be used for good."

"I promise, Dani. Good. Always good."

Epilogue

New Aideen beamed down to Earth from the space station, having just completed the journey from Terrene. She materialized in the time station in the Time Management building and was met by Annette and Danielle. Annette shook her hand, introduced herself, and welcomed her. Aideen knew who Annette was because Orla and Charles, back on Terrene, had told her about her, but she'd never met her, since New Aideen had not yet come to Brussels from Charles's time station at the moment she'd been cloned.

Danielle stepped forward, extending her hand. "Hi, I'm Danielle," she said.

Aideen pushed Danielle's arm aside and embraced her, kissing her fully on the lips, then pulled back, her hands on her lover's shoulders. "The hell you are," she said. "I haven't called you Danielle since the first time we met. You're Dani. Is that understood?"

Danielle looked to Annette for guidance and Annette nodded. "Understood," she said. "I've missed you, Aideen, so much."

"And I've missed you, Dani. Where can we celebrate?"

"Technically, you still need to go through the training program before you're released into society here in 2256," said Annette.

"Oh, hogwash," said Aideen. "Let's go out on the town. You and Dani can show me how to do everything."

Annette smiled and nodded. "Why not?" she said, always willing to make an exception for these two exceptional people. "This is a special occasion. I know a nice restaurant in town with great jazz music. I hope it's okay, but I'll have to bring a few security people with me. You know, my job and all."

"Yes, yes, of course," said Aideen. "You're the Minister of something or other, right?"

"Yes, the Minister of Time Management, although we don't do much with time travel anymore. In fact, nothing."

"It's a good thing you gave that up," said Aideen. "Nothin' but trouble ever came from time travel. Well, there was one good thing." Aideen reached over and took Dani's hand in her own.

The three of them left the building, followed discreetly by two security guards dressed in light blue skinsuits, and went to the restaurant. It was small and comfortable, and Aideen found the jazz relaxing, but at the moment she would have preferred some good old fashioned Irish music, with a violin, a banjo and maybe even some Irish bagpipes. But the jazz was good enough. The three shared some wine and small talk, but then Annette turned to a more serious matter.

"I realize you two have missed the last three years, and it will take some time to bring you up to speed. But I want you to know that your older 'sisters' were a very big part of helping this world stay out of harm's way during those three years."

"We know that," said Aideen. "And we'll be happy to do the same, if called upon."

"Well, I hope it won't be necessary, but something is brewing that could lead in that unfortunate direction."

"What on Earth is that?" asked Aideen.

"Do you know what OIM is?" asked Annette. "I can't remember when you learned about all of that."

"I know what it is," said Dani, "since I've been here a little longer than Aideen. Organic Intelligent Material. It's what almost everything here is made of and it can be programmed with AI to do just about anything."

"Well, I've known of the black stone for many years," said Aideen. "And when I saw that Base One on Terrene was mostly black stone, I asked Charles to give me a crash course on it."

"Ah, good," said Annette. "Did Charles mention the latest development with OIM? That it seems to be developing a collective consciousness all of its own, completely independent of AI, and sometimes able to override the commands of AI, if influenced by a more powerful source?"

Aideen shook her head. "No, he didn't mention that, but that would be like Charles, now wouldn't it?"

"Yes, you're more right than you know," said Annette.

"What's he done now?" asked Aideen.

"It's not so much what he's done, but what he might do. You see, Charles is the only biological human who can communicate directly with OIM. The rest of us can communicate with the OIM only through the Community of Minds."

"Those are the people who live in the big black box in the time station, right? Orla told me about that too."

"Yes, there are 100 million uploaded minds living in there," said Annette.

"That's a lot of brainpower," said Aideen.

"Indeed," said Annette. "But as I was saying, the Minds can communicate with the OIM. It also seems that messages come to the OIM here on Earth from the transit vessels, also made of OIM, that shuttle people and things back and forth from Terrene, where you just arrived from."

"And?" asked Aideen.

"Well, it seems the OIM from Terrene has informed the OIM on Earth, via the OIM in the shuttles, that Charles is up to something, and it might not be good."

"What is it?" asked Aideen.

"We don't know," said Annette. "He hasn't told the OIM yet. All he's disclosed so far is that he's immortal, which we already knew because he told Dani, the other Dani, and she told us. But the OIM claims he mentioned that someone as powerful as him deserves to go where he wants, when he wants. We don't really know what that means, but if he wants to return to Earth, where he is not allowed to be, legally, I suspect he'll come looking for you."

"Why?" asked Aideen.

"During the three years you missed, Charles has become quite close with both of you. He likes you, and he seems to even care for you."

"Hard to believe he cares for anyone, except himself," said Aideen.

"I will say," said Annette, "he seemed a different person when he left for Terrene than he was when you knew him three years ago."

"I suppose I'll have to agree with that," said Aideen. "My time with him on Terrene was brief, but he seemed a new man. He was always quite charming, but now he seems to be just glowing with happiness."

"Yes," said Annette. "Dani and Aideen on Terrene have reported that Charles has been doing a lot of good things there, and claims he intends to remain on the side of good. But I'm planning a diplomatic mission to Terrene so I can draw my own conclusions. I'm also aware that Charles built a time station there in order to create you, Aideen."

"Yes, everyone on Terrene knows that," said Aideen. "I wasn't there long, but it's a small community. Hard to keep a secret there."

"I imagine so," said Annette. "But Charles's new time station is a loose cannon the Earth needs to get a handle on, regardless of whether he's good or bad. Time travel has been far more trouble than it's worth for us, and EarthGov doesn't want that station to remain operable. I need to go there to shut it down, and while I'm there, I'll make my own opinion regarding Charles's disposition. There's no cause for alarm at this time, but I just thought you should know of my concerns. I tend to get a little paranoid when it comes to Charles, after all he's done."

"Thank you, Annette," said Dani. "We'll do whatever we can to help, should the need arise."

Aideen's reaction was a little different from Dani's. More direct. "If feckin' Charles is trying to take over the world again, Dani and I can handle him."

"I know you can," said Annette. "Let's hope we don't need you to."

Acknowledgments

Thank you to Sabrina Milazzo for her wonderful work on the cover design and on the inside of the book. I am also grateful to Claire Rushbrook for her editing and final polishing.

About the Author

Steven Decker lives and writes in a small town in Connecticut, although he spends a lot of time in other parts of the world, and sometimes those places appear in his books. In addition to writing, he enjoys time with his family, his dogs, and taking long walks in the countryside. *The Balance of Time* is his fifth novel and second in the *Time Chain* series.

Printed in Great Britain
by Amazon